B.Cooke

Alex Pine was born and raised on a council estate in South London and left school at sixteen. Before long, he embarked on a career in journalism, which took him all over the world – many of the stories he covered were crime-related. Among his favourite hobbies are hiking and water-based activities, so he and his family have spent lots of holidays in the Lake District. He now lives with his wife on a marina close to the New Forest on the South Coast – providing him with the best of both worlds! This is his third novel.

By the same author:

The Christmas Killer
The Killer in the Snow

THE
WINTER
KILLER

ALEX PINE

avon.

Published by AVON
A division of HarperCollins*Publishers*
1 London Bridge Street
London SE1 9GF

www.harpercollins.co.uk

HarperCollins*Publishers*
1st Floor, Watermarque Building, Ringsend Road
Dublin 4, Ireland

www.harpercollins.co.uk

A Paperback Original 2022
1

First published in Great Britain by HarperCollins*Publishers* 2022

Copyright © HarperCollins*Publishers* 2022

Alex Pine asserts the moral right to be identified as the author of this work.

A catalogue copy of this book is available from the British Library.

ISBN: 978-0-00-852026-7

This novel is entirely a work of fiction. The names, characters and incidents portrayed in it are the work of the author's imagination. Any resemblance to actual persons, living or dead, events or localities is entirely coincidental.

Typeset in Minion Pro by Palimpsest Book Production Limited,
Falkirk, Stirlingshire
Printed and Bound in the UK using 100% Renewable Electricity at
CPI Group (UK) Ltd

All rights reserved. No part of this text may be reproduced, transmitted, down-loaded, decompiled, reverse engineered, or stored in or introduced into any information storage and retrieval system, in any form or by any means, whether electronic or mechanical, without the express written permission of the publishers.

MIX
Paper | Supporting
responsible forestry
FSC
www.fsc.org
FSC™ C007454

This book is produced from independently certified FSC™ paper to ensure responsible forest management.

For more information visit: www.harpercollins.co.uk/green

This book is dedicated to my loving wife Catherine.
I couldn't have written it without her continued support.

Introducing DI Walker and his team . . .

This is the third book in the DI James Walker series. For those who haven't read *The Christmas Killer* and *The Killer in the Snow*, here is a brief introduction to the man himself and the key members of his team.

DETECTIVE INSPECTOR JAMES WALKER, AGED 41

An officer with the Cumbria Constabulary based in Kendal. He spent 20 years with the Met in London before moving to the quiet village of Kirkby Abbey. He's married to Annie, aged 37, who was born in the village and works as a teacher. The couple now have a young daughter, Bella.

DETECTIVE CHIEF INSPECTOR JEFF TANNER, AGED 47

James's boss and a highly experienced officer who prefers to delegate rather than investigate. He's married with a son.

DETECTIVE SERGEANT PHIL STEVENS, AGED 39

A no-nonsense detective who got off on the wrong foot with James because he was in line for the DI job when the man from London arrived on the scene and took it. But he is now a loyal colleague who is married with two children.

DETECTIVE CONSTABLE JESSICA ABBOTT, AGED 34

Youngest member of the team and of Irish and East African descent. She's sassy, as sharp as a razor, and not afraid to speak her mind. She has the closest working relationship with James. Her fiancé, Sean, is a paramedic.

PROLOGUE

The Fells Hotel stood on the edge of Cumbria's stunning Lake Windermere, with unhindered views across the placid water to the snow-capped hills in the distance.

As far as Jessica Abbott was concerned it was the perfect setting for a New Year's Eve wedding. She'd been gazing around in awe since she and her fiancé, Sean, had arrived an hour ago.

All the function rooms on the ground floor glowed with a variety of bright and colourful decorations, including balloons, eye-catching floral clusters, string lights that hung from the ceilings, and an impressive array of gilded candelabras.

When she was introduced earlier to the groom, Greg Murphy, she told him how impressed she was.

'You've done a really fantastic job,' she'd said. 'It's spectacular and yet intimate at the same time.'

'I'm glad you think so,' he'd replied. 'I wanted it to be special and memorable for everyone who came.'

Sean and Greg were members of the same golf club and saw each other fairly regularly – hence the invitation to the wedding – but Jessica hadn't met Greg before today and he struck her as friendly and approachable, despite his reputation as a hard and ruthless businessman.

She and Sean were due to tie the knot themselves in the summer, but no way would they be able to afford something so lavish. Sean was a paramedic and she was a detective constable with the Cumbria Constabulary based in the market town of Kendal. They were going to have to use most of their savings and take out a small loan to stage a far more modest affair for their nuptials.

Money, of course, was no object to Greg, who owned a chain of hotels across Cumbria, including The Fells.

He was now standing at the altar in his smart black suit and high waistcoat, waiting for the marriage ceremony to begin. He was tall and slim, with rugged good looks and the confident bearing of a successful man. He had a mop of dark, wavy hair and a deep baritone voice that suited him.

Jessica was looking forward to meeting the bride-to-be, Libby Elliott, who was due to make an appearance at any second along with her sister, the maid-of-honour, Rachel.

The ceremony itself was just the start of the celebrations, of course. It was going to be followed by a champagne reception and photo session in the Garden Room, then the sit-down wedding breakfast in the main hall. After that was the evening do and the countdown to midnight. Holding the wedding on New Year's Eve had been Greg's idea, as he wanted to enter the new year as a married man, and it meant that the guests could continue partying into the early hours.

The guy had really pushed the boat out to ensure that everyone had a great time, even to the extent of offering free accommodation in the hotel's forty rooms for those who wanted to stay the night.

Jessica and Sean had naturally taken up the offer and had already checked in to their second-floor room. It overlooked the landscaped gardens and the lake beyond.

Jessica was determined to make the most of the occasion and the weekend off as she'd been one of the officers on duty over Christmas and this was the first chance she'd had to get out and celebrate the holiday season.

The other guests seemed like a good bunch as those she'd already met had been friendly and welcoming. The first person to introduce herself had been Claire Prescott, a woman who got around with the aid of a heavy-duty walking stick and boasted that she was a sprightly seventy-one.

She and her son Ethan, who looked to be in his early to mid-thirties, had arrived at the same time as Jessica and Sean, and they'd all shared the lift going up to their rooms.

Claire had jokingly explained that she could have walked up the stairs, despite her arthritis, but wanted to conserve her energy so that she'd be able to see in the new year.

'This is a really special day for me,' she told them, and her voice rattled with emotion. 'I used to be a nanny to Libby and Rachel when they were little. They never knew their real grandparents who both died before they were born and I've always prayed that I would see at least one of them get married before I died. And thankfully my prayers have been answered.'

She went on to say that Ethan had known the girls for

years and used to work in a hotel himself, but now ran his own gift shop in Windermere.

The bride's parents had also made a point of introducing themselves. Denise and Fraser Elliott were a pleasant couple in their mid to late sixties, and it turned out they had once lived in Kirkby Abbey, a village that was very familiar to Jessica. Not only did her boss, Detective Inspector James Walker, live there, but it was also the location of a series of brutal murders three Christmases ago. And she'd been heavily involved in that investigation. Thankfully, this Christmas had been relatively crime free all across Cumbria.

It was three o'clock when things started to happen. Two young bridesmaids walked down the aisle followed by Libby's sister, Rachel. She wore a blush-pink dress and clutched a large bouquet of white flowers with both hands. She was a short, bespectacled woman with a full figure and a round face, and looked nothing like her sister.

Just as she took her place to the side of the altar, the room suddenly filled with the inimitable sound of Wagner's *Bridal Chorus*. All heads turned towards Libby and her father as they made their grand entrance.

The bride was radiant in a white, curve-skimming satin number with a lace capelet that was beaded with sequins.

'Wow, she looks fabulous,' Jessica said quietly to Sean. 'I'll have to find out where she got that dress.'

He turned towards her and grinned. 'I imagine it will be way out of our price range, my love.'

She pulled a face and gave a resigned nod. 'I expect you're right.'

The formal ceremony went off without a hitch as the couple

exchanged vows and rings and in no time at all they were pronounced husband and wife. Jessica knew that, at twenty-nine, Libby was thirteen years younger than Greg, but the age gap wasn't at all obvious when you looked at the couple.

'They look like the perfect match to me,' she whispered to Sean.

During the champagne reception that followed, guests mingled as waiters and waitresses moved around carrying silver trays bearing hors d'oeuvres, champagne flutes and various cocktails. Many of the guests went out into the garden where photographs were taken but no one stayed outside for long because it was bitingly cold unless you stood right next to the heaters dotted around the large, paved terrace.

The first indication Jessica got that it wasn't going to be a perfect day for everyone came when she left Sean downstairs and went up to their room to use the toilet and put on a wrap.

She was walking along the corridor when a door was flung open and a bearded man in a suit rushed out and almost bumped into her.

'*Mi scusi*,' he said in what Jessica knew to be Italian for *excuse me*.

Without waiting for her to respond, he strode towards the thickly carpeted stairs. A second later, a woman appeared – Rachel Elliott, the bride's sister.

She looked distinctly upset and after slamming the room door behind her, she hurried after the man without acknowledging Jessica.

Jessica assumed that it was a lovers' tiff and hoped that it would soon get resolved, for both their sakes, but half an hour later she spotted Rachel standing by herself at the bar and she looked as miserable as sin. There was no sign of the bearded man.

For a fleeting moment Jessica was tempted to approach her, but Rachel's sister suddenly appeared, so she held back. The siblings started talking and Jessica was happy to leave them to it.

Within minutes, she'd pushed it all to the back of her mind and didn't think about it again until an hour and a half later as the wedding breakfast got under way in the main hall.

That was when Sean drew her attention to the fact that the maid-of-honour had not taken her place at the top table.

The seat between Rachel's father and the groom was empty and it remained so throughout the meal. It was clear to everyone that Rachel's absence was a source of either concern or irritation for those closest to her as they were no longer smiling and laughing and her father and new brother-in-law kept getting up and leaving the hall for brief spells. Her sister, however, just sat there, rigid as a fence post, and the look on her face conveyed the impression that she wasn't happy.

It wasn't until the meal was over and the speeches and toasts were supposed to begin that Greg Murphy stood, his expression glum, and said, 'I'm afraid we're going to have to pause proceedings for a short while because our lovely maid-of-honour, who was due to make a speech right about now, appears to have gone AWOL. It shouldn't take long to find her, and once Rachel is back, we can continue to enjoy the rest of the evening.'

Jessica and Sean were among the dozens of guests who got up from their chairs and joined in the search. No one quite knew what to make of what was happening and an air of panic and confusion prevailed. Those who remained in the main hall spoke in hushed voices and Libby had to be comforted by her mother after breaking down in tears.

Twenty minutes after the search began Jessica was on the terrace when she spotted one of the wedding guests rushing across the lawn towards the hotel. The man started waving his arms in the air and calling to a security guard who was shining a torch into a bush.

'I don't like the look of that,' she said to Sean. 'You stay here while I go and see what's going on.'

She left Sean standing on the terrace as she dashed onto the lawn, approaching the security guard at the same time as the guest. By then she had taken her warrant card from her purse and was holding it up.

'I'm a police officer,' she said to the clearly anxious guest, a man she'd seen earlier during the ceremony. 'Am I right in assuming you've found something?'

He drew in a sharp breath and nodded before telling her what it was.

His words caused every muscle and sinew in her body to freeze. Turning to the security guard, she said, 'This is now a police matter and I'm going to have to call it in.'

CHAPTER ONE

There was a time when James Walker was rarely sober on New Year's Eve. Like millions of other revellers, he would shed his inhibitions and enter into the spirit of the occasion with great gusto.

But that was when he was single and living in London. Back then, he and his mates in the Met had used it as an excuse to de-stress after another difficult twelve months policing the capital.

Things changed when he met and married Annie. End of year celebrations became quiet, intimate affairs, usually spent at home or at the homes of close family members.

This year was the quietest yet because they had their new daughter to consider.

Annie had given birth to Bella six months ago after years of trying to conceive, and the little darling had become the centre of their world. Right now, she was on the sofa being breastfed by her mother and James was staring at them from across the room while reflecting on just how lucky he was.

He'd been unsure about their move to Cumbria just over two years ago, fearing the quiet life wouldn't suit him. But despite a difficult start he'd settled well into his role as a detective inspector at police HQ in Kendal. And since coming here he'd headed up two of the biggest investigations of his career. The first was the hunt for the serial killer who had struck in Kirkby Abbey. This was followed by the murders of an entire family on a nearby farm a year later.

Both atrocities were carried out during the Christmas periods and attracted worldwide attention. Thankfully, this Christmas had passed without any bloodshed, which had come as a huge relief to James and his colleagues.

He was now hoping that tonight would also pass off just as peacefully as he was the on-call detective and would have to respond to any major crime or serious incident that was called in. Sitting here with his family, that was the last thing he wanted to do but with just over four hours to go until midnight experience had taught him that there was still a chance that the phone would ring.

He'd drawn the short straw because most of the other senior detectives either had commitments or were on a break, including his boss, Detective Chief Inspector Jeff Tanner, who wasn't due back from his annual winter holiday in Scotland until late tomorrow.

'Is watching me feed the baby really more interesting than the film?' Annie said with a smile as her eyes remained fixed on the television.

James smiled back. 'Actually, it is. This film was your choice, remember? I wanted the other one.'

Now she turned towards him and her smile widened. 'No way was I going to spend New Year's Eve watching gormless gangsters killing each other. This film is all about lifting the spirits rather than chilling the blood. And if you really can't get into it, how about making us some more coffee? Then when I've finished feeding you can wind her.'

It was an offer James couldn't refuse, but before heading to the kitchen he crossed the room and kissed his wife and daughter on their foreheads.

'Do you want me to open the box of chocolates I bought for us?' he said.

Annie looked up and winked at him. 'I thought you'd never ask.'

She wasn't wearing make-up and there were dark circles beneath her eyes but to James she was still as beautiful as she had always been, with her soft facial features and bright blue eyes.

The challenges of early motherhood had taken their toll, however. She'd lost weight along with some of her hair and she'd been having difficulty sleeping. But despite that she was clearly enjoying her new role.

She'd already decided not to return to work as a teacher at the village primary school at the end of her maternity leave as she was determined to make the most of being a mum and was already wondering if they should try to provide Bella with a brother or sister.

James was keen to have more than one child, but he was also worried that they would be subjecting themselves to another long, drawn-out ordeal with no guarantee that things would turn out well.

He went into the kitchen and put the kettle on. While waiting for it to boil he picked up the box of chocolates he'd left on the worktop and placed it on a tray along with their coffee mugs.

He was reaching for the milk in the fridge when his phone rang, prompting him to exhale a loud expletive.

He closed the fridge and fished the phone out of his trouser pocket, frowning when he saw that the caller was Detective Constable Abbott. Wasn't she supposed to be at the wedding of some wealthy businessman at a plush lakeside hotel? James wondered if she was ringing to wish him a Happy New Year.

'I'm really sorry to bother you, guv,' she said when he answered, and the sombre tone of her voice sent a tremor of unease rippling through him.

'It's no problem, Jessica,' he replied. 'Aren't you and Sean at a wedding?'

'We are, but something has happened and I had to call it in. The team members who are on duty are otherwise engaged and so the controllers were going to ring you and I said I'd do it for them.'

'What's up? It sounds serious.'

'It is, guv, and I think you're going to want to come here. A young woman who happens to be the bride's sister and maid-of-honour suddenly disappeared in strange circumstances soon after the actual marriage ceremony. She was supposed to make a speech at the sit-down meal but was nowhere to be found. As she's been missing for almost two hours guests and staff are searching for her as we speak, but I fear that something bad might have happened to her.'

'Why is that?'

'Well, her purse and broken glasses have been found on the hotel's private jetty at the bottom of the garden.'

'Are you thinking she might have fallen into the lake?'

'That's a possibility, for sure. But it might not be as straight-forward as that. You see, her glasses are smeared with what looks like blood.'

James felt his stomach twist in an anxious knot.

'In that case, remind me which hotel it is and I'll head straight there,' he said.

'It's The Fells on Lake Windermere.'

'Okay, I know it. With luck I can be there in about forty minutes. Meanwhile, you need to lock the place down as best you can and call for uniformed backup.'

'Units are already on their way along with a forensics team. And I've enlisted the help of the hotel's staff and security officers who are making sure guests don't leave and no new arrivals are allowed in.'

'Good work. I suggest you also alert a diving team. From the sound of it we may well need them.'

'I'll get right onto it,' Abbott said.

'And before I hang up tell me who the woman is.'

'Her name is Rachel Elliott. She's twenty-five and the younger sister of the bride, Libby Elliott.'

'And the groom?'

'Greg Murphy. You've probably heard of him. He's a prom-inent businessman and CEO of a chain of hotels across Cumbria, including The Fells. His father died earlier this year and left him the business and a substantial amount of money, by all accounts.'

'And are you there because you're a close friend of either family?'

'No. Sean and Greg belong to the same golf club so we got an invite.'

'It's safe to say you're not emotionally involved then?'

'That's right, guv. Obviously, it's still quite shocking, but I'm confident I can remain impartial. To be honest, I'm just praying that Rachel turns up and that there's an innocent explanation for why she can't be found.'

'Well, keep looking and hopefully you'll call me with some good news before I get there so I can turn around and come back home.'

CHAPTER TWO

Annie wasn't at all surprised when James told her he was being called out.

'It's what I've been expecting, to be honest,' she said, as she moved Bella from one breast to the other. 'Just make sure that next year you put in an early request for leave over Christmas and New Year's Eve.'

He grinned. 'Consider it done. Will you be okay?'

'Of course. I'm used it, after all. Is it a bad one?'

'Not sure yet, but it could be. A woman attending a wedding over at Lake Windermere has gone missing and the circumstances appear somewhat suspicious.'

'That's awful. I do hope that no harm has come to her. Could it be she's simply wandered off or passed out after drinking too much?'

'Anything is possible, but there's evidence to suggest that she might have fallen or been pushed into the lake.'

'My God, I hope not.'

James glanced at his watch. 'I have to go. I'm really sorry.'

'Don't worry about it. I'll give Bella a kiss from you on the stroke of midnight.'

James hurried upstairs to change into a suit. When he came back down, he slipped on an overcoat and then stepped back into the living room to kiss his wife and daughter goodbye.

As he turned to leave, one of the framed photos on the mantlepiece caught his eye. It had been taken on their own wedding day at a hotel in Kent. They were standing either side of the cake and smiling at the camera.

He remembered how happy they were and how much fun all the guests had had. It made his heart go out to Greg Murphy and Libby Elliott whose special day had been wrecked, their memories of the occasion forever tarnished.

Kirkby Abbey, a village with a population of around seven hundred, was located on the eastern side of the county and was surrounded by spectacular peaks and sprawling moors.

James headed west out of the village in his Audi along a familiar route that would take him through Sedbergh and Kendal and then beyond to Lake Windermere, a journey of just under forty miles.

He had never been inside The Fells Hotel but had driven past it on numerous occasions. It was situated on the lake's eastern shore between the towns of Bowness and Ambleside.

The lake itself had always been one of Cumbria's most popular tourist attractions and weddings took place at venues around it throughout the year.

James had read somewhere that more and more couples were choosing to get married on New Year's Eve rather than during spring and summer. It didn't surprise him since it gave guests two good reasons to celebrate. However, it also increased the likelihood that excessive drinking by some could cause problems.

He wondered if that was what had happened to Rachel Elliott. Had she become involved in a nasty altercation fuelled by booze?

James was only too aware of the statistics in that respect. They showed that almost half the violent crimes in the UK each year – including rapes, sexual assaults and robberies – were committed by offenders under the influence of alcohol.

When he'd worked in London, call-outs to pubs, clubs and parties were a nightly occurrence. He lost count a long time ago of the number of stabbings he investigated where the assailant was pissed.

Sadly, even cosy Cumbria had seen drink-related crimes soar in recent years. Since moving here he had been directly involved in two serious cases. In the first, a man was shot and wounded on a farm by his inebriated partner. In the second, a young woman was badly beaten at her own birthday bash by a youth who was off his head on various spirits. In both cases the offenders claimed they didn't know what they were doing.

James could tell from the amount of traffic on the roads that it was going to be a busy night. No doubt the relatively calm weather had encouraged plenty of people to venture out. But it wasn't expected to last. Forecasters were already warning of heavy snow and high winds in the days ahead.

He drove across the M6 onto the A684. When he reached Kendal, he joined the A591, which would take him all the way to his destination.

He radioed Control to tell them that he was on his way and they informed him that a forensics team had already arrived at the scene.

The Fells Hotel was in a part of the county that attracted hordes of tourists during the summer months. Windermere was the largest natural lake in England and was surrounded by historical buildings and attractions such as The World of Beatrix Potter and the National Park Visitor Centre.

It prided itself on being a safe and scenic environment, and James knew that if something bad had indeed happened to Rachel Elliott then it was going to cause quite a stir among the local residents and business owners.

CHAPTER THREE

A police patrol car was parked at the entrance to the driveway that led from the main road to the hotel. Its emergency light was flashing and the uniformed officer standing next to it waved James through when he wound down his window and identified himself.

The driveway was lined with trees and the gardens on either side were consumed by darkness. The hotel, by contrast, was brightly lit and James could see that two more patrol cars and a forensic van were parked in front of it.

He pulled to a stop, switched off the engine, and took a few moments to make a mental note of the scene.

The building ahead of him was a three-storey Edwardian structure with steps leading up to the entrance and lots of windows. Off to the left was the guest car park, which looked to be full, and to the right a white-framed conservatory that appeared to house a swimming pool. It was much like many of the hotels in this part of the world – classy yet traditional, and designed to appeal to people with deep pockets.

James took out his phone and called DC Abbott to let her know that he had arrived.

'I'll meet you in reception, guv,' she said when she answered.

The reception area was smaller than he'd expected it to be and it was crammed with people and a large glittering Christmas tree. Uniformed police officers and staff members were doing their best to address the concerns of the smartly attired guests who all looked anxious and confused. James wondered how much they knew. Were they aware that items belonging to the missing maid-of-honour had been found on the hotel's private jetty? And that it was now highly unlikely that she would be found safe and well?

He looked around for Abbott as he moved slowly towards the reception desk, at the same time taking in his surroundings.

There was a wide, open staircase and a high-beamed ceiling from which hung glowing decorations. Framed paintings of Lake Windermere adorned the walls and through an arched doorway James could see a large lounge with armchairs, sofas and low tables.

The place had been decked out to a high standard for the wedding and New Year's Eve celebrations, but the joyous atmosphere that it would have conjured up had been well and truly trashed.

As James approached the reception desk, he felt someone tug at his arm and turned to see DC Abbott standing at his side.

'I'm glad you managed to get here so quickly, guv,' she said. 'This is not an easy situation to control.'

Abbott was one of the best officers on the team. She was smart, savvy and easy to work with, and he realised that this was the first time he'd seen her appear even slightly rattled. Her features were taut and her voice stretched with shock.

It was also the first time he'd seen her in anything other than a work suit, or casual clothes. She was wearing a low-cut red dress beneath a black overcoat that hung open, and like all the other wedding guests, had clearly been hoping to have a fun time.

'I'm afraid things haven't changed,' she said. 'Rachel still hasn't turned up and it's a mystery as to what might have happened to her. Meanwhile, word has got around that something belonging to her has been found down by the lake and everyone is jumping to the conclusion that she's drowned.'

It was difficult to hear what she was saying above the chatter around them so James suggested they go somewhere quiet.

'You can put me in the picture and then give me a quick tour of the place,' he said.

'I've been using the manager's office,' Abbott replied. 'Follow me.'

The office was at the end of a corridor off the reception area. The door was closed and a female staff member was standing outside. She greeted Abbott with a nervous smile and said, 'Miss Cornwall has gone back out into the garden to be with Mr Murphy. Do you want me to ask her to come back in?'

'No, it's fine,' Abbott told her. 'This is Detective Inspector Walker. He and I need to use the office for a few minutes. We'll talk to Miss Cornwall afterwards.'

The office was small and neat but the two detectives didn't

bother wasting time making themselves comfortable. They stood in the middle of the room as Abbott began by explaining that Karen Cornwall was the manager and reported to the hotel owner, Greg Murphy, who also happened to be the groom. She then repeated what she'd told James earlier, that Rachel Elliott had disappeared during the champagne reception in the Garden Room that followed the formal exchange of vows.

'Everyone was in high spirits as they drank, talked and helped themselves to the snacks that were provided,' Abbott said. 'The bride and groom posed for photographs in the various function rooms, and in the garden while it was still light outside. The garden is pretty big and leads down to the lake and the jetty, however, while all this was going on I bore witness to an incident involving Rachel and I think it might be relevant.'

Abbott filled James in on the scene she'd witnessed, starting with the unexpected collision with the bearded man, adding, 'I haven't had time yet to find out who he is, but he said sorry to me in Italian.'

'Really? So, you speak the language?'

'I spent a couple of years in Italy when I was younger and picked it up there.'

'I had no idea. So, what happened after he ran into you?'

'Rachel came out of the room and followed him along the corridor and down the stairs,' she said. 'She looked upset and I assumed they'd had an argument but when I saw her at the bar a little while later the man wasn't with her. I was actually going to ask her if she was all right when her sister turned up. They started talking so I didn't hang around.'

'Have you had a chance to ask the sister what they talked about?'

She shook her head. 'Not yet.'

'Okay, so how long did the reception last?'

'About an hour and a half, I reckon, and it was only when it came to the sit-down meal that we noticed that Rachel hadn't taken her seat at the top table with the rest of the wedding party. It soon became evident that the others were concerned.'

'And do the family members know about what was found on the jetty?'

'They do. I made sure I was the one to break the news to Libby and their parents as soon as it was brought to my attention. Up to that point, they were assuming she'd just wandered off somewhere or got drunk and passed out, so it came as a terrible shock. Now they're worried sick along with everyone else.'

Abbott had to pause there to catch her breath and James could see that she was feeling emotional. It didn't surprise him. As one of the wedding guests it would be difficult for her to remain detached or to treat it like any other case. This was personal.

'What have you done with Rachel's belongings?' James asked.

'They're with forensics. Unfortunately, the staff member who spotted them on the jetty picked them up so they're contaminated.'

'And is it definitely blood on the broken spectacles?'

'We won't know for sure until they get back to the lab, but I've seen them and I fear it could be.'

'What about her phone? You said it was in her purse.'

'It requires Rachel's fingerprint to unlock it so it will have to go to the techies. In the meantime, I've asked the manager to provide us with access to the hotel's surveillance system. There are cameras in the public areas, including the function rooms, the main entrance and some of the corridors. There are several in the garden, but unfortunately none of them covers the jetty, which can't be seen from the hotel because of various neatly trimmed hedges and low trees.'

'How many guests and staff are here?' James asked.

'Just over eighty guests and twenty staff. Guests include relatives, friends, colleagues of the bride and members of the hotel group's board of directors. Another thirty odd guests were due to attend the evening bash but they're either being contacted by the staff and told not to come or they're being turned away as and when they arrive. Most of the guests, including me and Sean, have rooms here courtesy of Greg Murphy.'

James blew out a breath. 'Then if Rachel does turn out to be a victim of foul play, we have an awful lot of suspects to choose from.'

Abbott nodded. 'I haven't managed to talk to many people yet, guv. In fact, all I've been able to do is respond to events. I've told the uniforms to try to encourage people to stay in the Garden Room so that we can talk to them, but a lot are insisting on taking part in the search. Others are too traumatised to do anything.'

'What about the divers?'

'I made the call and they're on their way.'

'Well, I think you've done all that could have been expected

23

CHAPTER FOUR

As soon as James stepped out onto the rear terrace, he realised why The Fells Hotel was such a popular venue for weddings. It provided an idyllic romantic backdrop for couples who wanted their day to be really special.

The landscaped gardens sloped gently towards the shoreline and the parts of the lake that he could see shimmered beneath a star-studded sky. Solar lanterns were spread among colourful herbaceous borders and along the pathways that criss-crossed the frost-covered lawns, lending an ethereal glow to the scene.

'There's a rear entrance to the grounds through the perimeter fence beyond that line of trees,' Abbott said, pointing to the right of them. 'It provides access to the hotel from a field that's used as an overflow car park on occasions when the place is really busy, such as now. The manager told me that it isn't covered by CCTV, but it is manned by a member of staff.'

'Then we need to establish whether or not it was left

unattended at any point during the reception,' James said. 'Are there any other entry points?'

'Only via the lake and the shoreline,' Abbott replied. 'Guests occasionally arrive by boat and disembark at the jetty.'

The hotel was positioned about two hundred yards back from the lake and a raw wind whipped at their faces as they walked towards it. Ahead of them and to either side, shadowy figures moved around, shining torches at the ground and into bushes.

'Rachel's friends and family are refusing to give up hope,' Abbott said. 'That's why they're determined to carry on with the search. But it does make it difficult for us to talk to them.'

'Do you know her well yourself?' James asked.

Abbott shook her head. 'I was expecting to meet her for the first time today, but I didn't get the chance.'

'Where does she live?'

'In Bowness with her parents. The family used to live in Kirkby Abbey apparently.'

'I've never heard their names mentioned.'

'I'm guessing it was quite a long time ago.'

'What about Libby and Greg?'

'Greg has a large house in Burnside. He was married once before, when he was in his twenties, but it only lasted a few years. According to Sean, Libby moved in with him about six months ago. Before that she lived in a rented flat in Kendal. And they've been together just over a year.'

'Tell me about Greg.'

Abbott shrugged. 'I'd never met him before today and he struck me as quite pleasant when we were introduced. He has a fearsome reputation as a hard-nosed businessman and boss, but Sean reckons that a lot of what he says and does is just for show. Greg's late father apparently drummed it into him that to be successful he needed to be ruthless.'

'Do we know what Rachel does for work?'

'I've been told she works at a café in Ambleside.'

'What about Libby?'

'She's MD of a property management company in Kendal. That was how she met Greg. He owns some cottages dotted about Cumbria that are let out to holidaymakers and Libby's firm looks after them.'

'Do you have any idea how wealthy the guy is?'

'I don't, but I gather his dad left him a couple of million in cash as well as the hotels and other properties.'

James was about to ask another question but got distracted as the path veered between two large bushes and more of the lake came into view.

The jetty lay directly in front of them beyond a small group of people that included two uniformed officers. It stretched about twenty yards out into the lake and looked to be eight or nine feet wide. It was supported by thick posts that poked up six or so inches through the wooden decking. Two forensic officers in white protective suits were on their knees examining one of the posts. James could see the scene clearly because a portable lamp had been set up on a stand to shed light on it for the forensics team.

James stopped walking and looked around to get his bearings. He saw that the shoreline here was low down and tucked behind a few trees and high mounds of shrubbery. It was why he hadn't seen the jetty before reaching this point, and it meant that if Rachel had got into trouble while standing on

27

it the other guests wouldn't necessarily have seen or heard anything.

He noted that more police officers were searching the shoreline on both sides of the jetty, some shining torches out onto the surface of the lake, looking for a floating body or any more of Rachel's belongings. They were keeping their voices low but that did nothing to mask the sense of urgency in their hushed tones.

'This is almost surreal,' James commented. 'What a way for a wedding to end.'

'I keep thinking she'll appear out of nowhere and accuse us all of overreacting,' Abbott responded. 'But in my heart, I know that's not going to happen.'

Gut instinct told James that she was right. Things were not looking good. And the questions were already piling up. Did Rachel have an accident or was she attacked? Did she come down to the jetty by herself or with someone? Did any of the wedding guests know what had happened to her but weren't saying? And was it possible that she would never turn up either dead or alive?

He started walking again, heading towards the jetty, and was glad to see someone had strung police tape between the first two posts to prevent unauthorised entry. Abbott stayed by his side and he couldn't help but feel sorry for her. This wasn't how she had envisaged the day panning out and he suspected that this might be a difficult case given she'd likely met – maybe even started to like – most of the guests who were now suspects. He would have to be mindful of the fact during the ongoing investigation.

As they drew closer to the group in front of the jetty,

Abbott said, 'I've just realised that the tall guy in the winter coat who's talking to the two uniforms is Greg Murphy. The woman next to him is Miss Cornwall, the hotel manager.'

Murphy towered above the others and he was the one doing the talking, his voice loud and strident as he complained about there not being enough officers. When he suddenly spotted Abbott approaching, he stopped speaking and jabbed an accusing finger at her.

'You told me that Rachel's disappearance would be taken seriously,' he said. 'But if that's the case, then why are there so few of you here?'

Abbott was about to respond but James beat her to it.

'More patrols are on their way, Mr Murphy, and I can assure you that we are taking this extremely seriously,' he said. 'I promise we'll do everything in our power to find your sister-in-law.'

Murphy broke away from the group and stood in front of James.

'And who might you be?' he asked.

'I'm Detective Inspector James Walker and I'll be the senior investigating officer on this case. I've just arrived and DC Abbott has been explaining to me what has happened. I can appreciate you're anxious and worried, but it takes time for a full-scale search to be organised.'

Murphy squeezed his lips together and dragged in a sharp breath.

'But she's already been missing for almost three hours,' he replied, and James noticed a trace of a Scottish accent tugging at his vowels. 'It seems bloody obvious that she's fallen into the lake, which, given the state she was in, is hardly a surprise.

You probably need to bring in boats and divers, not just a few plods to traipse around the grounds.'

'A search and rescue team will be here shortly, Mr Murphy,' James said. 'And we won't stop looking until we find her. For now, could you clarify what you meant about Rachel being "in a state" before she went missing?'

'I assumed you knew that she'd had a lot to drink, even for her. It's why she stormed out of the reception after Libby confronted her about it. We didn't want her to get drunk because as maid-of-honour she was supposed to make a speech and offer up a toast.'

James recalled what Abbott had said about seeing the two sisters having a conversation at the bar not long after the incident in the corridor involving Rachel and the bearded man.

'I know that Rachel is single, Mr Murphy,' James said. 'But she was seen coming out of her room with a man at some point during the reception. He spoke Italian and has a beard. Can you tell me who he is? We'd like to talk to him.'

Murphy shook his head. 'Your colleague there has already asked me that. As far as I know Rachel didn't invite any blokes and there were no bearded Italians on the seating plan. But you should ask Libby. She might know who he is. And check with Erika Chan. She's our wedding coordinator and was responsible for arranging everything.'

'I intend to speak to them when I go back into the hotel,' James said. 'I assume that's where they are?'

Karen Cornwall stepped up beside her boss and answered for him.

'Libby and her parents are together in the bridal suite,' she said. 'We thought it best if they waited for news there. I'll take you there if you like, Inspector. I'm the manager, Karen Cornwall.'

She was an attractive middle-aged woman with delicate features and black hair tied up in a bun.

'That's kind of you, Miss Cornwall,' James said. 'But first I need to spend a few minutes here assessing the situation. And I really think it would be best if you, Mr Murphy and the guests in the grounds return to the hotel so that it will be easier for my officers to carry out our interviews.'

James expected Murphy to object, but he didn't. Instead, he gave a resigned nod and said, 'I suppose that makes sense. It's time I got everyone together and brought them up to date. Karen can stay here to answer any questions you have and she can show you up to the bridal suite when you're ready.'

He strode off then with his hands thrust deep into his coat pockets.

'Mr Murphy is finding it hard to come to terms with what's going on,' Miss Cornwall said. 'This really shouldn't be happening on his wedding day and in his own hotel. It's a complete nightmare for him and everyone else.'

'Do you have any idea what might have happened to Rachel?' James asked her.

A shake of the head. 'I can only think that perhaps she came down here to sober up after being confronted by her sister. It's a pretty secluded spot and on cold nights like this you can be guaranteed some privacy.'

'Did you happen to see her during the reception?'

'No I did not. As the manager it's my job to make sure that things run smoothly while remaining in the background.

I spent most of the afternoon in my office and in the reception area.'

'I understand my colleague has told you that we'd like to see the footage from all the CCTV cameras,' James said. 'And we'll need to talk to the staff and get guests to let us see photos they've taken on their mobile phones.'

'I'm sure that everyone will be happy to cooperate, Inspector. And I'll do my best to provide whatever information and assistance you need.'

'Your boss mentioned the wedding coordinator, Erika Chan. I'd like to speak to her as well.'

'That can certainly be arranged.'

As she was speaking, a white-suited figure walking towards them seized his attention. He could see that it was Tony Coppell, the chief forensic officer, and realised Tony had been one of the pair who'd been kneeling on the jetty.

James thanked the hotel manager and then quickly stepped around her.

'I was about to come and look for you, Tony,' he said as Coppell approached. 'Have you got anything for me?'

'Indeed, I have,' Coppell replied. 'But it's not something you're going to want to hear.'

CHAPTER FIVE

Tony Coppell was one of Cumbria's most respected forensic officers. He was in his mid-fifties and had been doing the job for over twenty years.

He'd once told James that he relished the challenge that faced him at the scene of virtually every crime or serious incident he attended. No doubt that was why he excelled at what he did.

'This is a strange one,' he said as he led James and Abbott down towards the jetty. 'Granted, we haven't been here very long, but it's already obvious to me that it's not going to be straightforward.'

They stopped in front of the tape that stretched between the two posts at the start of the jetty.

'I'd rather you didn't step onto it,' Coppell said. 'There's already been too much contamination. First, there was the staff member who found and picked up the poor woman's purse and broken glasses. Then God only knows how many more people trampled on pieces of potential evidence before we got here.'

'What can you tell us, Tony?' James asked.

'Well, to begin with, there's no sign of the woman, but I very much fear that she's in the water,' he replied. 'You probably know that it's not uncommon for people to fall or be pushed from jetties such as these and when the water is as cold as it is now the shock to the system can be deadly in itself. Bodies can then get snagged on rocks and timber supports if they don't drift away from the shore. I've dealt with numerous similar cases all over the Lake District.'

'Have you come up with a theory as to what might have happened here?' This from Abbott.

Coppell shook his head. 'Like I said, it isn't straightforward, so let me explain.' He pointed to a spot about ten feet along the jetty. 'That's roughly where the purse and glasses were found, according to the staffer who spotted them. And having examined the glasses myself I do believe that there are traces of blood on the cracked lens and one of the temples.'

He then pointed towards the far end of the jetty where his colleague was still on all fours examining the decking. 'A few minutes ago, we discovered a significant amount of blood on top of the last post on the right and there are several drops on the wooden slats around it.'

'So do you think she could have fallen on it?' James said.

'I do. It has a sharp, splintered top and if it was her head that struck it, then it might have been hard enough to have rendered her unconscious or even killed her outright.'

Now James couldn't help but think the worst. From where he stood the jetty posts looked like thick black spikes jutting up through the decking. It was easy to imagine that falling on one could prove fatal.

'But if that's what happened then why were her glasses so far away from there?' Abbott asked.

Coppell nodded. 'That's a good point. One possible explanation is that she suffered a blow to the face or head before she hit the post. If so, the question is how did she get from this end of the jetty to the other? Was it under her own steam or was she dragged there and pushed onto the post before being shoved into the water?'

James felt the blood stir inside him, a hot flush through his veins. The more he learned about this case the more unsettling it became. And that was before they'd even drawn up a list of potential suspects.

'If our victim is in the water then she might well have sunk to the bottom by now,' Coppell said. 'But the lake is quite shallow at this point so it shouldn't take the divers long to locate her. However, I expect she would have floated for a while and could have drifted out or some way along the shoreline. The sooner a proper search can get under way the better.'

'Well, keep me posted on any further developments,' James told him. 'I need to go and talk to the sister and parents and try to get to the bottom of why she came down here during the reception and who might have been with her.'

As Coppell stepped back over the police tape onto the jetty, James asked Abbott to check on the progress of the search and rescue team and to find out if more officers could be sent to the hotel.

'I expect Control will tell you that resources are already

being stretched to breaking point,' he added. 'It is New Year's Eve, after all, and we're not far off midnight.'

Abbott took out her phone and started tapping at the screen as she followed James back to where the hotel manager was waiting.

By the time they re-entered the hotel, James had learned from Abbott that two additional patrols had already arrived and the search and rescue team were only minutes away. She was still waiting to hear if more officers could be made available.

It was less busy now in the reception area and one of the uniforms explained to them that most of the guests were gathered in the Garden Room where Greg Murphy was speaking to them.

'You go and let them know that I'll come and talk to them as soon as I've spoken to the family,' he told Abbott. 'I want to make it clear to them that we will need to speak to everyone individually and that as yet we're not sure what we're dealing with. They should be prepared to stay in the hotel until they've been granted permission to leave.'

He turned to Miss Cornwall. 'After you've shown me to the bridal suite, I'd like you to print off the details of all the guests and every member of staff. Did the wedding photographer come as part of the package?'

'Yes, he did. His name is Grant Fuller.'

'Then please arrange for him to show us all of his photos from the moment he started taking them. I'm hoping that along with the CCTV footage they'll help us to track Rachel Elliott's movements.'

James then spotted Dale Thomas, a uniformed sergeant

he'd worked with on many occasions. He called him over and told him in a hushed voice that the missing woman might well have been brutally attacked.

'We're dealing with a logistical nightmare here because there are so many people and some of them are likely to have consumed a fair amount of alcohol,' he said. 'It means that there's a strong chance that mistakes will be made and clues will be overlooked. So, make sure our people are fully alert to the possibility that if Rachel was the victim of an assault, then her attacker could be walking around in plain sight. I want them to pounce on anyone behaving suspiciously, whether it be a guest or a member of staff.

'I'm going to speak to Rachel's immediate family and afterwards I intend to call a team briefing. We have to be on top of this before we're forced to allow people to leave the hotel and go home,' he added.

'Leave it with me,' the sergeant responded. 'I'll spread the word and get things organised.'

James turned back to Karen Cornwall and apologised for keeping her waiting.

'Before we go up to the suite there are a couple of questions that I need to ask you. First, do you have any staff members who have a beard and could be Italian?'

She gave an emphatic shake of the head. 'No, we don't. We have one with a moustache but he's not in today.'

'Okay, now a second question. Do you happen to know the names of Rachel's parents?'

She nodded. 'Fraser and Denise Elliott.'

'Thank you. Let's go.'

CHAPTER SIX

James did his best to mentally prepare himself as he approached the hotel's bridal suite on the top floor, but he wasn't able to stop his stomach from churning with dread.

He felt so sorry for Rachel Elliott's sister and parents. This was supposed to have been one of the happiest days of their lives but instead they were bracing themselves for news that would break their hearts.

There was a smartly dressed man standing in the corridor outside the suite and Miss Cornwall introduced him as George Ross, the assistant manager.

'Mr Murphy asked me to remain here until he returns,' he explained. 'He wants someone to be on hand to get them anything they might need.'

'Is it just the three of them?' James asked.

'No. About ten minutes ago they were joined by an elderly lady who's a close family friend.'

'Aren't there any police officers with them?'

'There was to begin with, but they insisted he go and take part in the search.'

James told Miss Cornwall that he'd catch up with her when he was back downstairs and then knocked lightly on the door rather than ringing the bell. A voice from inside told him it wasn't locked.

He stepped into an elegant lounge area with two sofas, a coffee table, large TV and a small cocktail bar.

A knot tightened in his throat as three pairs of eyes stared up at him expectantly.

'I'm Detective Inspector James Walker,' he said. 'I arrived a short time ago and I'd like to ask some questions. Would that be all right?'

A couple he assumed to be Rachel's parents, Fraser and Denise Elliott, sat on one of the sofas and a woman who looked to be in her seventies sat on the other. All three appeared to be totally shell-shocked. There was no sign of Rachel's sister Libby.

'Has our daughter been found yet?' Fraser said, a faint note of optimism in his voice.

James closed the door behind him and shook his head. 'She's still unaccounted for but more officers have arrived and the search is being stepped up.'

Removing his overcoat, James asked the elderly lady if she was a family member.

'That's how I've always regarded myself,' she answered, with tears in her eyes. 'I used to be employed as a nanny to Rachel and Libby. My name is Claire, Claire Prescott, and I can't believe that this is happening.'

'Would you mind if I sit next to you?'

'Of course not,' she said, moving sideways slightly to make more room.

She had grey hair and a stocky frame, and her rheumy eyes nestled in tired folds of pale skin. Beside her, resting against the edge of the sofa, was a walking stick.

'I'm Fraser and this is my wife, Denise,' Rachel's father said, and then nodded towards a closed door. 'Our other daughter, Libby, is lying on the bed through there. She's a mess, but I can go and get her. I'm sure she'll want to hear what you've got to say.'

'There's no hurry,' James said as he sat down. 'It probably makes sense to ask you some questions first.'

Denise was clutching a crumpled hanky in her left hand and grasping her husband's knee with the other. She had a thin, angular face and pinched features, and James put her in her early sixties.

Her husband was about the same age and his blue suit looked too big on his small frame.

'If you've come to tell us that they've found Rachel's purse and glasses, we already know,' Denise said. 'But that was a while ago now. Have there been any further developments?'

'Not as yet, Mrs Elliott.' James decided that now wasn't the time to mention the blood found on the jetty post and boards.

She aimed unblinking eyes at him and he saw tears running down both her cheeks.

'Please be honest with us, Inspector. Do you think our baby is still alive?'

James cleared his throat before speaking. 'Given the circumstances, I really can't be sure, Mrs Elliott. But I must urge you not to lose hope. It's clear that your daughter was involved in some kind of incident on the jetty and it seems likely that she suffered an injury. But it's quite possible that it wasn't serious and she walked out of the hotel grounds afterwards through the rear gate or along the shoreline.'

'That's not what most people think,' Denise replied. 'Even Greg is convinced that she must be in the lake.'

Denise closed her eyes then and drew in a tremulous breath.

'We'll just have to keep praying then,' she said, her voice cracking as she spoke.

Her husband put an arm around her shoulders and pulled her closer to him.

'Do you know if Rachel was seen on the jetty or walking towards it during the reception?' Claire Prescott asked. 'Or even what possessed her to go down there when everyone else had come back into the hotel because it was so cold and getting dark?'

'As far as I know nobody has come forward to say that they saw her,' James answered. 'But Mr Murphy seems to think that she might have gone there to sober up after her sister spoke to her about her drinking.'

A look passed between Claire and Fraser and James decided to seize on it.

'Mr Murphy also gave me the impression that your daughter has a drink problem, Mr Elliott. Is that true?'

There was a long pause before Fraser spoke.

'It's not a problem as such,' he said. 'But she does consume more alcohol than is good for her when she's stressed.'

'And was she feeling stressed today?'

41

Fraser nodded. 'It was partly because she was uncomfortable being the maid-of-honour. It wasn't something she'd been looking forward to.'

'So why did she do it?'

'Because Libby insisted. They argued about it for weeks and Rachel eventually caved.'

'Was there a reason she didn't want to step into the role?'

Fraser bit his lip, trying to control the emotion in his voice.

'It's a long story,' he said, 'but essentially it was because today was always going to be a painful experience for her. You see, Rachel was supposed to get married in this very hotel just ten months ago, but the toerag she was engaged to dumped her just weeks before they were meant to walk down the aisle. Denise and I tried to persuade Libby to change the venue to one of Greg's other hotels, but he said they were all fully booked because it was New Year's Eve, which was when he wanted it to happen, and he wasn't prepared to waste money on a place he didn't own.'

'I can see why Rachel might have found it quite difficult,' James said. 'Did it put a strain on her relationship with Libby?'

'No more than usual,' Fraser said. 'They love each other dearly but they're like chalk and cheese. Libby is the outgoing one and has done so well for herself. She went to university whereas Rachel struggled academically and left school at sixteen. Libby now has a highly paid job in a property management company and Rachel feels like a failure because she works in a café and lives with us. So, naturally, they fall out from time to time, just as most sisters do.'

James then asked about the man Rachel was going to marry ten months ago.

'His name is Douglas Hannigan,' Fraser told him. 'You may have heard of him because he got involved in some scandal involving drugs. Rachel was heartbroken when he ended it. And when Libby started dating a local rich guy it was like rubbing salt into her sister's wounds, especially when she announced they were getting married here.'

'And what about Rachel's situation now? Is she dating anyone?'

'She did tell us a few weeks ago that she'd met someone and it must have been going well because she's seemed a lot happier lately. And she spent nights away from home so presumably she was staying with him. But, as usual, she kept the details of her love life to herself and she didn't like us asking questions about it.'

James brought up the subject of the bearded man Abbott had seen coming out of Rachel's room.

'The guest who spotted him told me it looked as though the pair of them had argued and he was rushing off,' James said. 'Rachel followed him down the stairs but when the same guest saw her in the bar soon after, he wasn't with her.'

'Well, that's news to us,' Fraser said. 'We don't know who the hell he is.'

'He was heard speaking Italian.'

Alarm suddenly shivered behind Fraser's eyes. 'Is it possible that this man went with her to the jetty and then harmed her?'

'We don't know, Mr Elliott,' James said. 'We're still trying to find him and I was hoping you'd be able to help us.'

'I wish we could, but it's a mystery, just like Rachel's disappearance.'

James then asked each of them if they could recall when they last saw Rachel.

'I can remember exactly,' Fraser said. 'I took a photo on my phone of my two daughters and Denise standing together. It was about five minutes after the ceremony itself had ended and the reception was about to start.'

'May I see the picture?' James asked him.

The photo showed three smiling women and James was surprised to see that Rachel and Libby bore no resemblance to each other. Libby was tall and slim and Rachel was perhaps a foot shorter and carried much more weight. She was wearing her glasses and clutching a small pink purse in her hands, presumably the one found on the jetty.

'I just hope that's not the last picture I'll ever take of our two daughters together,' Fraser said, tears shimmering in his eyes.

James started to ask another question, but at that moment the door to the bedroom was thrown open and Libby Elliott, still wearing her bridal gown, stepped into the room.

'I heard voices but I didn't realise that someone else was here,' she said, glancing at James. 'Please tell me that my little sister has turned up.'

CHAPTER SEVEN

James felt his throat thicken as he broke the news to Libby that her sister was still missing. She clamped her top lip between her teeth and shook her head as she walked further into the room.

'And who are you?' she asked, her voice small and gravelly.

James stood. 'I'm Detective Inspector Walker of the Cumbria Constabulary. Your parents were just telling me about Rachel. While the search for her is continuing I'm trying to find out what led her down to the jetty earlier and whether she was with anyone.'

'Well, it's a mystery to me,' she replied. 'I just can't help thinking that something horrible has happened to her. And if she did fall into the lake then we might not see her again.'

She stood in the middle of the room, her eyes puffy from crying, and James could see the emotions chasing across her face: shock, confusion, uncertainty.

She started to blink back more tears so he invited her to

take his place on the sofa next to Claire. As soon as she sat down her former nanny placed an arm around her shoulders, but that didn't stop the tears from flowing.

'I really do feel for you and your family, Mrs Murphy,' James said. 'What you're all going through is truly horrendous, but I want you to know that we're doing everything we can to find Rachel. And at this stage we shouldn't assume she's in the lake.'

'Then where else would she be?' Libby said as she looked up at him with pleading eyes. 'Surely she would have turned up by now if she's okay. And if she's still in the hotel somebody must have seen her since the place is full to bursting.'

'I understand you had a conversation with her at the bar after the marriage ceremony,' James said.

She nodded. 'It was obvious to everyone that she was taking a bit too much advantage of the open bar, probably because she was nervous. She was supposed to make a speech at the meal – one I wrote for her – but she would have been in no fit state if she'd continued drinking. I felt I had to intervene.'

'What did you say to her?'

'I hadn't seen her for a while because as soon as the formal photos were taken in the garden, she said she had to go up to her room to get something. It was Greg who spotted her at the bar and he wasn't happy. He told me to have a word with her. But as soon as I approached her, I sensed that she was upset over something because her eyes were red and it looked as though she'd been crying. I asked her what was wrong and she told me to mind my own business. Then I asked her to hold off on the booze until the evening do and she told me to leave her alone and stormed off. I didn't follow because I knew that if I did, she'd create a scene. I just hoped she'd go off somewhere to cool off and then show up in the hall. But now I can't help but feel guilty for not staying with her.'

'And was that the last time you saw her?'

Another nod. 'I don't know where she went after that, but when she didn't take her seat at the top table for the meal, I took it to mean that she'd either got legless and passed out or was hiding somewhere to get at me.'

'And why would she have wanted to get at you?'

'Well, I'm sure my parents have already told you that she wasn't happy that I was getting married here in the hotel and that she didn't want to be my maid-of-honour. And it gives me no pleasure to tell you that my sister has always felt hard done by. She's said more than once that she resents the fact that good things always seem to happen to me and not to her.'

People often thought of sibling rivalry as a childhood phenomenon, but James knew that adult sibling envy was just as common – and far more dangerous. It could bring out the worst in people and sour relationships to the point where one couldn't bear the idea of their sibling being successful or even happy.

'Are you aware that shortly before you talked to Libby in the bar she'd been in her room with a man?' James asked Libby. 'We believe they'd had an argument, which might account for why she appeared upset.'

Libby cocked her head on one side and frowned. 'No, I wasn't aware of that. Who was he?'

'We're still trying to find out. We know he has a beard and spoke Italian.'

Her frown deepened. 'We didn't invite any bearded Italians to the wedding. Could he be one of the staff?'

'Not according to the manager. None of her team has a beard.'

Libby raised a finger as though a thought had occurred to her. 'Actually, Rachel did ask me a few days ago if she could invite another friend. She'd already invited two of her mates who I've also known for years. But we'd had a couple of people pull out at the last minute so I said no problem. It was the least I could do since she'd finally agreed to be my maid-of-honour.'

'Did she give you a name?'

'I asked her and she said she hadn't decided who it would be, or if it was a guy or a girl.'

James turned his attention back to the parents who'd been listening intently to their daughter. Their faces were as grey as headstones and sheer terror was carved into their features.

'I think it's best if you all remain here for the time being,' he said. 'I'll make sure you're the first to know if there are any developments.'

'But shouldn't we be out there looking for our daughter along with everyone else?' Fraser said.

James shook his head. 'We're encouraging the guests to come in from the grounds, Mr Elliott. We need to limit the number of people outside so that the search effort isn't hampered in any way.'

'Does that mean you'll be looking in the lake?' Denise said.

'Of course, as well as along the shoreline and the land on either side of the hotel. You see, we have to consider the possibility that even if Rachel was involved in an incident on the jetty, she may well have wandered back into the garden or even into the overflow car park.'

James felt it was important to give them at least a shred of hope to cling to while their daughter's whereabouts were still unknown. Without it, the waiting would be even more unbearable.

Before leaving the suite James told them he would arrange for an officer to wait outside in the corridor.

'If you need to contact me for any reason then just ask the officer and they'll sort it,' he said. 'I'll get back to you with news as soon as possible.'

The reception area was almost deserted now save for a few uniforms. He instructed one of them to go upstairs and stand outside the bridal suite along with the assistant manager.

Handing the officer his card, he said, 'Call me on my mobile if you need to talk to me.'

He'd intended his next stop to be the Garden Room, where he assumed Greg Murphy was still speaking to his staff and guests, but instead he decided to go outside first to see if there had been any developments.

A door beyond the reception desk provided access to the terrace, which was being warmed by a bunch of pyramid gas heaters. But when he stepped onto the path beyond it, he noticed that the wind had picked up and was swirling and howling around him.

He was glad to see that more uniforms were searching the grounds now and there were fewer guests outside than there had been earlier. When he got to the jetty nothing much had changed. The SOCOs were still doing their best to gather evidence, but Tony Coppell informed him that no new clues had been found.

'It's hard going, James,' he said. 'I don't think we'll get to the bottom of what happened here until our missing bridesmaid either turns up alive and well or we find her body.'

It was a grim prognosis and it prompted James to shake his head in despair. He knew that the longer Rachel Elliott remained missing the more likely it was that her family would never see her again.

He told Coppell that he had spoken to her parents and sister and that he would now go and address the staff and guests.

'I'll let you know if and when we find something,' Coppell said.

As James stepped back inside the hotel his phone rang and he recognised the number as belonging to Detective Sergeant Phil Stevens, his second in command at Kendal HQ.

'I've only just been informed about what's going on up at Windermere, guv,' he said. 'Are you at the hotel now?'

'I am, along with a team who are still searching for the missing woman. Where are you?'

'In Carlisle. We came to spend New Year's Eve with the wife's brother and his family. I can't drive down tonight because I've had too much to drink but I can be there as early as possible in the morning.'

'I'd rather you went straight to the office,' James said. 'Get things organised there. DC Abbott is with me.'

'I remember her telling me that she was going to the wedding. How is she?'

'A bit shaken, but she's getting on with the job.'

'And how are things looking? I've heard about the blood found on the jetty.'

James updated him and said that he should get as much sleep as possible before setting out from Carlisle.

'I'm guessing that quite a few of the troops will have hang-overs tomorrow and I don't want you to be one of them,' he added.

After hanging up, James walked into the reception area where he came across Karen Cornwall heading towards her office.

'I'm just on my way to print off the guest and staff details for you,' she said. 'How are Rachel's parents?'

'Worried sick,' he told her. 'This is extremely hard for them.'

'I take it there's no news on Rachel?'

'Not as yet. Have you been in the Garden Room?'

She nodded. 'We're serving tea and coffee and Greg has been telling the guests that they should either stay there or return to their rooms.'

'I intend to go and have a word with them. Then I'd like to touch base with the wedding coordinator and photographer.'

'They're both in the Garden Room and they already know that you want to speak to them.'

'That's great. I'll talk to you again soon.'

James was approaching the Garden Room when he saw DC Abbott walking towards him along the corridor.

'I was just coming to find you, guv,' she said. 'The guests are all very anxious to know what's happening. Some are insisting that they should be allowed to go home.'

'Well, that's not going to be possible just yet,' James replied. 'There's still nothing to indicate that—'

He was interrupted by the ringing of his phone. This time it was Coppell on the line.

'What is it, Tony?' he asked.

'You need to come straight back down here, James,' he said. 'Something has just been spotted out on the lake. And they think it's a body.'

CHAPTER EIGHT

'That was Coppell,' James said to Abbott as he shoved his phone back into his pocket. 'There's been a sighting of something in the lake. It means the guests will have to wait.'

Her face tightened. 'Oh hell. It's what I've been dreading. Look, do you mind if I go to my room and change? Not only do I feel stupid prancing around in a dress and high-heels, but it's freezing out there.'

He grinned. 'Of course not. I'll meet you down by the lake.'

His whole body felt tight with tension as he hurried across the garden. When he neared the jetty the scene was very different to how it had been just a short while earlier.

The atmosphere was now electric, and he could almost feel the sparks. There were quite a few more officers, some of them in reflective yellow jackets, and the air was filled with raised voices and the crackle of police radios.

He could see what was going on before he reached the

shoreline as spotlights were pointing at a small vessel in the lake about fifty yards out from the end of the jetty.

'It's a warden patrol boat,' a uniformed officer informed him. 'It got here just as one of the lights picked up something floating out there. The crew have confirmed by radio in the last few minutes that it's a woman's body and it's remained afloat because it's caught between the branches of a couple of sunken trees. They're liaising with our own diving team on how best to bring her ashore.'

The news was like a punch in the gut to James even though it was what he had been expecting. His mind flashed on an image of Rachel's parents and sister waiting in the bridal suite. It was going to be his job to tell them and although he'd broken such horrendous news countless times it never got any easier and the thought of it filled him with dread.

He dragged in a breath and told the officer to make sure that the hotel grounds were cleared of all civilians.

Then, as he stared out over the lake, he saw a police dinghy arrive on the scene. Thanks to the searchlights he was also able to make out a small, bright shape bobbing up and down on the water between the two vessels.

He was so focused on what was happening that he wasn't aware that Tony Coppell had sidled up beside him until the SOCO spoke.

'I've already been on to Control and requested they send a forensic pathologist right away,' he said. 'You'll be glad to hear that Pam is on call tonight.'

Many considered Dr Pam Flint to be the best forensic pathologist in the north and James had a good working relationship with her.

'At least that's one piece of good news,' he said.

They both knew it wouldn't be long before the body was brought ashore. And there was no doubt in their minds that it would be that of Rachel Elliott.

'It's fortunate for us that she drifted into those submerged trees,' Coppell said. 'There are a few of them in this part of the lake apparently.'

Around them the night felt heavy and subdued. James checked his watch and was surprised to see that it was eleven o'clock already. He couldn't believe how quickly the time had passed. Just one more hour until the country welcomed the new year and celebrations reached a crescendo.

But one thing James knew for certain was that here at The Fells Hotel there would be no kissing and cheering and the guests would not be bellowing out the words to *Auld Lang Syne*.

DC Abbott arrived in time to see the police dinghy approaching the bank. She was now wearing a heavy waterproof coat over a polo sweater and jeans and looked much more comfortable.

'They're just bringing the body in,' James told her. 'Are you sure you want to be here?'

She nodded. 'I'm fine, guv, honestly. Sure, I was one of the wedding guests and saw Rachel earlier, but I didn't know her or the family so I can remain detached.'

'What about Sean? Is he all right?'

'I just spoke to him and he's doing okay. He's in the Garden Room with the other guests and on hand to help anyone who might need a paramedic.'

Another twenty minutes passed before the dinghy reached

the shore and the divers in wet suits stepped into the water and carried out the delicate task of lifting the body out. It was placed on a plastic sheet that had been laid out on the grass.

As soon as James stepped up to it, he saw that it was indeed Rachel Elliott. At the same time, Abbott caught her breath beside him and said, 'There's no question it's her, guv.'

Rachel was on her back and beneath a white cardigan her pink maid-of-honour dress clung to her frame like an extra skin. Her face was frozen in a fearful grimace and even from a distance James could see the damage that had been inflicted on it.

Coppell was the first to kneel next to the body for a close look. He moved her head to check the back of it and examined her neck and bare arms. It wouldn't be up to him to determine cause of death, but his preliminary findings would give James an idea of what they were dealing with.

After a minute, Coppell invited James to join him on the ground and pointed to two facial wounds that Rachel had sustained. One was just below her left eye, a deep gash about two inches wide.

'She was found floating on her back so it's unlikely it was caused by any of the tree branches,' he said. 'The pathologist will provide you with a more accurate assessment, but experience tells me that it's from a sharp blow to the face that was delivered while she was on the jetty, and that was when her spectacles were broken.'

He then pointed to a huge, dark bruise in the middle of her forehead.

'This clearly indicates that she was attacked more than

once and with a great deal of force,' he went on. 'But I very much doubt that either blow would have been hard enough to have killed her.'

'Then what did?' James said.

Coppell leaned forward and tilted Rachel's head to one side, then moved her wet hair so that James could see a large lump behind her ear with a gaping hole in it.

'I reckon that this was the fatal wound, and that it was caused when she fell or was pushed onto the sharp edge of the jetty post,' he said. 'In all probability she was dead before she hit the water. However, it's possible she was still alive but unconscious and then left to drown.'

But that wasn't the end of it. Coppell then showed James several more bruises on Rachel's right arm.

'I've seen enough of these in my time,' he said. 'And I suspect you have too.'

James nodded. 'They look like defensive bruises from where she raised her arms to try to protect her face.'

'Precisely.'

James exhaled a long breath and felt a cold shiver run down his spine.

'There's no doubt in my mind now that Rachel Elliott's death wasn't the result of an accident or suicide,' he said. 'There's enough evidence to suggest that she was murdered. But did she know her attacker or was it the work of a stranger?'

CHAPTER NINE

James hauled himself to his feet and turned to DC Abbott. She was staring down at the body, her expression one of shock.

'Did you hear that?' James asked her.

'Every bloody word,' she replied, her voice husky with emotion. 'I can't believe that only hours ago I saw her walking down the aisle with the bridesmaids. And when this was being done to her, I was inside the hotel swigging back the booze with everyone else. It's hard not to feel bad about that.'

'Don't even go there, Jessica,' James said. 'You can't blame yourself for not stopping something that you didn't know was happening.'

'I just wish I'd spoken to her after I saw her hurrying after the bloke with the beard. She might have opened up to me and maybe I could have said or done something that would have changed what turned out to be a tragic course of events.'

James shook his head. 'Come off it, Jessica. There's no

reason for you to feel in any way responsible. And the same goes for all the other wedding guests and hotel staff who had no idea that Rachel had come down to the jetty. Guilt lies with the assailant.'

She inhaled deeply. 'I know and I'm sorry. It's just so horrible to see her like this.'

'I can appreciate that, but this is now a murder investigation and I need you to be fully focused on it.'

She lifted her head, threw back her shoulders. 'You don't have to worry about that, guv. I won't rest until we've collared the bastard who did this. So, what's our next step?'

'I need to break the news to the family,' James said. 'I want you to go and tell the manager what's happened and enlist her help to get all the guests and staff into the Garden Room. When I come back down, I'll put them in the picture and explain why we need their full cooperation.'

He told Coppell to erect a tent over Rachel's body and to prepare for Dr Flint's arrival.

'It's all in hand, James,' Coppell said. 'You just concentrate on how to deliver the news that no family ever wants to hear.'

On the way back to the bridal suite James encountered Greg Murphy again, this time on the terrace. The hotel owner was involved in another spat with uniformed officers because they were stopping him from going down to the lake.

'This is my property and I demand to know what's going on,' he yelled at them in a loud, ill-tempered voice. 'If you want my help, then it makes no sense to keep me in the dark.'

Murphy switched his attention to James as soon as he saw him approaching.

'Is it true?' he shouted. 'Have they found Rachel's body in the lake? We can see the boats from here so we know that something has happened.'

James walked straight up to him and placed a hand on his shoulder.

'I was actually coming to find you, Mr Murphy,' he said. 'Would you accompany me up to the suite so that I can talk to your wife and her parents at the same time?'

The man's whole body stiffened and his eyes grew large like those of a startled animal. 'Please. I want to know now so that I can prepare myself. I'll be more helpful to them that way.'

James saw the sense in that and said, 'Well, I'm sorry to say it is true.'

'My God, this is t-terrible,' he stuttered. 'Libby will be devastated. Do you know if it was an accident, or did she kill herself?'

James saw no point in withholding information that would soon have to be shared with everyone.

'It pains me to have to tell you, Mr Murphy, but we strongly suspect that Rachel was murdered,' he said.

Murphy clenched his eyes shut as though struggling to process the news. It didn't surprise James. After all, not only had the man lost his new sister-in-law and had his wedding ruined, a murder had also been committed in the grounds of one of his hotels and that was bound to have a negative impact on the business once the news got out.

After a few seconds Murphy opened his eyes and let out a loud sigh.

'Let's go and get this over with,' he said, then quickly turned on his heels and headed into the hotel. James followed close behind and they both remained silent as they walked up the stairs together.

The vision of Rachel's body raged in James's mind as he arrived outside the bridal suite. The officer on the door informed him that only Rachel's parents and sister were inside, Claire Prescott having returned to her own room.

As soon as he stepped inside the look on his face and the fact that Murphy was with him gave the game away before James had even opened his mouth.

'It's her, isn't it?' Denise Elliott cried out. 'They've found our baby in the lake.'

As James started to speak, she let out a cry of anguish and then buried her face in the nape of her husband's neck.

At the same time, Murphy rushed across the room towards his new wife who was sitting on the sofa.

But Libby sprang to her feet before he reached her and her eyes flared with emotion as she stared at James.

'Please tell me it's not true, Inspector,' she said. 'Rachel can't be dead. She just can't be.'

James felt his jaw go tight, making it hard to speak.

'I'm really sorry, but yes, it is true,' he managed. 'Her body has been brought ashore and is now in the care of the forensic officers.'

Libby clapped her hands over her mouth as Murphy put his arms around her and pulled her against him. Her father, Fraser, spoke then, a tortured expression on his face.

'I want to go and see her,' he said. 'I need to be sure that it's not a mistake.'

'That won't be possible right now, Mr Elliott,' James replied.

'In time we will have to ask you to carry out a formal identification, but for now my team need space to do their jobs. It's standard procedure, I'm afraid.'

Fraser's face crumpled then and tears were pushed out by racking sobs.

'How did she die, Inspector?' Libby asked, her voice laced with despair.

James felt he had no option but to be totally honest with them all.

'The exact cause of death will have to be determined by the pathologist,' he said, 'but it appears that Rachel suffered several blows to the head and face from an unknown weapon before she fell or was pushed into the lake. We're therefore treating her death as murder.'

Libby's face froze and tears pooled in her eyes.

James went on to explain that all the guests and staff would be questioned before being allowed to leave the hotel.

'Statements will be taken and we're asking everyone to share with us any photographs they've taken on their mobile phones,' he said. 'We have to find out everything we can about Rachel and try to piece together her precise movements during the reception. Pictures taken by the official photographer and by guests will be a huge help in that respect along with the hotel security footage. I will also need to talk to each of you at some point.'

'What about the man you told us was seen coming out of her room?' Fraser asked. 'Shouldn't you be talking to him?'

'Yes, and we will as soon as he's been identified,' James answered. 'Hopefully, one or more of the guests will shed some light on who he is. And we'll also be checking to see if he left anything in Rachel's room.

'I have to ask, can any of you think of anyone who might have wanted to harm Rachel?'

Fraser shook his head. 'She had no enemies that we knew of. She was a sweet girl who tried her best to lead a happy and fulfilling life,' he said. 'But it was a struggle for her at times and she had more than her fair share of bad luck.'

He broke down again then and slumped back onto the sofa next to his wife, who buried her face in her hands.

James told them that a family liaison officer would arrive soon and suggested they stay together in the bridal suite for now.

'I'm sure Mr Murphy can arrange for you to get anything you might need,' he said.

As he stepped out into the corridor he glanced at his watch and saw that it was five minutes past midnight on Sunday morning.

New Year's Day had arrived but no one in The Fells Hotel was going to be celebrating.

CHAPTER TEN

As James was heading down to reception his mobile phone
rang again. He tugged it from his pocket and saw the call
was coming from the constabulary press office team at
Carleton Hall in Penrith.

'Detective Inspector Walker, hello, you need to know that
the media are now onto the story,' the woman on the other
end of the phone said. 'Someone tipped off the *Cumbria
Gazette* and they've been calling incessantly. So far, they only
know that a bridesmaid has gone missing, but I understand
from Control that there's been a significant development in
the last half an hour so I wanted to warn you that you may
have media arriving shortly.'

James had known it wouldn't be long before the press pack
descended like vultures and the usual media frenzy ensued.
After all, it was a belter of a story for the tabloids. The young
maid-of-honour at her sister's New Year's Eve wedding is

badly beaten on the venue's private jetty and ends up dead in Lake Windermere.

James quickly briefed the PR liaison on the details that were safe to be released. Hopefully, they could use the press attention to their advantage and prompt anyone who might know if Rachel had any enemies to come forward.

After hanging up, he noticed he had a text message from Annie.

Happy New Year from me and Bella. Please take care and let me know when you'll be coming home. Love you xxxx

A wave of sadness washed over him because he hadn't been able to spend this special night with his wife and new daughter. But there was no way he was going to feel sorry for himself given what had happened to Rachel Elliott and what her family were now going through.

He quickly tapped out a reply.

Happy New Year to you both. Sadly I won't be home any time soon. Sleep tight and I'll keep you posted. Love you both xxxx

DC Abbott and the hotel manager were waiting for him in reception when he arrived downstairs and he told them that he had broken the news of Rachel's death to her family and that Greg Murphy was with them in the bridal suite. He also mentioned that the media had got wind of what had happened and that reporters and TV camera crews would soon be turning up at the hotel.

To a clearly shocked Karen Cornwall, he said, 'As I mentioned, my officers need to view the surveillance footage and the pictures taken by the official photographer. Can you see to it that everything is made available so they can get started asap?'

'Of course, Inspector,' she said. 'And on my desk is the information you requested on all the guests and staff.'

'Thanks. I'd also like to speak to the staff member who was manning the rear gate that leads to the overflow car park during the reception. I want to know if he or she left the post for any reason and if so for how long.'

She nodded. 'That won't be a problem. His name is Neil Sherwood and he'll be in the Garden Room.'

'I also want the crime scene investigators to examine the room that Rachel was staying in, so no one else is allowed access to it. And your people need to cancel the reservations of those who have booked to stay here for the next few days. The property will effectively be locked down while the forensic work is carried out.'

James noticed a glint of sweat on the manager's brow as she scuttled away to get things done.

Turning back to Abbott, he said, 'Are they ready for me in the Garden Room?'

'They are,' she replied. 'But be prepared because they're all very much on edge and I think they must already suspect what you're going to tell them about Rachel.'

'That doesn't surprise me. I don't suppose you spotted any blokes with beards in there?'

'There are a couple, but not the man I saw with Rachel.'

'How many officers do we have here now?'

'Just over thirty, including two more detectives from Kendal. There are about a dozen in the Garden Room. Others are manning the front and rear gates while several are dotted about the grounds and car parks. More patrols are on their way.'

'That's good. We'll need them all if we're to get this investigation off to a solid start.'

He looked beyond her to the corridor that led to the Garden Room and felt a clutch of apprehension.

'Rachel's killer might be among the people waiting in there for me to come and speak to them,' he said.

'That thought has occurred to me as well, guv,' Abbott said.

'Come on then,' he said. 'We've kept them all waiting long enough.'

The whispered conversations and anxious faces were strikingly at odds with the bright and joyful decorations that greeted James when they stepped into the Garden Room and he was surprised at how quiet it was given that about seventy people were crammed inside.

A bar ran along one wall and there was an area with chairs and sofas, a circular dance floor, a small stage packed with DJ equipment and lots of glass tables surrounded by stools.

As he stood facing the guests in front of the stage and swallowed the saliva that had gathered in his throat, James pictured in his mind how loud and lively it would have been now if tragedy hadn't struck.

Most of the guests were seated or standing in front of him

on the dance floor. There appeared to be an equal number of men and women and several looked to be in their teens. James was pleased that there weren't any children present. The staff members in their hotel attire were gathered in front of the bar, and the police officers were standing either side of the entrance.

The room wasn't so large that James needed a microphone to make himself heard. But before speaking he raised an arm in the air to get everyone's attention and took a deep breath.

'I'm Detective Inspector Walker with the Cumbria Constabulary, and I'm the senior investigating officer here,' he said. 'I'm sorry you've had to wait for so long and that your movements have been somewhat restricted but it's been necessary to take certain measures in view of what has happened.'

'So what exactly has happened?' someone called out. 'We've been told that Rachel has been found dead. Is that true?'

'Unfortunately, it is,' James said. 'Her body was found a short time ago in the lake and we have reason to believe she was murdered while standing on the jetty.'

There were gasps all round and some shouted expletives. A couple of women burst into tears and one teenage girl dressed as a bridesmaid fell to her knees and wailed hysterically.

James felt a frisson of guilt even though he was convinced that being brutally honest with them from the off was the right approach to take, especially as it was the only time he would have them all together and be able to see them react with each other.

If Rachel's killer was among them then there was a small chance that they'd give themselves away with an awkward interaction, an out-of-place gesture, or by drawing attention to themselves in some other way.

'We don't believe that anyone else is presently at risk from whoever did this to Rachel,' James continued. 'And we're determined to find the perpetrator. As such, it's essential that you come forward now if any of you have any information that you think might help us as we don't yet know if Rachel knew her assailant or if it was someone who entered the grounds uninvited through the back gate or along the shoreline.'

'Does that mean that whoever did it to her could be here in this very room with us?' The question came from a middle-aged man in a suit.

James pursed his lips. 'We have to accept that it is a possibility, but let me stress again that I'm confident that no harm will come to anyone else.'

'Well let's hope you're right,' the man said.

'We will need to take statements from everyone – guests and staff members both – to determine where each of you was when the crime was committed,' he said. 'At the same time, we'll be reviewing the video footage from the hotel's surveillance cameras and all the photographs that have been taken. I would therefore ask you to share any pictures you have on your mobile phones with my officers and flag up any that include Rachel.'

He paused for a few moments to let it sink in and then carried on.

'Today was supposed to be a happy occasion and I completely understand how distressing this is for everyone. Please be assured that we'll be providing you with information on how to access support in the coming days. I suspect most of you knew Rachel and some of you were no doubt very close to her. Please bear with us as we try to get to the bottom of what happened to her. I know it's a lot to ask but we really do need your help and cooperation. And that means we will have to disturb you into the early hours as we take statements and ask questions. I'm afraid that in these unusual circumstances it can't be avoided.'

Questions started to come thick and fast from both guests and staff members then.

'How can you be sure that the rest of us are not going to be targeted?'

'Why would anyone want to hurt Rachel?'

'Shouldn't the hotel have better security?'

'When can we all go home?'

Most of the questions James couldn't or didn't want to answer so he focused on doing his best to assure everyone that they were safe. He then made a point of asking about the bearded man.

'We are also hoping one of you can help us in identifying a man who was seen with Rachel earlier this evening. He's a person of interest to us and is known to have a beard and an Italian accent. And just to put your minds at rest I can confirm that the individual in question is not among those men in this room who are sporting a beard.'

Several people immediately raised their hands.

The first – a woman in her twenties – claimed a man with a beard had sat next to her during the marriage ceremony. 'He told me his name was Carlo and that Rachel had invited him to the wedding,' she said. 'And he definitely had an accent.'

James then called on the second woman, who identified herself as wedding coordinator Erika Chan. A petite thirty-something with black hair pulled back in a tight braid, Erika told James, 'Rachel asked me to make a place available in the name of Carlo Salvi on a table at the wedding breakfast. She told me that Libby had okayed it so I went ahead and arranged it.'

The next person to speak up was a close friend of Rachel's and she revealed something that Rachel had told her in confidence over the phone the night before the wedding.

It clearly came as a surprise to most of the guests in the room, but James suspected that to Rachel's parents and sister it would come as a complete shock.

CHAPTER ELEVEN

Rachel's friend gave her name as Emily Straus and said she had known both sisters since they were at school together. She'd phoned Rachel the night before the wedding to check what time she needed to be at the hotel.

'She was very excited,' Emily told James when he took her to one side after she'd dropped her bombshell. 'I couldn't wait to talk to her about it but I knew it would have to wait until after the ceremony. Unfortunately, I never got the chance.'

James took out his notebook and pen and wrote down Emily's name, address and phone number.

'Now can you please repeat exactly what Rachel told you during your telephone conversation?' he asked her, pen at the ready. 'I need to make sure I've got it right.'

Emily stared up at him, her eyes fearful as the words tumbled out between quivering lips.

'She told me that she was going to surprise everyone at the wedding by announcing that she would soon be moving to Italy with her new boyfriend. She said he'd be there and we would all be able to meet him for the first time, including her family. I wasn't even aware that she'd been seeing someone! She said his name was Carlo and she told me that she was in love with him.'

'Did you mention this to anyone before now?'

She shook her head. 'She asked me not to, and I wouldn't be telling you if …' Emily lost it then and started sobbing. Thankfully, DC Abbott was on hand to put an arm around her.

'That's all for now, Miss Straus,' James said. 'Are you here with someone?'

'No. I came by myself. But I do have a room.'

'Then I suggest you go there and try to get some rest. You've been most helpful.'

Abbott signalled for one of the uniforms to accompany Emily to her room.

James then raised his voice to grab the attention of everyone else again.

'It's time for those of you who are staying here to return to your rooms,' he said. 'At some point in the coming hours you'll be visited by an officer who will take down your statement and ask you some questions. Those who are not staying here should make themselves known to one of my officers who will speak to you before you go home. The same applies to staff members. It's necessary for us to interview all the individuals who were on the premises when the attack on Rachel Elliott took place. But to make things quicker and more straightforward, family groups and couples can provide joint statements.'

As the guests started trooping forlornly out of the Garden Room, Erika Chan informed him that all but a couple of them had rooms to go to.

'Mr Murphy's offer of free accommodation was taken up by virtually everyone,' she said.

'Of course,' James said. 'I need to know – did you yourself speak to Rachel at any time during the day?'

'The only time I spoke to her was when she arrived with her sister and the other bridesmaids on Friday,' she said. 'I got them together in the lounge for a talk through of the schedule and then gave them a tour of the hotel.'

'And how did she seem then?'

'In pretty high spirits, as I recall. They all were. And I believe they all went to bed quite late after a few drinks in the bar. The next time I saw Rachel was when she walked down the aisle during the ceremony. After that, I don't recall seeing her at all. I think if she had spent much time in the Garden Room during the reception, I wouldn't have been able to miss her in that lovely pink dress she was wearing.'

'Thank you. Miss Cornwall has given us a list of guests and it would be useful if you could break it down into couples, families and singles for us.'

'The majority are here as couples who are friends and work colleagues of Mr and Mrs Murphy,' she said. 'There are a few families and I believe about fifteen people who came alone. Mr and Mrs Murphy decided they didn't want any children to attend, which is the reason that several people turned down invitations.'

'And as a matter of interest, who from Mr Murphy's family is here?'

'Sadly there's no one. You may know that Mr Murphy's father died fairly recently. His mother passed away some years ago and he has no siblings.'

A bald man in a light grey suit then came up and introduced himself to James.

'I'm Grant Fuller, the wedding photographer,' he said. 'Miss Cornwall has spoken to me, Inspector, and I can show you all the photographs I've taken when you're ready. I've had a look and there are quite a few of Rachel.'

'Where's your camera?'

'In Miss Cornwall's office. I've already transferred the photos to a USB stick so you can view them on the computer.'

'Then could you perhaps go and wait for me there? I'll be along shortly.'

As the photographer nodded and hurried away, James flipped open his notebook and started writing down a list of questions that he wanted answers to.

Can we pinpoint the exact time when Rachel was last seen?

Who is Carlo Salvi and where is he now?

Had the pair actually made plans for her to move to Italy with him?

Did they argue about it in her room and is that why she appeared upset and started drinking heavily?

And did they end up on the jetty together where the argument got out of hand and he attacked her before fleeing the hotel?

James was about to tell Abbott to pass on the name 'Carlo Salvi' to Control when he was approached by a young man in a staff uniform.

'My name is Mike Lynch and there's something I need to tell you, Inspector Walker,' he said.

'I'm listening, Mike,' James replied.

'During the reception I was collecting bottles and glasses that had been left in the garden. I was walking back towards the terrace when I heard voices and saw three people on a path that ran between some high bushes. They were standing between a couple of solar lamps so I was able to recognise two of them immediately as the bride and her sister,' he said. 'There was also a man I'd seen earlier but I don't know who he is.'

James's interest was immediately aroused because Libby had never mentioned being in the garden with Rachel.

'What time was this, Mr Lynch?'

'It must have been about half five.'

'Did you hear what they were saying to each other?' James asked him.

'I only heard the tail-end of the conversation because it was obvious that they were arguing and I didn't want to be accused of eavesdropping. So, I carried on walking.'

'What did you hear then?'

'Well, I saw and heard Ms Elliott – or rather, Mrs Murphy

– tell her sister that if she ruined everything, she would never forgive her.'

'And did her sister respond?'

'She did, and I can remember the exact words. She said, "Do you really think that bothers me?"'

CHAPTER TWELVE

Eager to quickly establish the identity of the man seen in the garden with Rachel and her sister, James asked Mike Lynch to accompany him to the manager's office so that he could view the pictures taken by the wedding photographer.

DC Abbott went with them and on the way, they bumped into her fiancé, Sean, who was hanging around the reception area.

'I don't envy you guys with this one,' Sean said. 'I still can't get my head around what has happened.'

James nodded. 'You and me both. I gather you're a friend of Greg Murphy?'

'That's right. We play golf together. He's a nice guy.'

'Then I might need to pick your brain a little later if that's okay.'

'Sure thing. Jessica can always reach me.' He turned to her then and added, 'I think it's best if I go to the room now. I

78

don't want to be in the way. I don't suppose you'll be coming up any time soon?'

'You must be joking,' she told him with a smile. 'You try to get some sleep.'

He smiled back. 'Now who's joking? My brain feels like it's on fire and my nerves are shot to pieces.'

They left him standing in reception and hurried to the manager's office. Karen Cornwall was with Grant Fuller and the first thing James did was explain why Mike Lynch was joining them.

She raised an eyebrow and asked him why he hadn't already mentioned it to her.

'It didn't really occur to me that it might mean anything, boss, until the detective here spelt things out to us,' he said. 'Then I thought it might be relevant to what's happened.'

'Well, let's hope the man you saw had his picture taken at some point,' she said.

James then told her that the bearded guy seen with Rachel was believed to be named Carlo Salvi.

'Do you know if he was registered here as a guest?'

She gave an emphatic shake of the head. 'I've been through the list several times and his name's most definitely not on there.'

'Then the plan must have been for him to sleep in Rachel's room.'

Miss Cornwall nodded. 'Would you like me to get you all something to drink?'

'Abbott and I could both do with a caffeine fix,' James told her. 'Milk and no sugar for me.'

'And I'll have mine black with one sugar,' Abbott said.

As she left the room Grant Fuller held up a USB memory stick.

'The photos are all on here,' he said. 'There are quite a few to go through. I've also got some video footage that I've yet to download.'

James found it hard to look at so many happy scenes and smiling faces knowing what had transpired later on. There was the bride and groom taking their vows. The couple with the bridal party. Shots of the three-tiered wedding cake. The maid-of-honour beaming at the cameras while clutching either a bouquet or her purse.

Most of the shots were taken inside the hotel, but some showed groups of guests posing in the garden and on the terrace. Many more had been randomly snapped during the ceremony and the reception.

'I didn't take any during the meal, but I did intend to video the speeches and toasts,' Fuller explained.

It didn't take long for them to find the bearded man Abbott had seen coming out of Rachel's room as he had been photographed standing with Rachel in the Garden Room at the start of the reception, both smiling and pointing glasses of champagne at the camera.

'The guy is quite good looking,' Abbott commented and James couldn't disagree.

Carlo Salvi, if indeed that was his name, was probably in his early thirties. He was about six inches taller than Rachel and had thick black hair, prominent cheekbones and a strong jaw. He was wearing a tapered grey suit and bright yellow tie.

He appeared once more, this time in the background of

a photo that featured Rachel with her arms around two bridesmaids.

They had viewed countless photos when Mike Lynch pointed at the screen and said, 'That's him. He's the guy who was with the two women in the garden.'

James judged the man to be in his early to mid-thirties. He had unruly, fair hair and was wearing an open-necked white shirt beneath a black jacket.

'My God, I know who he is,' Abbott blurted. 'I met him when Sean and I arrived at the hotel. We shared the lift going up to our room with him and his mother. His name is Ethan and his mum is Claire Prescott, who used to be a nanny to Rachel and Libby.'

James felt his pulse escalate. 'So, what the hell were the three of them doing in the garden together?' he asked.

CHAPTER THIRTEEN

Mike Lynch and Grant Fuller left the office and James and Abbott continued to scroll through and scrutinise the photos while James made a note of all the time codes.

He noticed that the wedding ceremony began at 3 p.m. The champagne reception got under way half an hour later, at around 3.30 p.m., and at 6 p.m. the guests started making their way into the main hall for the meal.

The last photo of Rachel showed her standing on the terrace by herself at ten minutes past five.

'That must have been taken after I saw her in the bar with her sister,' Abbott said.

'At least now we've got some idea of the timeline,' James said. 'After the ceremony, Rachel posed in the garden for photographs with the bride and groom for maybe half an hour. She then went up to her room, where we believe she got into an argument with her Italian friend, before coming back downstairs and ending up at the bar where her sister had words with her. At just after five she was photographed on the terrace and about half an hour later, she was seen on the garden path with Libby and Ethan Prescott.'

'The search for her began at about seven and her belongings were found on the jetty at around seven thirty,' Abbott pointed out.

James thought about it for a moment. 'It's likely then that she was murdered between half five and half seven. And we might be able to pinpoint a more accurate time if she shows up on any photos taken by the guests or on the hotel security footage.'

Karen Cornwall arrived back with their coffees in plastic cups just then, accompanied by another man wearing a staff uniform, who she introduced as Neil Sherwood.

'Neil was in reception so I asked him to join us,' she said, handing them their coffees. 'As I mentioned earlier, Neil's job this afternoon was to man the rear gate between the hotel grounds and the field we use as an overflow car park,' she said. 'I've told him you want to ask him some questions.'

Sherwood was a squat, bullish man with a nasal edge to his voice. Once Miss Cornwall left them he explained that he took up his post on the gate as soon as the main hotel car park became full at about eleven o'clock on Saturday morning.

'By about two o'clock all the wedding guests had arrived and nothing was happening so I spent some time helping out in the garden and on the terrace. I went back to the gate frequently but I knew the overflow wouldn't get busy again until the evening guests started to arrive.'

'Does that mean that between about four and seven the gate wasn't constantly manned?' James asked.

Sherwood nodded. 'It does, but I'm pretty sure that nobody arrived during that time.'

'But someone could have left without being seen. Is that correct?'

'Of course. Nobody left while I was there, though. It was dead quiet.'

James puffed out his cheeks. It wasn't what he'd wanted to hear because it meant the killer could have fled the premises without anyone knowing since the overflow car park wasn't covered by CCTV cameras.

He thanked Neil Sherwood and dismissed him, mulling things over as he sipped at his coffee.

'So where do we go from here, guv?' Abbott asked him.

He thought about it for about thirty seconds and said, 'I have to go and talk to the family again. I think it's going to come as a real shock when I tell them that Rachel was planning to move to Italy. And I want to know why Libby didn't tell us that she had words with her sister in the garden after their encounter at the bar. But first let's get the team together for a quick briefing. There's a lot of work to be done and it's going to take some organising.'

It was 2 a.m. when the briefing got under way in the now empty Garden Room. Most of the uniformed officers were present along with two detective constables from Kendal HQ.

James brought them all up to speed and then assigned various tasks.

He told Sergeant Dale Thomas to make sure the entire hotel, including all the rooms, was checked over. He was also to make arrangements for statements to be taken from all the guests and staff, even if they didn't have much to say.

'And get the guests to show you what pictures they took on their phones,' he said. 'DC Abbott will print off and circulate the picture we have of Rachel and Carlo together and one of Ethan Prescott as we need to track the movement of both men during the reception. Grab a copy of any guest photos you see that you think might be helpful to us.'

He turned to Abbott. 'You and Sean will also need to provide statements but we can sort those out when we're back in the office,' he said. 'In the meantime, I need you to view the hotel surveillance footage and the video sequences shot by Grant Fuller. With any luck they'll tell us when our prime suspect, the Italian guy, arrived and left as he presumably arrived at the hotel by car and if he parked in the main car park he'll probably be on CCTV.'

He then told the third DC to start the process of digging up information on Carlo Salvi and to pass on the name to all units in the county and all transport hubs, especially airports. Did the guy have a criminal record? Was he a UK resident or here on holiday?

'We need to act quickly and gather as much information as we can and to get on top of this before we come under pressure to let everyone leave the hotel,' James stressed to the team. 'Once they do it will slow the pace of the investigation considerably.'

He finished the briefing by saying he would be returning to the bridal suite to talk to Rachel's family again.

'After that I'll be heading for the jetty, by which time I hope the pathologist will have arrived and be able to shed some more light on what happened to Rachel.'

CHAPTER FOURTEEN

James was walking across reception to the stairs when the lift doors opened and Greg Murphy stepped out. He saw James and walked up to him.

'It doesn't feel right to just stay in the suite,' he said. 'This is my hotel and I need to show support for the staff and be on hand to help the guests. Libby and her parents can cope without me for a while.'

'I'm just on my way up there,' James said. 'There are some things I need to tell them.'

'Do you know who killed Rachel?'

'Not yet. But we do know that the man who was seen with her goes by the name of Carlo Salvi. She invited him to the wedding. Is he known to you, Mr Murphy?'

His eyebrows shot up inquisitively. 'I've never heard of him. And it's not a name I would easily forget.'

James told him what Rachel said to her friend about moving

to Italy. 'She was apparently going to announce it during the wedding and at the same time introduce Carlo as her boyfriend.'

Murphy's face took on a thoughtful expression as he slowly shook his head.

'That's news to me and it will be to Libby,' he said. 'Are you sure that Rachel didn't make it up?'

James shrugged. 'The friend was in no doubt that she was telling the truth.'

'When was she intending to go?'

'Soon, apparently. I'm guessing she was going to reveal all at the meal, probably after making her speech. But it seems that something happened between them and whatever it was may have encouraged her to go down to the jetty during the reception.'

Murphy scrunched up his face. 'This is all so fucking unreal. I can't help wondering if the state she was in played a part in what happened to her. Perhaps she offended someone, the boyfriend maybe, and he lost his temper with her. She had no filter when she drank too much and that was why I asked Libby to speak to her. I feared she was on course to make things difficult for herself and everyone else.'

'Am I right in thinking that you didn't have much time for Rachel?' James said carefully.

'I've never made a secret of the fact that I wasn't her biggest fan,' he replied. 'She was quite jealous of Libby and would sometimes say things that really upset her sister. And I know she never liked me. If she really was planning to unveil her boyfriend at the dinner then I suspect it was with the aim of upstaging Libby and me on our big day. But that doesn't mean

I don't care that she's dead. Most of the time she was pleasant and easy to get on with. But she simply couldn't take her drink. What's happened is a tragedy and my wife is heart-broken. She'll never get over this.'

He closed his eyes for a couple of seconds, teeth tugging at his bottom lip. When he opened them again, they were glistening with unshed tears.

'I'm sorry, Inspector,' he said. 'It's just that I'm so worked up and emotional. I'm not thinking straight.'

'That's understandable, Mr Murphy. It's a lot to deal with.'

Murphy pressed the heels of his hands against his eyes, trying to regain his composure. 'Is it all right if I go to speak to the staff before going back upstairs?' he asked.

'I will need to talk to you again later,' James said. 'But it can wait.'

Murphy nodded, turned away and walked towards his manager's office, leaving James wondering just how much of a problem the man had had with the woman who was murdered on the day she became his sister-in-law.

There was only the PC outside the bridal suite when James got there as the assistant manager had been summoned to the impromptu staff meeting Murphy was holding.

When he stepped inside the suite, James found Fraser, Denise and Libby sitting together on a sofa, Libby in the middle and being hugged by both parents.

Their faces were still stricken with shock and bewilderment, and screwed-up tissues littered the floor in front of them.

Before James even spoke, Fraser asked again if he could go to the lake to see his daughter.

'That's not going to be possible, Mr Elliott,' James said. 'We can't allow anyone to go near to Rachel at this stage. A forensic pathologist is about to carry out an examination.'

The poor man's nostrils flared and he started blinking rapidly, crushing tears with his eyelids.

James had always empathised with the families of murder victims, but this time it felt like his emotional response was off the scale. And he knew why. It was because he now had a daughter of his own and was therefore more sensitive to the pain that Fraser Elliott was having to endure. He couldn't even imagine how he would feel if anything happened to Bella.

James lowered himself onto the other sofa so he was facing them.

'I just met with most of your wedding guests,' he said. 'And a couple of things were mentioned that I need to ask you about.'

His eyes settled on Libby and she gazed back at him, her face pale and drained.

'Firstly, the man who was seen coming out of Rachel's room is believed to go by the name of Carlo Salvi,' he said. 'Did Rachel ever mention that name to any of you?'

'No, she didn't,' Libby said, and her parents shook their heads.

'The wedding coordinator told me that she was asked by Rachel to make a place available for him at the wedding breakfast,' James went on. 'And that it was done with your blessing, Mrs Murphy. Is that correct?'

The muscles around Libby's eyes tightened and she rubbed a hand over her face.

'I've already told you that I had no problem with her

inviting another friend,' she said. 'But she never gave me a name. Who the hell is this bloke?'

'That's what we're trying to find out. We've been told that Rachel told Emily Straus over the phone on Friday evening that Carlo was her boyfriend and that she intended to introduce him to everyone at the wedding.'

'Then why didn't she do it when he arrived?' Libby asked.

'It could be because she wanted to do it at the end of her speech when she had everyone's attention,' James answered. 'Miss Straus also said that Rachel was going to announce that she was moving to Italy.'

Both parents recoiled in shock and it was obvious to James that they hadn't known.

'I don't believe it,' Fraser said. 'She wouldn't have kept that secret from us.'

'Apparently, she did,' James said.

It was a tough one for the family to process on top of everything else and James felt every sympathy for them.

Denise started sobbing again and her husband struggled to hold it in. Libby just stared at the floor, her pale blue eyes desolate.

'Something else came up during the meeting with the guests,' James said, and all three looked up at him, as though dreading what he was about to say.

He nodded towards Libby. 'One of the staff reported seeing you in the garden arguing with your sister, Mrs Murphy. He said that Mrs Prescott's son, Ethan, was with you. But you told me that you didn't see her again after the conversation you had with her at the bar.'

Libby held his gaze for a few moments, and then shrugged.

'I was in shock, Inspector. I wasn't thinking straight and I just forgot. But now I remember that I was talking to Ethan on the terrace and spotted Rachel on the path heading towards the lake. She was alone so I thought I'd try again to get her to pull herself together. But she refused to talk to me and told me to bugger off. So, I did.'

'And what about Mr Prescott?'

'He returned to the terrace with me.'

'And as far as you know Rachel carried on walking towards the lake?'

'I suppose so. But that wasn't my fault. She was pissed and in a foul mood.'

Her mother reacted sharply by removing her arm from her daughter's shoulder and leaping to her feet.

'I can't believe you're prepared to talk about your sister like that,' she snapped. 'Or that you couldn't recall the last time you actually saw her. That's important information.'

Libby shrugged. 'Well, I'm sorry. But I was in a state and it slipped my mind.'

Denise jabbed a finger at her. 'But it's not just that,' she exclaimed angrily. 'You should have done more to stop her walking away.'

As Libby stared at her mother, her face seemed to collapse in on itself.

'Jesus, Mum. It sounds like you're actually blaming me for what's happened.'

Denise lowered her arm and shook her head. 'Well, let's be honest. You are indirectly responsible. If you hadn't insisted on getting married to that man even though we didn't want you to your sister would still be alive.'

It was an explosive remark and Libby responded by getting up and rushing into the bedroom, slamming the door behind her.

Denise dropped back onto the sofa where her husband wrapped his arms around her.

'If it's all right with you, Inspector, could I have some time alone with my wife?' Fraser asked quietly.

James took that as his cue to halt the interview, but before leaving the suite he asked Fraser if he knew which room Mrs Prescott was staying in.

'It's at the other end of this corridor on the left, room number twenty-two,' Fraser answered. 'She called to check on us just before you arrived so I expect she's still up.'

CHAPTER FIFTEEN

It was 3 a.m. when he tapped the door to Claire Prescott's room and James got a surprise when the door was opened by her son, Ethan.

'Detective Inspector James Walker,' he said, showing his ID. 'Would it be possible to speak to Mrs Prescott if she's still up? I spoke to her earlier.'

Ethan nodded. 'I know. She told me. Is there any—'

He was interrupted by his mother's voice from inside the room.

'Let the inspector in, Ethan,' she called out. 'He might have some news.'

Ethan stepped back, saying, 'I'm her son, by the way. My room's next door, but I don't want to leave her by herself right now.'

Close up and in the flesh, Ethan Prescott struck James as a rough-looking individual. His eyes were small and deep set and his jawline was coated with stubble. He was wearing a tight blue shirt and James detected firm muscles bunched beneath it.

Ethan's mother was in an armchair next to the large double bed. Her eyes were inflamed from crying and blood vessels bulged out of her neck.

'Hello again, Mrs Prescott,' James said.

'I know about Rachel,' she replied, her voice hoarse. 'Fraser told me. It's the worst news possible and I don't see how any of us can ever come to terms with it.'

'Do you really think she was murdered?' Ethan asked.

James nodded. 'That appears to be the case.'

Claire covered her face with her hands and began to sob.

'It makes no fucking sense,' Ethan said. 'I can't imagine why anyone would want to harm her.'

James wanted to explore why Denise Elliott had accused Libby of being indirectly responsible for Rachel's death, so he said, 'I got the impression from something Rachel's mother just told me that not everyone was happy to see Libby marry Greg. Is that so?'

Ethan started to answer but his mother beat him to it after removing her hands from her face.

'We were all against it, Inspector,' she said. 'Greg Murphy is not right for our Libby. He gives the impression that he's a kind and caring person, but behind the mask he's a bully and a control freak. And in that respect, he takes after his father, Michael Murphy, who all but ruined my life.'

James narrowed his eyes at her. 'How do you mean?'

She took a breath. 'My late husband, Kyle, used to manage a hotel near Sedbergh. He really enjoyed it until it was sold to Greg's dad who was in the process of building his little empire. Kyle was kept on but he was treated like a slave and the pressure my husband was put under was relentless. He got depressed and unwell and eventually had a stroke that killed him. As far as I'm concerned, Michael Murphy was to blame. He was an arrogant arse-wipe who acted like a tyrant. Most of the people who worked for him hated his guts.'

Ethan invited James to sit on the side of the bed and said, 'That's why Mum is angry as well as grief-stricken, Mr Walker. If Libby had broken up with Greg and called off the wedding when she threatened to then this wouldn't have happened.'

'Are you telling me that Libby had had second thoughts about getting married?' This was quite a surprise for James to process.

Once again, it was Claire who answered. 'They split up and got back together a couple of times, but three months ago Libby decided she'd had enough and seemed determined to end it once and for all. That came as a huge relief to me and her parents, who feel the same way as I do about Greg. But then his father died suddenly from a brain aneurism and she changed her mind. I'm convinced it was out of pity more than anything else.'

James was reminded of how often tragedies exposed the dark underbelly of relationships, whether it be within families or among friends. From the outside everything seemed fine, while below the surface lives were blighted by brooding resentments, festering hostilities and mutual mistrust.

Rachel Elliott's untimely death was proving to be a case in point, revealing the fact that the Elliott sisters had serious problems with each other, that Greg Murphy was not well liked by his new in-laws and that Claire Prescott and Libby's parents hadn't wanted her to marry him at all. None of this would have been obvious from the wedding photos James had just seen, which showed lots of smiling faces, loving looks and affectionate gestures.

'We'll never stop regretting that the wedding went ahead and that Rachel is now lost to us forever,' Claire said, the deep wrinkles carved into her face suddenly seeming more pronounced by her grief. 'But what's important now is finding out who did it. Is that why you're here, Inspector, to tell us you know the person responsible?'

'I really wish that were the case, Mrs Prescott,' James said. 'But our investigation is only just getting started and I fear we've got a long way to go.'

He turned to Ethan. 'Mr Prescott, were you in the Garden Room earlier when I spoke to the guests?'

Ethan shook his head, his expression guarded. 'I've been in my own room for a while. I didn't know it was happening.'

'Well, some matters came to light that I need you both to know about.'

He told them about Carlo Salvi and Rachel's plans to introduce him to everyone as her boyfriend.

'We also learned that she disclosed to a friend that she was moving to Italy with him,' James went on. 'Were either of you aware of any of this?'

They exchanged looks, both foreheads knotting.

'As you can probably appreciate, I haven't seen much of the girls in recent years,' Claire said. 'They got on with their lives and popped over to see me very infrequently. And who can blame them? Why would they want to spend time with an old woman who constantly moans about her crippling arthritis? So, the answer to your question is no, I didn't know she had a fella or that she was going to move abroad.'

'What about you, Mr Prescott?'

Ethan ran a hand along his jawline. 'It's been the same for me. I had no idea.'

'Do you live and work locally?' James asked him.

He nodded. 'I live with Mum in Windermere and run my own small gift shop there.'

James had no reason not to believe what they were telling him but when he moved on to the incident in the garden with Libby and Rachel, Ethan's face became tense and when he responded it sounded as though he was choosing his words carefully.

'I was talking to Libby on the terrace and she was fretting because she didn't know where Rachel had got to,' he said. 'Then she spotted her sister on the path and rushed after her and I followed. But Rachel made it clear that she didn't want to talk to us. So, we left her alone and returned to the terrace. From there, I went back into the hotel. But despite what happened I was as surprised as everyone else when Rachel didn't turn up for the meal. As soon as Greg announced that she was missing I joined in the search for her.'

'Going back to when you went after Rachel,' James said. 'Did you happen to spot the bearded Italian on the terrace or in the garden, or anyone else acting suspiciously?'

'No, I didn't, but then I wasn't really paying that much attention to what was going on around us.'

CHAPTER SIXTEEN

James knew he'd need to speak to the Prescotts again but it could wait as there were plenty more things he needed to accomplish before the night was out.

A wave of tiredness washed over him as he left Claire's room.

This was already proving to be a challenging case. Yes, they had at least one potential suspect in Rachel's Italian boyfriend – though he appeared to have scarpered from the hotel – however, James knew that putting all their eggs into one basket would be a serious mistake. There were other possibilities. It had already been established that the victim had ruffled some feathers, including those of her new brother-in-law, Greg Murphy.

Going down in the lift, James made more notes and added to his list of questions. He wanted a background check carried out on Ethan Prescott. Did he have form? Was he in a relationship? What did people think of him?

At the same time James felt it necessary to do some digging into Greg Murphy as well. At this early stage nothing could be ruled out and the hotelier had already made it clear that he hadn't much liked his new sister-in-law.

James was also intrigued by what Claire had said about Murphy's father, Michael. It seemed a bit much to blame the man for causing her husband's death from a stroke, even if he had been a hard taskmaster, but it did appear that Greg had inherited some of his father's unpleasant genes and was making enemies of his own.

But Rachel hadn't been one of his employees and it was hard to see why he would have wanted to harm her. Unless, of course, she had known something about him, something that he feared she might reveal in her inebriated state and ruin his wedding day.

Perhaps he'd followed her down to the jetty to warn her to keep her mouth shut and when she told him to bog off it provoked a violent reaction on his part. Maybe he hit her with an object he was carrying or something he picked up, such as a rock.

James knew it was all just wild speculation at this point, but it was often wild speculation that eventually led to the solving of the most difficult cases.

Claire Prescott had aroused his curiosity in respect of the Murphy family so when he stepped out of the lift, he took a moment to run a quick search on his phone to find out a little more about them. And there was plenty of information to be found online.

Michael Murphy had made a name for himself as one of Cumbria's most successful businessmen. His big break came over thirty years ago when his career as a tax consultant ended with redundancy and he received a significant payoff, which he then used to buy a small hotel in Cockermouth.

It proved a hit with tourists and encouraged him to buy another and then another. When he died three months ago at the age of sixty-eight there were seven hotels in the Murphy chain. In addition, he owned a bunch of other properties in the county.

In the photos James came across he looked nothing like his son. He was short and plump with a flat face and sunken eyes.

There was one newspaper story from five years ago that James found particularly interesting as it appeared to confirm what Claire had said about Michael Murphy and how he had allegedly treated her husband. It reported that a female member of the company's board of directors had taken Michael Murphy to court claiming that she was forced to give up her job because he made her life a misery. She won the case and got damages.

In contrast, James didn't spot any negative reports about Greg. Quite the opposite in fact, with the hotel owner having been written about in glowing terms and described variously as 'dynamic', 'forward-thinking', 'shrewd' and 'handsome'.

'So, has anything turned up on the surveillance footage?' he asked DC Abbott as he stepped inside the security office.

She was sitting at a desk on which rested a large TV screen and was scrolling through a video that had been recorded during the wedding, showing the guests mingling and enjoying themselves in the Garden Room. To her left was a bank of smaller monitors showing live feeds from cameras dotted about the hotel.

Standing behind her was a man in his fifties with a long, sullen face framed by shapeless brown hair that was streaked with grey. He introduced himself as Andrew Nolan, one of the hotel's security team.

'I've marked up a few useful clips, guv, and they've been copied onto a memory stick,' Abbott said. 'But there's quite a lot more to sift through.'

'Have you come across anything that might help us crack the case?' James asked.

'Not so far. And I should warn you that the system might not yield as much as we've been hoping for as there are quite a lot of blind spots.'

'Why is that?'

'For one thing, there are fewer cameras than I expected there to be. Only fifteen covering the hotel and grounds, including the entrances, reception, function rooms, service areas and terrace, plus two in the garden. But one of the cameras in the garden hasn't been working for over a week and the image quality on the one covering the terrace is really poor. Everything is a blur. Mr Nolan here explained that the fault developed on Wednesday and they weren't able to get it fixed before this weekend's wedding.'

'It's not an uncommon problem with the system we have,' Nolan said. 'Rough weather causes the outside cameras to malfunction from time to time. The supplier is busier than usual because of Christmas and can't get an engineer out to us until Thursday.'

'What a bugger,' James said. 'Does that mean we won't be able to see who was on the terrace and when?'

'I'm afraid it does.'

'And presumably anyone can walk from the terrace to the back gate, which is not always manned, without being caught on camera.'

'Yes, that is the case,' Nolan said.

'Does the camera in the Garden Room cover the door that opens out onto the terrace?'

Nolan shook his head. 'It's actually on the wall above the door so as to take in the bar area.'

James felt a stab of disappointment. 'So why aren't there more cameras here?'

Nolan shrugged. 'Like most hotel owners, Mr Murphy endeavours to strike a balance between security and privacy. If you have too many it can make guests feel uncomfortable. And crime has thankfully never been a problem here.'

James turned back to Abbott. 'Can you show me what you do have?'

Two of the clips Abbott had bookmarked featured the bearded man. In the first he was walking across the hotel reception a few paces behind Rachel, a smile on her face.

'You'd never guess they were in a relationship,' James observed.

'Probably didn't want the big reveal to come before the dinner,' Abbott said. 'Now check this out.'

The next clip showed Abbott getting into the lift in reception.

'This was when I went up to get a wrap because Sean and I were going into the garden.'

She then fast-forwarded a few minutes and they watched the Italian come back down the stairs.

'This was seconds after I saw the pair of them come out of Rachel's room and it was less than an hour after they went upstairs.'

James watched as the Italian strode purposefully across reception, his head lowered the whole time. Rachel appeared just as he walked out of shot and she seemed quite distressed as she looked around for him. Then she hurried in the same direction he had been headed.

The guy was then picked up on the Garden Room camera making his way between the other guests as he headed towards the terrace.

'I reckon he must have parked his car in the overflow field,' Abbott said. 'I know he didn't enter the hotel through the front because I skimmed through the footage from that camera. And he also wasn't picked up by the car park camera, which clearly shows people arriving.'

'So, what did Rachel do after he walked off?'

'I expected to see her enter the Garden Room after him, but instead she came back into reception before going upstairs, presumably to her room. See for yourself, guv.'

James saw Rachel moving fast in the footage, ignoring a couple of people who tried to talk to her.

Nodding, he said, 'For now, we work on the assumption that they had an argument in her room that led to him storming off. She followed but soon realised it was a wasted effort and so returned to her room, probably to have a cry or to get her phone so she could call him. I noticed she isn't carrying a purse.'

'But she didn't stay in the room for long,' Abbott said, and played yet another clip that showed Rachel reappearing before heading for the Garden Room. Now she was wearing a white cardigan and carrying her purse.

'Looks like she planned to go outside the hotel, maybe in search of Carlo.'

'But I think she went to the bar first. I was just about to check and see.'

James told her to go for it and minutes later they spotted Rachel and her sister at the bar, but the camera was too far away to see their faces and zooming in didn't help.

But they did see Rachel wander off in the direction of the terrace after a while.

'That's as much as we've got so far,' Abbott said. 'It's a shame about the terrace camera, but at least we know she went outside about twenty minutes before the staff guy saw her having words with Libby and Ethan.'

'But we don't know if she made her way down to the jetty where her boyfriend was waiting.'

'Or if someone other than him followed her.'

'And that's what we need to find out,' James said. 'But anyway, you've done a cracking job here. I can't believe you've got through so much footage in such a short time.'

'It makes a big difference if you're searching through hours of video rather than days, guv.'

'True. Well, keep at it. I'm going to get the team together for a debrief after I've paid another visit to the jetty. I need to check what progress they're making down there and see if the pathologist has arrived yet,' he said.

CHAPTER SEVENTEEN

The temperature outside had dropped dramatically and the cold wind lashed at James's face as he made his way across the garden towards the lake.

It was darker too, thanks to the dense clouds that had been blown across the fells, blocking out the glow from the moon and stars.

In a few more hours it'd be daylight and James was hoping that by then they'd have interviewed most of the guests and staff and would have more of a handle on what had happened to Rachel Elliott.

The poor woman had been savagely beaten only a short distance from where her family and friends were celebrating, though it was precisely because the hotel had been buzzing with music and laughter that the murder had gone unnoticed.

They were lucky in the sense that the killer had been careless, leaving behind Rachel's purse and broken glasses. It suggested that the killing hadn't been premeditated, as the police often found more evidence when a crime was committed in the heat of the moment, the perpetrators often too shocked to think straight and so would flee in a panic without checking to see if they'd left anything behind.

That said, James wasn't expecting much in the way of fingerprints and incriminating fibres to turn up on Rachel's belongings or on the jetty itself. And if the weapon had been lobbed into the water, which was a strong possibility, then any evidence on it would probably have been washed away.

He decided not to go straight to the jetty after all. Instead, he veered off to the right along a winding path that he knew would take him to the rear gate. He wanted to check it out for himself and have a look at the overflow car park.

The gate was now being manned by a uniformed PC who informed the inspector that in the two hours he'd been stationed there only his colleagues had passed through.

It was a wooden gate set into a high hedge and James counted ten cars in the field beyond it, which had a row of three solar lamps at its centre. It might well have been convenient when the venue was particularly busy, but it clearly wasn't very secure and would have provided an easy escape route for Rachel's killer, assuming they weren't still in the hotel.

And it would also have been a quick and easy way for someone who wasn't a wedding guest or member of staff to have gained access to the grounds.

The level of activity down by the lake had increased when James returned as a tent had been erected over Rachel's body and the search for the weapon used to kill her was progressing in earnest.

More officers with torches were now searching the shore-line, bushes and grass, while members of the dive team were using spotlights to scour the water around the jetty.

The task would become much easier once visibility had improved, but delaying the operation was not an option as the first twenty-four hours of any murder investigation were crucial and if there were clues lying around they needed to be found as quickly as possible.

Dr Pam Flint emerged from the tent as James was approaching it. She acknowledged him with a flick of the head and lowered her mask.

She was in her late forties with a pointed nose and narrow eyes. As usual, her expression was composed and neutral and there was no indication that she found the job she did too unpleasant or demanding.

'Good morning, Detective Inspector Walker,' she said. 'I won't wish you a Happy New Year because I don't think it would be appropriate in the circumstances.'

'I couldn't agree more,' he replied. 'How long have you been here?'

'Just long enough to have carried out an initial examination of the body.'

'And?'

She worked her jaw in circles for a few moments as she considered her response.

'It's a nasty one for sure,' she said. 'The cause of death is almost certainly blunt force impact, and the fatal blow was to the back of the head. If you want me to take a guess, I'd say it was when she struck the jetty post with what would have been extreme force.'

'And the other wounds?'

'She was certainly attacked with a weapon that was hard enough to have pierced the skin and caused extreme bruising. It could have been a smooth stone or a metal bar, or something similar.'

'Can you tell me if she was dead before she fell – or was pushed – into the lake?' James asked.

'Not yet I can't, and I'm not sure I'll be able to.'

'Is it possible she drowned then?'

'It is, but only because she must have been unconscious when she hit the water. She wouldn't have been able to save herself.'

None of this came as a surprise to James as Dr Flint was echoing what the chief forensic officer had already told him.

'I gather she was the maid-of-honour at the wedding that was taking place here?' Dr Flint said.

James nodded. 'Her name is Rachel and her sister was the bride. She went missing after the pair had words during the reception.'

'What was it over?'

'Rachel had apparently drunk a little too much and was due to make a speech at the dinner. There was concern that she wouldn't be able to.'

'At least you've got a good idea of when the attack took place.'

'We have, but despite the hotel being full there don't appear to have been any witnesses.'

'Any suspects?'

James told her about the Italian boyfriend.

'It sounds like a promising lead,' she said. 'Now all you have to do is find him.'

'I know it's New Year's Day and all that but is there any chance you can fast-track the post-mortem?'

'I should be able to fit it in later today. Would it be okay for me to arrange for a coroner's office vehicle to take the body away?'

'Of course, but before you do is there anything else you can tell me that might be helpful?'

She shook her head and was about to speak when someone behind her began yelling.

James spun round and saw Fraser Elliott hurtling towards them along the path while being chased by a uniformed PC.

'Oh shit, it's the victim's father,' he said for Dr Flint's benefit.

CHAPTER EIGHTEEN

'I want to see my daughter,' Fraser yelled. 'You have no right to stop me.'

He got to within about ten yards of the forensic tent before the uniforms closed in and blocked his path.

'This is not fair,' Fraser screamed. 'I want to tell her that I love her.'

The officers held onto his arms and he tried to struggle free but gave up after only a few seconds. Then his head dropped along with his shoulders and he started to cry.

James rushed forward and told the officers to let him go.

'I'll escort Mr Elliott back to the hotel,' he said.

He then gently placed a hand on Fraser's shoulder. 'It's simply not possible for you to see Rachel at this time, Mr Elliott. Delicate forensic work is being carried out, which we hope will help lead us to whoever did this to her.'

Fraser lifted his head and stared at James, his breath coming in short, sharp bursts.

'But I can't accept that she's dead, Inspector. If I can just see her for myself, I might be able to.'

'Rachel is no longer alive, Mr Elliott,' James said and realised that he was finding it hard to keep himself professionally detached. 'Please believe me.'

Fraser swallowed hard and wiped the back of his hand across his eyes. Then he gave a nod and said, 'You're right. I know that. But it's so hard.'

He allowed James to lead him back towards the hotel. On the way, James informed him that his officers would have to visit the Elliotts' home.

'We know that your daughter lived with you so we need to search her room for possible clues,' he said. 'And any of her digital devices, such as laptops and tablets, will have to be taken away and examined by our technicians. Do you want to accompany us or would you rather stay here in the hotel for the time being?'

'I'll have to ask my wife,' he replied. 'I'm not sure she's ready to leave just yet.'

As they stepped back into the hotel, James asked Fraser if he was up to answering some more questions.

'I'll do whatever I can to help,' he said, more composed now, his voice steadier.

James steered him into the Garden Room, which was thankfully empty, and invited him to sit down on one of the sofas.

'I want to find out as much about Rachel as I can, Mr Elliott,' he said as he sat opposite. 'All I really know from what you've told me is that she was somewhat insecure and that she and her sister didn't always get along.'

'Both true,' Fraser replied. 'But she was also a very warm

and caring person, and it's just such a pity that life wasn't kinder to her.'

'I understand that your new son-in-law wasn't very fond of her. Were you aware of that?'

He nodded. 'It was Libby's fault. Rachel told her that she didn't like or trust the man and said she was mad to marry him. Libby then made the mistake of telling Greg and it soured the relationship.'

'But I gather that Rachel wasn't the only one who thought that Libby was making a mistake. Claire Prescott was of the same opinion and she suggested to me that you and your wife were too.'

'The honest truth is that none of us thought that this marriage was a good idea, Inspector. And not just because of the obvious age difference, which some would say isn't a big deal. We've just never felt that they're right for each other. Libby insists that he makes her happy but we're not convinced. It seems more likely that he has some kind of hold over her. It's such a shame that she and Ethan didn't stay the course. They were good together.'

James couldn't conceal his surprise. 'Are you saying that Libby was in a relationship with Ethan Prescott?'

Fraser nodded. 'That's right, and it was after he had a fling with Rachel.'

'Really? I didn't realise that. No one has mentioned it before now.'

'Why would they? It's in the past.'

'So, when were Rachel and Ethan a couple?'

'A few years ago,' Fraser said. 'They dated for just over three months. But then he ditched her and moved on to Libby.'

'Then what happened between Ethan and Libby?'

'They split up after about six months, which was unfortunate because despite what happened we like Ethan.'

'Do you know why they broke up?'

'They just grew apart as Libby's job took up more and more of her time. They both agreed that it wasn't working and decided to go their separate ways. I think they might have got back together if Libby hadn't met Greg through her work.'

'And how did Rachel cope with it all?' James asked.

'When Ethan dumped her, she was upset but not heart-broken. However, when she was told he had moved on to her sister she was mortified. She wouldn't talk to Libby for weeks and continued to hold a grudge, which of course didn't help their relationship.'

'Did Rachel remain on speaking terms with Ethan?'

'They've not seen much of each other in recent years, but when they were brought together on various occasions, she was always civil to him and there were no fireworks.'

'And was it the same with Ethan and Libby?' James asked.

'Yes, that's why Libby had no hesitation in inviting him to the wedding along with his mum. And before you ask, Inspector, I don't believe he's the one who killed Rachel.'

'Then who do you think did?'

He locked eyes with James and there was a sudden gear change in his voice when he spoke. 'Now that I know about the mysterious boyfriend, I'm assuming it must be him. So rather than wasting your time talking to me and the other wedding guests, I think you should be putting all your efforts into trying to find the bastard!'

CHAPTER NINETEEN

James accompanied Fraser Elliott up to the bridal suite only to be told by the officer on the door that his wife had returned to their own room, leaving their daughter alone inside.

'I half expected this after Denise's outburst,' Fraser said, and James was reminded of how his wife had lost her temper with Libby and more or less blamed her for what had happened to Rachel. 'I just hope it doesn't mean we'll lose our other daughter as well.'

Fraser once again started sobbing suddenly, unable to contain his anguish, and James asked him if he wanted to go in to see if his daughter was okay.

'I think it best if I leave her by herself for a while,' he replied in a shaky voice and so James walked with him to his room, which was on the next floor down.

When they reached it, he said, 'I'll be back soon, Mr Elliott. In the meantime, would you please ask your wife if she wants to stay here or go home so that she's there when we search Rachel's room?'

'Very well,' he replied, wiping tears from his eyes.

'And is there anyone you want us to call for you? A relative or a friend?'

He shook his head. 'Our closest friends and relatives are all here in the hotel. But right now, we would rather be alone.'

The door wasn't locked so Fraser let himself in and James waited until he'd closed it behind him before going back downstairs.

There was a lot going on in the hotel now and the noise level had increased as uniformed officers went from room to room interviewing guests and asking to view photographs taken on their mobile phones.

James spotted Greg Murphy holding court in the lounge area with a group of staffers, including the hotel manager and the wedding coordinator. To one side of him stood a PC who was making notes of what was being said.

James headed for the security office where DC Abbott was still viewing the surveillance footage, her tongue poking through her teeth in concentration. She was by herself now and she looked exhausted, her eyes glinting from tiredness.

'Where's the security guy?' James asked.

'Greg called a staff meeting and he was told to attend,' Abbott replied.

'Yeah, I saw them in the lounge. So, how is it going?'

'Nothing new to report, guv. Rachel doesn't appear on any of the footage after she left the bar.'

'What about the bearded boyfriend?'

She shook her head. 'He almost certainly left the hotel after he came down the stairs, and he wasn't picked up on the one garden camera that is still in working order.'

James rubbed his temples and scowled at the screen.

'Anything from the video footage shot by the wedding photographer?'

'DC Hall went to view that on the laptop in the manager's office,' Abbott said. 'I assume he's still at it.'

James was silent for a minute or so as he tried to marshal his thoughts while looking at moving pictures of the ill-fated wedding. He then filled Abbott in on his conversations with Claire Prescott and Fraser Elliott, and how Denise Elliott had blamed Libby for what had happened.

Abbott's eyes grew wide. 'My God, that's not something I would have expected. Libby must feel awful.'

'I'm sure she does, and I can't help feeling sorry for her.'

'Me too. It seems grossly unfair to hold her even partly responsible just because she decided to marry a man they didn't approve of. But then, we both know from experience that people deal with grief and trauma in different ways, guv. It can trigger unexpected emotions as well as some unpleasant reactions.'

'That's true enough. Anyway, that's not the only surprise that's been sprung on me. Did you know that both Libby and Rachel dated Ethan Prescott?'

'Are you serious?'

He recapped what Fraser had said to him, adding, 'I don't see how it could relate in any way to what's happened here but it does help us to understand why the sisters had such a fractious relationship.'

'It certainly does,' Abbott said. 'And poor Rachel then

suffered another blow when the guy she was going to marry ditched her just before their planned wedding.'

James nodded in agreement. 'Anyway, how are you coping, Jessica? Looking at that footage showing how things were before Rachel disappeared can't be easy for you.'

Abbott hesitated before she responded. 'Well, if I'm honest, guv, it's bloody difficult, but it's got to be done. And since I was among the guests, I reckon I'm best placed to do it.'

James gave her shoulder a squeeze. He was full of admiration for the way she was handling things.

He checked his watch, saw it was almost 4 a.m., and decided it was time for another team talk.

'We'll have it in the Garden Room again,' he told Abbott. 'Let's say in half an hour. I'll round up the troops and see if the hotel can lay on some coffee and snacks to help keep us going. Daylight may only be four and a half hours away, but that doesn't mean that any of our shifts will be coming to an end then. We've got a full day ahead of us.'

CHAPTER TWENTY

James went first to the hotel manager's office where DC Hall informed him that the video clips from the wedding photographer were not very useful.

'They're focused mainly on the marriage ceremony and the photo session in the garden,' Hall said. 'There are plenty of shots of Rachel with the bride and groom and family members, but none that show the bloke with the beard.'

James gave Hall the job of getting the key team members together, including the chief forensic officer, for the briefing in the Garden Room.

'I'll be waiting there,' he said. 'I need to make a couple of calls first.'

The first call was to Central Control to provide them with an update and to find out if anything new had come in at their end. He was told that the name Carlo Salvi was not on the criminal records database, and that his photograph was now in circulation.

'The press team want to know if you'd like them to put it out there with an appeal.'

'The sooner the better,' James answered. 'But I'll contact them now and tell them myself.'

When he got through to the press office, he spoke to the same person he'd spoken to earlier.

'By all means, send out one of the photographs you've been sent,' he told her. 'But make it clear in the release that we understand his name is Carlo Salvi and that we want to talk to him as a possible witness, not a suspect.'

'That won't be a problem,' she replied. 'Meanwhile, as you would expect, there's growing interest in the story. The Chief Constable's office thinks it would be a good idea to stage a press conference as soon as is practical. You won't have to come to Penrith though as we can arrange for it to take place in Kendal if you'd prefer.'

James said he would give it some thought. He was never keen on fronting pressers, but they often proved invaluable in generating fresh leads.

After ending the call, he checked some of the online news feeds on his phone. Even though only a matter of hours had passed since Rachel's body was found the story was already making headlines.

He was surprised to see that there was more information available than what had been officially released and James suspected that reporters had been in touch with hotel guests and staff.

The BBC News homepage appeared at first sight to have the most comprehensive coverage.

Breaking News: Missing maid-of-honour found dead at wedding.

A murder investigation is under way after a young woman's body was found in Cumbria's Lake Windermere.

The discovery came only a short time after Rachel Elliott disappeared during her sister Libby's wedding at The Fells Hotel, which is owned by the groom, local businessman Greg Murphy.

Miss Elliott, 25, was the maid-of-honour and early reports suggest she was beaten about the head. It's believed the attack took place on a private jetty in the grounds of the hotel near Ambleside as, according to a wedding guest who wishes to remain anonymous, several items belonging to Miss Elliott were found on the jetty during a search for her.

Soon after police divers found her body floating close to the shore.

Detective Inspector James Walker, who is based in Kendal, is leading the investigation and he and his officers have been at the hotel since before midnight.

Guests and staff are being questioned and the property, one of the most popular wedding venues in the county, has been locked down.

James raked a hand through his hair and let a breath out between his teeth. He felt sure that the day ahead was going to be immensely challenging.

The media would update the story as soon as the photo of

Carlo Salvi was released and with every development the pressure on him and the team would be ramped up until they got a result.

Just before the briefing got under way in the Garden Room, three members of the hotel staff arrived with trays containing pots of coffee, sandwiches and cakes.

'Help yourselves,' James told the nine team members who were present. 'This is the only sustenance you're likely to get for a while.'

He poured himself a coffee and chewed on a ham sandwich before kicking off with a summary of what the pathologist had said about Rachel's wounds. Tony Coppell also added his thoughts and findings before James relayed the various conversations he'd had with the Elliotts, Greg Murphy and Claire and Ethan Prescott, and the interaction he'd witnessed between Libby and her mother.

'None of this points to any discernible motive for murder,' he went on, 'but it does highlight the fact that the wedding wasn't the joyful occasion that most people attending thought it was. Behind the scenes there was a great deal of dismay, bitterness, animosity and ill will.'

They then discussed the possibility that Rachel might not have been attacked by a guest or member of staff, but by someone who entered the hotel through the garden gate.

'I, for one, think this is the most unlikely scenario,' James said. 'But nevertheless, we have to give it full consideration.'

He then read from his notes a list of tasks he wanted carried out, including speeding up the background check on Ethan Prescott.

'We know he runs his own gift shop in Windermere and lives with his mum, but there's a lot we don't know. Is it significant that he and Libby Elliott might well have been the last people to have seen Rachel before she was killed?

'Based on what we've seen in the photos and videos of the event, we've concluded that the murder must have been committed between half five and half seven. The sit-down meal began about six but throughout it the surveillance camera shows people getting up and leaving the room for various lengths of time. In addition, quite a few tables in the room are not covered by the camera. Plus, Grant Fuller stopped taking pictures during the meal and was waiting to video the speeches and toasts.

'All of this means that any number of people could have slipped out of the hotel during those two hours and carried out the killing as it takes only a few minutes to get from the terrace to the jetty. It was also dark and there are lots of bushes and hedges in the garden so the killer could easily have got there and back without being spotted if they so chose.

'We also need to know more about Greg Murphy. DC Hall, I need you to dig up information on the man, including details of his hotel business. He's been described as a bully and a control freak so I suspect he has more than a few enemies,' James said. 'We know that Rachel didn't much like him so perhaps she had something dodgy on him that she was going to share with others. If so, did he follow her to the jetty to confront her and things got violent?'

James then passed on what Claire Prescott had said about Murphy's father, Michael.

'Her late husband worked for Michael Murphy for a time and she claims he treated him like a slave. She even blames

123

Murphy senior for the stroke that made her a widow. I'd therefore like someone to delve into this just in case it has a bearing on what's occurred. There's quite a bit of info about the man online so let's start there.'

He then asked Sergeant Dale Thomas how things were progressing with taking statements from guests and staff.

'It's slow going but we're getting there, sir,' Thomas said. 'As you can probably guess, they haven't got much to say except that they all saw Rachel during the ceremony and at the start of the reception but only a couple of them spoke to her. They say she appeared anxious and it was obvious she was a little tipsy.

'Thankfully, the guests have been happy to share the photographs they'd taken on their phones and a couple of dozen have already been emailed over to Kendal HQ.'

James was about to end the meeting when two more officers entered the room to provide updates.

The first said that the search for the weapon used on Rachel was continuing and the coroner's office vehicle had arrived to transport her body to the mortuary.

The second officer delivered some news that sent a rush of adrenaline through James's body.

'I've just spoken to a female guest who claims that she had to fend off the advances of a man when she went for a smoke in the garden,' the officer said. 'She says he was harassing her and when she pushed him away, he got nasty.'

'What exactly did he do?' James asked.

'He called her an ugly slag. She called him a name back and he raised his hand and told her to fuck off if she didn't want a slap.'

'Why didn't she report this earlier when everyone was gathered in here?' This from a shocked DC Abbott.

'Because she didn't want to ruin her friend's wedding,' the officer said. 'You see, the bloke in question is Mark Slade. He was the best man and also happens to be the groom's closest mate.'

CHAPTER TWENTY-ONE

What best man Mark Slade said to the young female guest amounted to a threat, and quite possibly sexual harassment too. If it was true. But before James confronted him, he wanted to get a first-hand account from the alleged victim.

The officer who spoke to her told him that she would likely be awake as she was anxious to leave the hotel as soon as she was allowed to and since it was almost 6 a.m. she didn't intend to go to bed.

Her name was Belinda Travers and she was a friend of the bride. She'd told the officer that she was a twenty-four-year-old nurse, single, and lived in Carlisle.

'Let's not get too excited about it,' James said to DC Abbott, who was going with him to speak with Belinda.

'But it's hard not to, guv, given what we've just learned,' she replied, referring to the result of a quick Police National Computer search that James had carried out, which had revealed that Mark Slade, aged thirty-two, had a criminal record. Three years ago, he was convicted of punching his then-girlfriend in the face during an argument and breaking her nose.

The attack had taken place in a flat the couple shared in Keswick. Slade pleaded guilty to the assault charge, claiming he was drunk and lost control, and the court gave him a six-month jail sentence, suspended for two years.

A year before that incident, he had been fined and ordered to attend an anger management programme for smashing the windscreen of a car with a golf club during a road rage incident with a female driver who ran into the back of his car at traffic lights.

'Miss Travers says he approached her at about four o'clock, during the champagne reception,' Abbott said. 'It could be that after that encounter he went looking for someone else and came across Rachel on the jetty.'

James nodded. 'It's an interesting theory and one we need to explore. But it's best not to jump to conclusions until we've heard both sides of the story.'

Belinda Travers answered the door to her room on the first floor and as James started to introduce himself, she interrupted. 'I know who you are. I was downstairs when you spoke to everyone.'

'Well, my colleague and I need to ask you some questions about what happened to you in the garden, Miss Travers,' James said.

'But there's nothing to add to what I told the other policeman.'

'Then this shouldn't take long. You see, as the senior

investigating officer it's important that I hear your story straight from you.'

She let them in and sat on one of the two chairs next to the single bed. James sat on the other while Abbott stood with her back to the door, notebook in hand.

Belinda was wearing jeans and a jumper, and James could see the tension in her face. She was a pretty young woman with soft eyes set in olive skin and a small, pointed nose dusted with dark freckles.

'I'm sorry we're having to disturb you for a second time,' he said. 'I realise how difficult all this is for you and the other wedding guests.'

She bit down on her bottom lip and breathed in sharply through her nose, and it looked to James as though she was trying to stifle a sob.

'I can't think what else to do with myself. It's like being trapped in a horrible nightmare,' she said. 'I want to go and see Libby, but I wouldn't know what to say to her, and I'm sure she's too upset to talk to anyone anyway.'

Tears were threatening the corners of her eyes now so when he next spoke, James lowered his voice, using a gentler tone.

'How long have you known Libby?' he asked.

'We were at university together. She's one of my best friends and I was so happy for her. I thought it was going to be the perfect wedding and I'd been really looking forward to it.'

'And did you know Rachel?'

A nod. 'Of course, but not very well. We never hung out together, but I liked her. She was nice.'

'And I take it you don't know who might have wanted to kill her?'

A shake of the head. 'I have no idea. And please don't go telling Mark Slade that I think he did it. That's not why I told the other officer what happened to me. I just felt that, in the circumstances, it was something the police needed to know.'

'But you didn't think it was serious enough to report it earlier.'

'I knew that if I did it would have caused a huge fuss and spoiled Libby's big day,' she said. 'And I had to bear in mind that I might not have been believed. It would have been his word against mine, and since him and Greg are so close, I thought it best to keep schtum.'

'Had you met Mark Slade before yesterday?'

Another nod. 'I was introduced to him early last year at a party at his house, which Libby invited me to, and we've met at several events held in Greg's hotels since. But I don't like the guy. He's arrogant and thinks he's God's gift to women.'

'Has he tried it on with you before?'

'Several times, and I've always made it clear to him that I'm not interested.'

'So, it didn't come as a great surprise when he approached you in the garden yesterday?'

'It did because I didn't hear him walk up behind me. When he grabbed me by the shoulders and kissed me on the cheek, it was a big shock. I instinctively pushed him away, but he reacted badly.'

'Had he been drinking?'

'Probably. Most of us had already had at least a couple of glasses of wine or champagne by then. But I don't think he was drunk.'

'Tell me exactly what happened,' James said.

'Well, like I told the other officer, he called me an ugly slag and threatened to slap me if I didn't "fuck off". I saw him lose his temper once before at a birthday bash in a restaurant,' she said. 'He got really angry and swore at a waitress because she spilled some wine over his suit. Libby was appalled and embarrassed, but Greg defended him and told her the waitress should have been more careful. In that sense, the pair of them are very much alike. They both think they're better than the rest of us because they have money.'

'You've never warmed to Greg Murphy then?' James said.

She hesitated before answering. 'He's not my cup of tea, but don't get me wrong – he's never been anything but polite and respectful towards me. I just don't get what Libby sees in him …'

'Does she know how you feel?'

'It's … not my place. She loves the guy and if I ever told her what I think of him I fear it would damage our friendship.'

'How well do you know Ethan Prescott?' Abbott asked from where she was standing by the door.

'I regard him as a friend even though I've hardly seen him since he and Libby broke up,' she replied. 'He was always a gentleman and it was a shame they didn't stay together.' Then she frowned, adding, 'Why are you asking me about Ethan? Surely he's not a suspect.'

'Everyone is a suspect at this early stage, Miss Travers,' James said. 'We know that Mr Prescott had relationships with both Elliott sisters and it seems he was one of the last people to have seen Rachel before she went down to the lake. It follows, therefore, that he's one of the individuals we would like to eliminate from our inquiry as soon as we can.'

'Well, then it might help you to know that I sat at the same table as Ethan and his mum during the dinner. He was his usual quiet and unassuming self and he certainly didn't seem anxious or flustered. And as I recall, when he left the table to go to the loo or the bar, he was only ever gone a matter of minutes.'

'That's useful to know,' James said. 'Now, before we leave, can you please tell us what else you know about Mark Slade?'

'I know that he was married but his wife left him after only a year amid rumours of domestic abuse and they haven't yet divorced. He lives in Kendal and has made pots of money over the years as an online market trader. Oh, he also co-owns the golf course and club where Greg plays.'

At that, James saw Abbott start and remembered that she'd told him that Sean was a member at the same club as Greg Murphy.

CHAPTER TWENTY-TWO

'Sean has never mentioned Slade's name to me,' Abbott said once they'd left Belinda Travers's room. 'But then, whenever he comes back from golf, he only talks about how the game went and whether he's won or lost. He knows I'm not hugely interested in the specifics.'

'Well, we can sound him out now before we go and talk to Slade,' James said. 'See if he knows the guy and what he makes of him. Belinda certainly painted an unpleasant picture.'

'Did you believe her?'

'Absolutely. He sounds like a bad 'un. And it's easy to imagine that he could be our killer.'

'I agree. Based on his record and the suggestion that he was an abusive husband during a pretty short marriage, he clearly has no qualms about attacking women.'

'It seems it doesn't take much to ignite his temper,' James agreed.

Abbott nodded. 'A few years ago, I worked on a case involving a bloke just like him. He went from stalking women to beating up a teenage girl who refused to have sex with him. But we didn't manage to collar the bastard until after he'd put another woman in hospital.'

'I've got a bunch of similar stories from my days in the Met,' James told her. 'But we'll save those for another time. For now, let's go check in with your fella.'

On the way, Abbott took out her phone and showed James a photo she'd snapped just after the marriage ceremony had concluded.

'That's Mark Slade,' she said, pointing at the screen.

He was a bulky man, James noted, with a head of thick brown hair and a square-jawed face. Interestingly, he was standing next to Rachel in the photo and it looked as though he had an arm around her waist.

It was almost 7 a.m. by now and Sean was watching the news on the TV in their room. He looked like he hadn't been to bed and told Abbott that he'd just given a statement to a PC.

'The officer was taken aback when I told her that I was your fiancé and we were among the wedding guests,' he said to Abbott.

'I don't think word has got around yet,' she replied. 'What else did you tell her?'

'Only that I didn't witness anything suspicious and that I didn't go down to the jetty at any point before Rachel was declared missing and the search for her began.'

'I'm sure that almost everyone else will be saying much the same thing,' she said.

Sean turned to James. 'Am I right in thinking that you've come to ask me about Greg Murphy? You said that you wanted to pick my brain since we're members of the same golf club.'

'Actually, it's not just Murphy we'd like your take on,' James said. 'We're about to go and question Mark Slade, who as you know was Murphy's best man. He's also part-owner of your golf club. Did you know?'

Sean's face registered surprise as he shook his head and switched his gaze back to his fiancée.

'Start with Slade, Sean,' Abbott said to him. 'What do you know about the man?'

'I've met him three or four times in the bar there, but I've only had one round of golf with him,' he said. 'I was part of a four ball back in the summer with Greg, Mark and another member.'

'So how would you describe him?' James asked.

Sean flashed an uncertain smile. 'To be honest, as someone I wouldn't like to meet up with on a regular basis.'

'And why is that?'

He shrugged. 'He's a bit of a loud mouth, always boasting about how much money he's got and how many women he's bedded. And he can be quite rude to the staff.'

'We've been told that him and Greg are best buddies.'

'No question. They go back a long way apparently as Slade helped Greg's dad out once when his hotel business had some serious cash flow problems.'

'Is Slade in a relationship now?' James asked.

'I wouldn't know. Before yesterday, I hadn't seen him in months. I usually only take to the fairways in the summer.'

'And did you speak to him yesterday?'

'We had a quick word when I was on the terrace.'

'I don't remember that,' Abbott said.

'That's because it was when you popped upstairs to get your wrap. But we didn't have an in-depth conversation. He was too busy circulating to stop for long.'

'And was anyone with him?'

'Not that I noticed.'

'Have you ever witnessed Slade acting violently towards anyone, including women?' James asked.

'No, I haven't,' he replied. 'But whenever I've been in his company it's only been for a short time and Greg has always been with us. So perhaps he was on his best behaviour on those occasions.'

'How would you best describe Greg Murphy, Sean?' James queried.

Sean thought about it for a moment. 'He's not half as arrogant as Slade, but he does like to be in control of things, and he doesn't suffer fools gladly. But as I've already told you, I reckon he's a fairly decent bloke who has unfortunately inherited some of his father's more unsavoury traits.'

'What do you mean by that?' James said.

Sean shrugged. 'Well, he likes to get his own way and is a sore loser. Many a time he's blown a fuse when he's had a bad day on the golf course. But he once told me that his dad helped shape the way he is by trying to control his life and making him do things as his deputy that he didn't want to do. And it got much worse apparently after his mother died three years ago. Michael Murphy was quite an unpleasant man by all accounts and Greg clearly didn't enjoy working for him, but he stayed because it was the family business and he knew that one day he'd be expected to take charge.'

'That's as good a reason as any, I suppose,' James said.

'And it's probably worth mentioning that Mark Slade and myself both attended Michael Murphy's funeral. Greg delivered the eulogy and got quite emotional. I remember how he cried in Libby's arms after.'

'Thanks for your help, Sean,' James offered.

'Of course. Can I ask, do you think Mark Slade killed Rachel?' Sean asked.

Abbott gave him a playful punch on the arm. 'You know better than to ask that, my sweet.'

He nodded. 'Right. Sorry.'

She leaned forward and planted a kiss on his mouth.

'I'll be back as soon as I can to update you,' she said. 'Meanwhile, try to relax. And if you decide you'd rather go home then it's not a problem. Take the car and I'll get a lift back later.'

CHAPTER TWENTY-THREE

Before heading to Mark Slade's room, James sought out Dale Thomas, who was keeping a list of all the guests and staff members who'd so far been questioned. The best man wasn't among them.

'Then leave it to me and DC Abbott,' he told Thomas. 'We're on our way to talk to him now. You can get a formal statement later.'

They had to ring the bell twice before Slade answered the door to his room.

'I'm so sorry, Detective Inspector Walker,' he said. 'I fell asleep on the bed while waiting for someone to come and talk to me.'

'Well, we're here now, Mr Slade,' James said. 'May we come in? This is my colleague, Detective Constable Abbott.'

Slade waved them inside and invited them to be seated on two small armchairs. His room was a large double and had a balcony overlooking the rear garden. The TV was on and muted, tuned to the BBC News channel.

He perched himself on the edge of the bed and on the table next to him James noticed a half-empty bottle of vodka and a glass piled high with ice cubes.

'I would offer you both a drink,' Slade said, pressing out a grin as he looked at Abbott, 'but I don't suppose you're allowed to partake while you're on duty.'

James took an instant dislike to the guy and he had to remind himself that just because someone was a knob, it doesn't mean they were capable of murder.

Slade had changed out of his wedding garb and into a crew-neck sweater and loose-fitting jeans. His eyes were small and unfriendly, and his voice rough and clipped. He'd obviously been drinking but seemed sober enough and wasn't slurring his words.

'I was there in the Garden Room when you put us all in the picture, Inspector,' he said, returning his gaze to James. 'It's a terrible bloody business. I can't believe Rachel is dead. She was a lovely girl and a great character.'

'How well did you know her, Mr Slade?' James asked.

'Not very well at all. I was hoping to get to know her better here at the wedding. Before today, our paths only crossed a few times when we attended the same functions, but we've always hit it off. I've met her sister more often, though, because Greg and I are mates. That's why he had me as his best man.'

'We're asking all the guests the same three questions,' James said. 'Did you see anyone acting suspiciously around Rachel before she disappeared? Did you go down to the lake and jetty at any time during the reception and meal? And do you have any thoughts as to who might have committed the murder?'

'My answer to all three questions is an emphatic no,' he responded. 'I've been racking my brain to recall when I last saw Rachel and I'm pretty sure it was on the terrace during the reception. She was moving around saying hi to people and posing for photographs.'

'Did you take any pictures on your phone?' Abbott asked him.

'I didn't see the point. There was an official photographer and Greg told me he'd send me copies of all the photos so that I could choose which ones I wanted to keep.'

'Were you aware that Rachel had invited a man to the wedding?' This from James.

'You mean the Italian bloke with the beard?'

'That's correct.'

'No, of course not. Like everyone else, I was surprised when her pal let it be known downstairs. Have you found him yet or has he done a runner?'

'We believe he left the hotel,' James said, 'but I'm sure we'll be talking to him soon enough. Did you have any contact with him during the wedding?'

'None at all, although I think I saw him a couple of times. First, while we were waiting for the ceremony itself to start, and then again on the terrace. But he was by himself both times. I just assumed he was a family member or friend on Libby's side.'

James studied the man's face as he spoke. He obviously wasn't nervous, or if he was, he was doing well to hide it.

Both detectives asked a few more general questions about his personal circumstances and his relationship with Greg Murphy.

'We've been friends for years,' he answered. 'I knew his father too, before he died not long ago. Like Greg, he was a regular at the golf club I own.'

He didn't refer to Sean so James took it to mean that he wasn't aware that Abbott was engaged to one of his club members.

James finally got around to asking him how well he knew Belinda Travers.

At the mention of her name the blood seemed to retreat from his face.

'What's she got to do with anything?' he snapped.

'I'm sure you're well aware of what I'm alluding to, Mr Slade,' James said. 'Miss Travers has made an accusation against you. She says you approached her in the garden and kissed her without her consent. You then threatened to slap her when she pushed you away and told you to leave her alone. And the reason it's significant is that this allegedly occurred not long before Rachel was killed only a matter of yards away on the jetty.'

Slade shook his head, his mouth agape, fury in his eyes.

'I don't fucking believe this. That bitch is trying to stitch me up. And it sounds to me like you believe her.'

James leaned forward. 'Are you telling us she's lying?'

'That's exactly what I'm telling you. Yes, I saw her when I went into the garden to smoke a joint away from prying eyes. And not for the first time she started flirting with me. She even tried to kiss me. When I pulled away, she got angry and told me to fuck off. I didn't want to cause a scene so I did just that.'

James had been here before – having to balance one person's word against another. And as usual, it was hard to know which one of them was telling the truth.

Right now, it was Belinda's story that sounded the most convincing to James, but he would need to speak to her again, and find out more about her, in order to be certain.

Meanwhile, a hot rage continued to burn in Slade's eyes and his hands were clenched tightly into fists on his lap.

'If you've got it into your heads that I killed Rachel then you really are as daft as you look,' he seethed. 'I had no reason to harm her and you won't find any evidence linking me to it because it wasn't me. I swear to God.'

'But surely you can see why you've become a person of interest to us?' Abbott said. 'It's not just because of what Belinda Travers has told us. It's also because you have a history of violence against women. We've checked your police record and it makes for disturbing reading.'

'That's all in the past,' he said. 'I'm not like that anymore. People who know me will testify to that, including Greg Murphy. I've been through treatment programmes and I've learned my lesson.'

'Then you won't object if we bring in forensic officers to search this room and your belongings,' James said. 'We can't simply ignore what Miss Travers has alleged. And given where and when the encounter you had with her took place it has to be an avenue of enquiry in respect of the murder investigation.'

'Does that mean I'm under arrest?' Slade asked, his eyes popping.

James shook his head. 'Of course not. Miss Travers has given no indication that she wants to press ahead with a case against you. And provided you're prepared to cooperate fully with us, and that you're telling the truth, then there's no reason for this to drag on.'

Slade sat there steaming for several seconds, his jaw pulsing, his face white with anger.

Then, in a voice stretched with tension, he said, 'So what next?'

James sat back in the chair. 'I'll go and arrange for a forensics team to come here. And I'll get an officer to take a statement from you. Would that be all right?'

'I suppose it will have to be. Should I call my lawyer?'

'That's up to you. But I don't think it's necessary at this stage.'

'Then get on with it,' Slade said, his tone icy.

James stood up. 'One other thing, Mr Slade. Stay well clear of Miss Travers. It would be a big mistake to try to confront her regardless of whether what she's told us is true or not.'

CHAPTER TWENTY-FOUR

'I reckon he's lying through his teeth about what happened with Belinda Travers, guv,' Abbott said when they were back in the corridor outside Slade's room. 'He adopted the usual tactic of going on the offensive in the hope it would confuse the issue.'

James nodded. 'That's what I'm inclined to believe too. But I felt he was a tad more convincing when it came to saying that he had nothing to do with Rachel's death.'

'True, but that doesn't mean it wasn't him who killed her. Belinda gave the impression that he was acting like a dog in heat and if so then he may well have gone sniffing out another woman after she rejected him and come across Rachel.'

'The tricky thing will be proving it if we don't come up with any forensic evidence,' James said. 'I'm sure that if any of the guests or staff had seen or heard anything they would have come forward by now. Without any credible witnesses or physical evidence this is likely to be a difficult case to solve.'

Every floor of the hotel had at least one uniformed officer patrolling it so there was someone on hand to stand outside Slade's room while James and Abbott went downstairs and put other wheels in motion.

Sergeant Thomas was tasked with obtaining formal statements from both Slade and Belinda Travers and DC Hall was told to go back over the photos and CCTV footage, this time searching for the best man.

'We now have a new person of interest in Mark Slade,' James said. 'So, let's see where he crops up on the recorded images.'

While Abbott went to speak to Tony Coppell about assigning a couple of SOCOs to Slade's room, James called Control to check if there had been any developments in the search for the Italian, Carlo Salvi. There hadn't, but he did learn that police resources across the whole of Cumbria were under extreme pressure because the early hours of New Year's Day had arrived with a spate of other serious crimes and incidents.

A man had been stabbed to death outside a pub in Carlisle, two youths had been hospitalised after a street brawl in Whitehaven and a large warehouse in Milnthorpe had been razed to the ground in what was believed to have been an arson attack. There had also been several road accidents in which a total of seven people had been injured, and one of the accidents was being treated as a hit and run.

James was also told that the pressure was likely to grow over the rest of the day as the Met Office had just issued a severe weather warning for northern counties, including Cumbria. The heavy snow and gales they'd predicted for later in the week would now arrive sooner than expected.

James knew that it did not bode well for the investigation. One thing he had learned since moving to Cumbria was that extreme weather invariably slowed things down. Staff couldn't get into work. Roads were closed. Emergency services became overwhelmed. And sometimes entire communities found themselves cut off.

When he came off the phone, he took a moment to organise his thoughts and update his notes. He had no choice but to leave it to his team to carry out the majority of the interviews with guests and staff. This wasn't a run-of-the-mill case with only a handful of people needing to be questioned. The murder of Rachel Elliott had been committed at a hotel that happened to be full and so everyone had to be spoken to.

But this was a task fraught with difficulties because Rachel's family and friends were struggling to deal with the grief and shock while having to answer questions about what they saw or didn't see during the wedding. Guests and staff alike would also inevitably become impatient sooner rather than later and eager to depart the scene of the crime.

It was all very stressful for everyone and unlikely to get easier any time soon.

The next item on James's to-do list was a visit to the home Rachel shared with her parents as he wanted to be among the first to search her room in the hope it would contain valuable information about Carlo Salvi.

Despite what they now knew about Mark Slade, the Italian remained their prime suspect. Who was he and where had he gone? Was he proving hard to trace because he didn't live in the country? Was it possible that he was already on his way back to Italy?

James decided to go and tell Fraser and Denise Elliott that he was ready to travel to their home in Bowness and that they were welcome to go with him or they could give him the keys and remain here at the hotel.

But on his way back up the stairs, he decided to go to the bridal suite first. He wanted to find out if Libby was okay and at the same time ask her how much she knew about her husband's best man.

CHAPTER TWENTY-FIVE

The officer outside the bridal suite informed James that Libby was no longer alone. She'd called Claire Prescott's room and asked her former nanny to come and be with her.

'Has her husband or anyone else paid a visit since I was last here?' James asked.

'The hotel manager popped up to see if she needed anything,' the officer said. 'Mrs Murphy came to the door and said she didn't. She also told the manager to tell Mr Murphy that she was fine and that there was no need for him to hurry back.'

When James rang the bell, it was Claire who answered. Her face was still lined with emotion and fatigue, and when she spoke her voice was scratchy.

'Hello again, Inspector,' she said. 'I came to help comfort Libby. I gather you were in the room when her mum lost it with her?'

James nodded. 'How is she now?'

'Come in and see for yourself. I've at least managed to get her to change out of her dress.'

He followed her inside and she limped across the room without the aid of her walking stick. James felt as sorry for her as he did for Rachel's immediate family. By the sounds of it, the old lady had played a big part in all their lives for some years.

Libby was seated on one of the sofas, warming her hands around a mug of what looked like black coffee. She was now wearing a thick, baggy sweater and her long, dark hair was tied in a knot at the nape of her neck. She hadn't yet removed her make-up and rivers of mascara ran down her cheeks from bloodshot eyes.

Claire planted herself next to Libby and placed an arm around her shoulders.

'Support and counselling can be made available to you, Mrs Murphy,' James said, sitting opposite them. 'And we'll arrange for you to leave the hotel whenever you're ready to.'

Libby sipped her coffee, then licked her lips. 'I won't need counselling, Inspector. And Greg will be back soon and I'll let him decide when the time is right to go home. He needs to be on hand to help his staff and the guests to get through this.'

'Of course, I understand,' James said. 'I've actually come here to let you know that I'm about to go to your parents' home so that I can look around your sister's room. With luck, we'll find something there that will lead us to Rachel's Italian boyfriend who we're very keen to talk to. I'll be inviting your parents to go with me and if they decide to, then they might want to see you before they leave here.'

Her bottom lip quivered and tears welled up in her eyes.

'Claire just rang Dad on my behalf to tell him I think we need some time apart,' she said. 'My mother's head is all over the place and I couldn't bear it if she shouted at me again. It really hurts that she believes I'm to blame for what's happened.'

'I'm sure she doesn't think that,' James said. 'Like everyone else, she's in a state of shock and that can make people say things they don't mean.'

'I'm well aware of that and it's why it wouldn't be a good idea for me to see her any time soon. Either one of us might say something that will make things very much worse than they already are.'

'Fraser was upset but he said he understood,' Claire broke in. 'And I told him that I'll be staying with Libby until Greg takes her home.'

James decided not to tell her that according to Fraser the family had been bitterly opposed to the wedding. He felt it would serve only to make Libby even more upset. He had no choice but to mention the best man, though.

'One of your female guests is claiming that Mr Slade behaved inappropriately towards her in the garden during the reception,' he said. 'I've spoken to Mr Slade and he says she isn't telling the truth and that she was the one who came on to him and he turned her down. I thought you ought to know about it from me because it does mean we'll have to look into it and find out as much as we can about both parties, particularly Mr Slade.'

James saw the shock on Libby's face but it was Claire who responded first.

'Do you think this could have had something to do with Rachel's death?' she said, her eyes wide. 'I don't know the man personally, but I've heard stories about him. Didn't he get done for beating up his girlfriend and then his wife left him because he was violent towards her?'

James started to answer, but Libby got in first.

'It doesn't surprise me that Mark upset someone because he can never keep his grubby hands to himself,' she said. 'But I'm not sure he could have killed my sister. He was sitting at the top table with the rest of us from the very start of the meal and before that he spent most of the time close to Greg and me in the Garden Room and on the terrace.'

'Do you know if he had any feelings for Rachel?' James asked.

Libby put her mug down on the table between them.

'He probably fancied her, but then he fancies anyone in a skirt. He's been like that ever since I've known him and it's true what Claire just said about what he's done. He has a short fuse and a fierce temper, but me and Rachel have always been safe from his groping hands because he would never dare upset Greg.'

'But it's still possible that he made a move on her?'

She shrugged. 'I suppose so, but I doubt it. It wouldn't have been worth it to him to risk his relationship with Greg over Rachel.'

'In at least one of the wedding photos I've seen he's got his arm around Rachel's waist,' James said.

'He put his arm around me as well, Inspector. It's what people do when they're posing together at weddings.'

'Did any aspect of his behaviour yesterday give you cause for concern?'

'Not that I remember. For once he acted like the perfect gentleman and I suspect Greg had told him not to play up.'

'I understand that Slade and your husband are close friends.'

'They are. Greg knows that I don't much care for the man, but he won't hear a bad word said about him. And I'm sure that he won't believe for a minute that Mark killed my sister.'

James fell silent for a moment, unsure whether or not to pursue this line of questioning. Before he'd made up his mind Claire said, 'I thought it was the boyfriend you suspected of the murder. Isn't that why you're looking for him?'

'He is someone we need to talk to, for obvious reasons, and we're doing everything we can to find him,' James said. 'But in the meantime, we have to explore every other avenue of enquiry.'

Libby suddenly dissolved into tears and covered her face with trembling hands. She continued to sob and shake her head as she spluttered words that were unintelligible.

'Could you please stop there, Inspector?' Claire pleaded. 'This is all too much for her. You can see for yourself that she's in no condition to answer your questions.'

'Of course,' James agreed as he stood. 'As I said earlier, family liaison officers will be assigned and will keep you all updated on the police investigation. As soon as I know who they are I'll pass on their details to your husband and your parents,' he said to Libby.

After he exited the suite, James experienced a pang of guilt for having left Libby in such a state. The poor woman had so much to deal with. Her sister had been murdered. Her wedding had been ruined. And her mother had turned against her. Surely that was more than anyone should have to bear?

CHAPTER TWENTY-SIX

James had now been at the hotel for about nine hours and he could feel exhaustion gnawing at his bones.

He knew he was in for a long, gruelling day and that he wouldn't be able to return home to his wife and daughter until at least early evening.

He also had his doubts about how much he and his team would manage to achieve by then. It would all depend on how quickly things developed and how lucky they were.

Would they get a breakthrough with the discovery of some solid piece of physical evidence? Would a guest or member of the hotel staff suddenly recall seeing something that would point them in the direction of the killer? Would Rachel's Italian lover turn up in the coming hours and confess to the crime?

So many thoughts were gnashing in his head that he feared that it was only a matter of time before it brought on one of his tension headaches. He'd long ago come to accept that it was one of the downsides of his demanding job as they were usually triggered by tiredness and stress, and it was why he always carried a pack of painkillers with him.

There were things he needed to do before setting off for the Elliot house in Bowness, which was luckily only a couple of miles away, but first he needed to visit their room to see if they wanted to go with him.

Fraser answered the door and invited him in. His wife was lying on the bed fully clothed and hugging a pillow, her eyes squeezed shut.

'We've discussed it and would prefer to go home,' Fraser said. 'We see no point in staying here and Libby has made it clear that she doesn't want to see us again today.'

James then asked Fraser how long it would take them to get ready.

'Half an hour at the most,' he replied. 'We haven't got much to pack.'

'Did you use your own car to get here?'

'No, we came by taxi.'

'Then I'll take you and someone will help you with your bags when we're ready to go.'

'Will we be permitted to take Rachel's things with us?' Fraser asked.

'I'm afraid not,' James said. 'It all needs to be examined and tested by forensics. But I can assure you that nothing will get lost and I'll personally see to it that everything is returned to you.'

James then set off at a brisk pace for his next port of call – Rachel's hotel room. The door was ajar and inside two SOCOs were giving it the once-over under the watchful eye of a PC. The double-bedded room was strewn with black plastic bags containing Rachel's belongings.

'There's no evidence to suggest that she was planning to share the room with someone last night,' the officer told him. 'All the clothes are hers, along with the clutter in the bathroom, and there's only the victim's one overnight bag.'

James was confused. The manager had confirmed that Carlo Salvi had not booked a room in the hotel so surely the intention had been for him to sleep with his girlfriend, in which case his things should still be in the room, especially as he wasn't carrying a bag of any kind when he headed out of the hotel in the CCTV footage James had viewed earlier with Abbott.

'Call me if anything does turn up,' he said to the officer before going in search of DC Abbott.

He found her in the reception area where she was briefing two forensic officers who had been instructed to check out Mark Slade's room. As soon as she was finished, he filled her in on what Libby and Claire had said about the best man, and how Libby had broken down. Abbott shook her head, compassion in her eyes. He then told her about the search of Rachel's room and why he thought it was odd that there was nothing belonging to Carlo Salvi in there.

'Maybe he hadn't planned on staying, guv,' she said. 'Or, if that had been his intention before they fell out, it could be that all he brought was a toothbrush and razor. That wouldn't be so unusual.'

'That's true. Okay, I'm headed to oversee things in Bowness so I want you to take charge here while I'm gone. Keep an eye on Slade and if the SOCOs find anything incriminating in his room then take the guy into custody and phone me,' he said. 'When I get back, we'll have a catch up with the team and set out plans for the day ahead.'

CHAPTER TWENTY-SEVEN

It was still dark when James drove away from The Fells Hotel with Libby's parents in the back seat.

They were followed by a patrol car with a police constable at the wheel and a forensic van driven by a SOCO. It had been arranged for a family liaison officer to meet them at the Elliotts' home in Bowness.

The estimated journey time was only about five minutes and thankfully the roads were empty, unlike during the summer months when traffic congestion was always a major problem.

The town of Bowness-on-Windermere had for some time been the most popular visitor destination in the Lake District. It was filled with cafes, pubs, gift shops and attractions such as The World of Beatrix Potter, which used the latest technology to bring the stories of Peter Rabbit and other lovable characters to life. James and Annie had spent a weekend there not long before Bella was born, staying in a town centre hotel and taking a cruise on one of the lake steamers.

During the drive, Denise remained silent, the pain raw and visible on her face. But Fraser dutifully answered James's questions even though he clearly found it difficult. He revealed that both he and his wife had retired two years ago – him from his job as a dentist and Denise as one of the town's GPs. He also gave James the name and address of the café in Ambleside where Rachel had worked, but pointed out that it wouldn't be open until Monday.

'The owner's name is Mary Wilson and I can give you her number,' Fraser said. He also confirmed that Rachel owned a laptop but she had never shared the password with them. And as far as he knew she hadn't kept a diary.

James then asked him how long they had lived in Bowness.

'We moved here from Kirkby Abbey thirty-one years ago, shortly before the girls were born,' he replied. 'Because we both had careers, we employed Claire to help out as a visiting nanny when they were young. She lived a couple of minutes away, in Windermere, but spent most of her days with us.'

James let it be known that he himself lived in Kirkby Abbey. 'My wife moved to London fifteen years ago. But when her mother died and left her the house in the village, we decided to move there. It was one of the best decisions we ever made.'

Fraser couldn't recall ever meeting Annie's parents and when he asked Denise if she remembered them, she simply shook her head and continued to stare out of the window.

They entered Bowness along the Rayrigg Road and well before the town centre they hung a right into a smart residential area close to the lake.

The house was a two-storey detached property with stone walls and a slate roof. It had a driveway on which two cars were parked, a Peugeot and a Mini. Fraser explained that the Mini had belonged to Rachel and she'd used it mainly to go to work in Ambleside.

A woman wearing a heavy grey overcoat was standing in front of the gate and James recognised her straight away as Victoria Hartley, the Family Liaison Officer.

He introduced her to the couple as soon as they stepped out of the car, but Denise responded by breaking down in tears again. Thankfully, Officer Hartley was highly experienced and immediately took control of the situation.

'Once we're inside I'll make you a cup of tea, Mrs Elliott,' she said. 'And I'll explain to you how I hope to be of assistance during this very difficult time.'

Moments later they were inside the house, which was modern and spacious. Fraser guided his still-sobbing wife into the living room where a three-piece suite was arranged around an open fireplace.

Once Denise was seated on the sofa alongside Officer Hartley, Fraser led James and the others up the stairs to his daughter's bedroom. But as soon as he pushed open the door his eyes flared with emotion and he shook his head.

'If I go in now, I'll lose it,' he said. 'Please try to leave it as you find it.'

'We will,' James assured him, before entering the room followed by the forensic officer and constable.

It was a large and tidy room with cinnamon-coloured walls, a double bed and fitted wardrobes. There was also a desk beneath the window, and on top of it a laptop and printer.

As James pulled on a pair of latex gloves, he said, 'We're looking for information on Rachel's boyfriend, Carlo Salvi.

Phone number, address, place of work. Also, anything that indicates that she might have been having issues with people other than him.'

The first thing to draw James's attention was a multi-aperture photo frame on the wall above the dressing table. There were pictures of Rachel with her sister and her parents at various stages in her life. And several of the two girls with nanny Claire Prescott when they were quite small. But there were no photos of Rachel with any boyfriends.

The forensic officer quickly established that the laptop was password-protected so would have to be taken to the lab along with Rachel's phone. The same applied to a Samsung tablet they found in one of the drawers.

One item was of particular interest to James. It was a page torn from a recent edition of *Cumbria Life* magazine. It contained a feature on a woman James had met a year ago during the investigation into the murder of an entire family on a farm near Kirkby Abbey.

Lisa Doyle was a psychic medium and clairvoyant, and something of a celebrity in the county. She lived in Ravenstonedale and had a popular website through which she carried out online readings and publicised events she held.

The feature profiled her life and work, but what intrigued James was a note that had been scrawled on the page.

December 27 2pm

Did this mean that Rachel had met up with her just four days ago? he wondered. If so, then it struck him as a weird coincidence since one of those murdered in the farm massacre last Christmas had previously attended several seances with the psychic.

Miss Doyle was never implicated in those killings and James could not imagine she'd had anything to do with Rachel's death, but he would speak to her nonetheless to find out if Rachel did indeed go to her for a reading.

After twenty minutes they'd found Rachel's passport and a guidebook on Italy but nothing that alluded to Carlo Salvi. There was no diary and no notes with his name on but James wasn't surprised since most personal information these days was stored on phones, tablets and computers. It meant they would have to wait until the techies had unlocked Rachel's digital devices to find out what she kept on them.

Just as they were about to call it a day, the constable found a birthday card that had been tucked beneath underwear in a drawer.

'You need to check what's inside, sir,' he said. 'It seems Miss Elliott had made at least one enemy.'

James took the card and felt his stomach clench when he saw that the warm-hearted printed greeting had been scrubbed out and replaced with a handwritten message that read:

I hope you have a rotten birthday Rachel because I know it was you who gave those pictures to the paper and fucked me over.

Revenge might seem sweet now but I'm going to make sure that you come to regret what you did.

160

CHAPTER TWENTY-EIGHT

The birthday card was a major development and it raised a number of questions.

Who sent it? When was it sent? Did Rachel show it to the police? And was the writer of the threatening message the person who killed her?

The first thing James needed to find out was whether Rachel's parents knew about it. They were sitting side by side on the sofa when he went back into the living room, with Officer Hartley on an armchair facing them. Denise had stopped crying and was sipping tea from a cup.

'I need to ask you if you've seen this birthday card before, Mr and Mrs Elliott,' he said.

He showed them the front of it first, a picture with bells either side of a fancy birthday cake.

They both shook their heads and Fraser said, 'I thought she had thrown all her cards away. Where did you find it?'

'In a drawer beneath her underwear,' James replied. 'When was her birthday?'

'It was in early December; the eighth,' Fraser said. 'She turned twenty-five and received quite a few cards, as I recall.'

'And she never drew your attention to this one in particular?'

The couple looked at each other, their brows creasing. This time it was Denise who asked the question.

'Why do you want to know about the card, Inspector? What's so special about it?'

'Take a look at the message inside,' James said. He held the card so that Fraser could see it but not touch it and Fraser read the message out loud.

The words sent a shockwave through his wife and she started shaking so much that Officer Hartley had to carefully remove the cup from her hands before she dropped it.

'Rachel obviously didn't want you to see it, but it would surely have upset her. Have you any idea who might have sent it?'

Once again, the couple turned to look at each other, both their faces registering alarm.

It was Fraser who broke eye contact after several seconds and switched his gaze first to Officer Hartley, and then to James.

'There's only one person it could have been,' he said. 'But that piece of shit wasn't a guest at the wedding and wouldn't have dared to show his face there.'

'You need to tell me who you're referring to,' James said.

'Douglas bloody Hannigan, of course,' Fraser barked back. 'Her ex-fiancé.'

James nodded. 'I remember. You said he was involved in a drug scandal that was covered by the papers.'

'That's right. He was standing as a candidate in a by-election and as a former Marine and now a well-known documentary film maker he was a favourite to win. But he had to pull out because of it. The story brought a smile to our faces because we felt that he got what he deserved for dumping Rachel the way he did so close to the wedding.'

'Do you know why he decided to end the relationship so suddenly?' James asked.

'He told her that he realised that he didn't love her enough, but she suspected he was cheating on her with someone else.'

James took out his notebook and pen. 'Can you recall when this story appeared in the news, Mr Elliott? His name certainly rings a bell with me.'

'It was back in October.'

James made a note. 'I will be looking into the details, but for now can you tell me what exactly he was accused of?'

'Well, the story first appeared in the *Cumbria Gazette*, and it exposed his habit of taking illegal drugs,' Fraser said. 'They even managed to get a photo of him snorting cocaine at a party.'

James reread the message in the card, and said, 'So you believe that this could be from him and he's accusing Rachel of leaking the story.'

'I can't think who else would have sent it,' Fraser responded. 'And before you ask, Rachel knew about his drug habit. She told us after they split up and we were livid because she said he encouraged her to take them as well.'

'And did she?'

Fraser shrugged. 'She claimed she occasionally smoked a cannabis joint when she stayed at his place but steered clear of the cocaine. Unfortunately, we couldn't be sure she was being truthful with us.'

'I see.' James scribbled some notes, before adding, 'Is it possible that your daughter did tell the paper what she knew about him in order to get her own back?'

Fraser lowered his gaze, as though out of embarrassment, and it was left to his wife to answer the question.

'When it was announced that Hannigan was going to stand as a candidate in the by-election, she told us she was thinking of doing just that to scupper his chances,' Denise said. 'We urged her not to because we didn't want her to get involved. She promised us she wouldn't and when the story appeared she insisted that she wasn't responsible.'

'Thank you for this,' James said. 'We will be talking to him but as you've already pointed out, he wasn't a wedding guest and he'll probably be able to prove he was somewhere else when it happened. We shouldn't leap to the conclusion that Douglas Hannigan is the person who killed your daughter.'

James went on to ask more questions about Rachel's relationship with Hannigan, learning that they'd met through an online dating site and were together for seven months. She often stayed overnight at his house in Kendal, and she had been planning on moving in with him after they married.

'We only met him twice,' Fraser said. 'He was always smartly dressed and polite, and struck us as quite pleasant. Rachel thought the world of him. But as we all know, appearances can be deceiving. When Rachel said he'd proposed and she'd accepted we were shocked because they hadn't been together long. But we put our concerns to one side because she seemed so happy.'

James showed them the page from the *Cumbria Life* magazine and the article on psychic medium Lisa Doyle.

'We found this in Rachel's room,' he said, pointing to the date and time scribbled on it. 'This looks like she might have made an appointment to see her. Do you know if she did?'

It was Fraser who answered. 'I subscribe to the magazine and Rachel picked it up one evening just before Christmas. She said she had often thought about having her fortune told and asked if she could tear out the page. I'd finished with it so I said no problem. But she didn't mention it after that so I have no idea if she ever went to see the woman. Just as we had no idea that she was planning to move to Italy with some bloke we had never met. It turns out there was a lot we didn't know about our daughter.'

Once again it proved too much for Rachel's mother. Her lips trembled and tears formed in her eyes. Before long she was sobbing into her hands again, but as James got up to leave the room, she managed to spit out a single, heart-wrenching sentence.

'Please find the monster who murdered our daughter, Inspector. And then make sure they spend the rest of their life behind bars.'

CHAPTER TWENTY-NINE

Cold air rushed into James's lungs as he walked out of the Elliott house. He stood on the pavement for a few minutes, his mind spiralling with fresh thoughts and questions.

They now had another potential suspect in Douglas Hannigan, assuming it actually was him who sent the birthday card to Rachel. If he believed she had exposed him as a druggy, thus wrecking his chance of becoming a Member of Parliament, then it would have given him a clear motive for wanting to harm her.

But James found it hard to believe that he would have risked doing something during her sister's wedding. For one thing he would have had to sneak into the hotel without being seen, which would require prior knowledge of the hotel and grounds, and then he would have had to lure Rachel to the jetty during the reception. It was, of course, possible that he'd arranged to meet her beforehand, perhaps by phone or text. It was also possible that his intention had been to confront her and not to kill her but, as often happened, an argument flared into violence.

It was agreed that Officer Hartley would stay with Fraser and Denise for at least the next few hours, offering support while trying to elicit as much information as possible about both of their daughters. The SOCO would leave as soon as he had finished up in Rachel's room and Mini.

As James climbed into his car, he could feel adrenaline searing his senses. The case was suddenly moving at a rate of knots and there were already three people in the frame – Douglas Hannigan, Carlo Salvi and Mark Slade. And he still considered several other individuals to be persons of interest, including Ethan Prescott, Greg Murphy and even his new wife, given the somewhat turbulent relationship that had existed between the two sisters. And with so many people moving around the hotel and its grounds while the reception was taking place it was possible that any one of them could have slipped down to the jetty unnoticed and got involved in an altercation with Rachel that resulted in her death.

Daylight was fast approaching as James drove back to The Fells Hotel and during the short trip he used the hands-free to call HQ in Kendal. He assigned one of the duty officers to gather information on Douglas Hannigan, including his address.

'And find out if the victim, Rachel Elliott, came to us in recent weeks to report that she'd received an anonymous threat,' he said.

When he arrived back at the hotel, James saw a TV news satellite truck parked opposite the entrance and two press photographers on the pavement. He knew it wouldn't be long before he'd be expected to make himself available for an interview and that wasn't something he was looking forward to.

Once parked up he stayed sitting in the car and tapped *Douglas Hannigan* into his internet browser. There were lots of men with that name, but only one who had attracted a significant amount of media attention during the past year.

He was thirty-three and ran a multi-award-winning TV production company based in Kendal. According to its website, it produced wildlife documentaries, corporate and promotional videos, and commercials. Hannigan was currently single and had spent nine years in the Army, including a stint in Afghanistan. He was until recently a prominent local councillor and had planned to run for Parliament in a by-election but he was forced to withdraw after the *Cumbria Gazette* ran its exclusive exposé.

James found the story easily enough. It was written by Gordon Carver – a journalist he often came into contact with – and it had dominated the paper's front page.

There were two photographs: one showing Hannigan sniffing lines of coke from a tray on a coffee table during what looked like a party in someone's living room, and another where he was lying on his back on a sofa with his eyes closed and his mouth wide open, seemingly unconscious. Resting on his chest was an ashtray containing what looked like the remains of a joint.

James recalled how the story had dominated the local headlines at the time.

SHAME OF THE WOULD-BE POLITICIAN

By Gordon Carver

This is not the behaviour one would expect from a man who wants to represent our community as a Member of Parliament.

Kendal film maker and ex-Marine Douglas Hannigan is standing as an independent candidate in the forthcoming Westmorland and Lonsdale by-election, but these exclusive pictures now cast doubt on his fitness for office.

They were taken at a house party earlier this year and one shows him sniffing what's believed to be cocaine. A source close to Mr Hannigan, who wishes to remain anonymous, revealed to us that he frequently attends get-togethers where drugs are consumed and also buys illegal substances from local dealers.

One man who was jailed last year for drug trafficking revealed to this newspaper that Mr Hannigan was among his customers.

James went on to read several follow-up stories on various online news sites in which Hannigan admitted to taking drugs on occasion but denied that it was an addiction.

In the days that followed the revelations he came in for so much flak from people in the constituency that he withdrew from the by-election. James watched a video clip in which Hannigan read out a pre-prepared statement, saying that he very much regretted his past actions and understood why people felt that he had let them down.

In the video he was dressed in a smart grey suit, his dark

hair slicked back with gel, and James couldn't help wondering if he would have become an MP had those photographs not been leaked to the paper.

Among the many questions that needed to be answered was whether his former fiancée attended that same get-together and took those incriminating photos.

And whether she then passed them on to the *Cumbria Gazette* to punish the man for what he had done to her.

CHAPTER THIRTY

Back at the hotel, things were much the same as when James had left, though the reception area was now busy with uniformed officers, staff, and guests who were preparing to go home.

It was noisier than it had been earlier, probably because for most people the shock had worn off and they were finding it easier to talk about what had happened the day before.

Sergeant Dale Thomas was standing at the front desk speaking to the young female receptionist and taking notes on what she was telling him.

James crossed the room to join them. 'Thomas, how are things going?'

'We've now interviewed most of the staff and guests,' he said. 'I'll collate the statements and notes as soon as I get a chance but unfortunately no new leads have emerged and everyone is saying more or less the same thing. They didn't go to the jetty, they saw little of Rachel Elliott after the ceremony, and they did not engage with the bearded Italian guy.

Several of them are in a rough way because of too much drink and too little sleep.

'Mark Slade's room has now been searched but officers found nothing to incriminate the best man. Meanwhile, DC Hall is still scrolling through the photos and security footage and DC Abbott has just gone to the jetty to check on progress there,' Thomas continued.

'I'm going to pop down there myself,' James said. 'Can I leave it to you to get some of the team together for a catch-up in about fifteen minutes? In the Garden Room, if it's still empty.'

'I'll get right on it.'

The darkness had at last retreated from the sky as James strode through the garden towards the jetty, and daylight revealed the setting in all its glory. The view across the lake to the less populated western shore was awe-inspiring.

The Cumbrian landscape never ceased to amaze James and he felt that its reputation as one of the most beautiful places in the country was well deserved. He couldn't imagine living anywhere else now, and he didn't think he would ever contemplate moving back to London under any circumstances.

But at the same time, he had to accept that even in a place of such beauty and charm, bad things would continue to happen, and no one could ever be completely safe.

He could see that officers and SOCOs were still searching the area around the jetty, their job made easier thanks to the natural light, and that the forensic tent had been removed along with Rachel Elliott's body. Crime scene tape fluttered in the wind and the air was polar cold.

A police patrol boat floated just offshore, there to stop

vessels containing press photographers from getting too close to the jetty, but James knew it would prove ineffective against the drones that were bound to arrive soon in order to transmit video footage to newsrooms or online news sites.

DC Abbott was talking to Tony Coppell, who was reading from his notes. As James approached, he noticed how tired she looked. Her eyes were pouchy and raw and there was no colour in her cheeks.

'You're back sooner than I expected you to be, guv,' she said. 'How did it go?'

'I've got a new lead that needs to be followed up,' he replied. 'There'll be a catch-up in the Garden Room in fifteen minutes. I'd like you both to be there and I'll go through it then. Meantime, has anything new been turned up here?'

It was the chief forensic officer who answered. 'Still no sign of a weapon, but we're about to widen the search to cover the entire garden and the overflow car park. The divers gave up searching the bottom of the lake around the jetty because it's covered with rocks and large branches and any one of them could potentially have been used to attack our victim.'

'Have you found any more blood traces on the decking?'

Coppell shook his head. 'No, we haven't, and I've been giving more thought to how it might have played out. I'm still certain that the attack took place at this end of the jetty, where the victim's glasses were knocked off and she dropped her purse. And the bruises on her arm are a strong indication that she was trying to defend herself. I think she was backing away from her assailant and while doing so she fell or was knocked onto the post, which delivered the fatal blow to the back of her head.'

'So, what happens now?' James asked. 'Is there much more to be done?'

'We'll be here for another few hours at least,' Coppell said. 'But I'm not too optimistic about finding anything else that will shed more light on what happened. And if I'm honest, I don't believe that forensic evidence will solve this case for you. There's just too little of it. Plus, the whole scene has been compromised by the weather and the number of people who trampled over it before we were able to seal it off.'

During the catch-up, James learned that every room in the hotel had been checked and all the footage from the surveillance cameras had now been viewed. Guests and staff were beginning to leave and the only person still unaccounted for was Rachel Elliott's Italian boyfriend.

'Carlo Salvi remains our prime suspect and we need to do all we can to track him down,' James said. 'But Mark Slade, the best man, cannot be ruled out. We know he has a history of violence against women, but as there were no witnesses and he denies threatening Belinda Travers in the garden, it's his word against hers. He has also denied killing Rachel and right now there's no evidence to prove that he did.'

James then told them about the birthday card found in Rachel's bedroom at home and why her parents were convinced that it was sent to her by her ex, film maker Douglas Hannigan.

'As soon as I have his address, I intend to pay him a visit,' he said. 'In the meantime, we need to find out as much as we can about him. A good place to start is the *Cumbria Gazette* story that exposed him as a drug taker and forced him to pull out of the parliamentary by-election. I know the journalist who wrote it so I intend to call him to find out if it was Rachel who gave them the photos from the house party.

'DC Hall, I'd like you to go back through the surveillance footage to see if Hannigan appeared on any of it. It seems extremely unlikely that he would have come into the hotel, but we need to be sure,' he said.

'Now, I'm going straight from here to Kendal HQ but I want us to maintain a strong presence here throughout the day,' he went on. 'No new guests will be checking in and the media are to be kept at bay. Those of you who've been working through the night will be relieved as soon as possible. DC Abbott, it's time you went home and got some rest. All credit to you for holding it together and getting on with the job despite the strain you've been under. It can't have been easy.'

'Thank you, guv,' Abbott said. 'I appreciate it. And I think I'm about ready for a little nap.'

As the group dispersed, James decided to check on Libby and have a quick word with the manager, Karen Cornwall, before leaving the hotel.

But just as he was about to exit the Garden Room he was confronted by an irate Greg Murphy.

'I've been looking all over for you,' Murphy seethed as rage burned in his eyes. 'I've just seen Mark. How dare you accuse him of being a murderer? Mark did not kill Rachel and I know that for sure because he was with me and my wife when it's supposed to have happened.'

CHAPTER THIRTY-ONE

'You need to calm down, Mr Murphy,' James said. 'We most certainly have not accused Mr Slade of killing Miss Elliott. He's simply been asked a number of questions about his movements during the reception, the same as everyone else.'

Murphy's jaw tightened and bulged. 'Well, that's not what Mark just told me. He said you also accused him of threatening one of the other guests and then went and turned his room upside down.'

James held Murphy's stare as he signalled for his colleagues to carry on walking out of the Garden Room. Once they were alone, he said, 'You must appreciate, Mr Murphy, that we could not ignore the allegation made by the other guest. We have a duty to follow it up.'

'But why the hell would you believe her word over Mark's? Belinda Travers is a flirt and everyone knows it.'

James shook his head. 'At this stage I don't know who is telling the truth about the incident. Regardless, it has to be treated seriously given the fact that it took place in the garden and so close to the jetty.'

'Then why not subject Belinda's room to the same thorough search? I know you haven't because I've been to see it for myself.'

James felt a surge of irritation. 'Please don't tell me you went there to confront her about what she told us.'

'Of course I bloody well did. You made it clear to Mark that he had to steer clear of her, but I wanted to hear for myself what she had to say. And guess what? She couldn't bring herself to repeat it. Instead, she started blubbering, which was enough to convince me that she was the one who came on to Mark and then got shitty when he rejected her.'

James managed to supress his anger, but a wave of unease swelled in his chest.

'I'm not at all surprised that she got upset,' he said, his voice raised an octave. 'You should not have gone to her room or spoken to her about it.'

'I don't see why not,' Murphy replied, defiant. 'This is my hotel and she was a guest at my wedding. I'm not prepared to let her get away with making such an outrageous allegation while we're all trying to deal with what has happened to Rachel. It's the last thing we need.'

James was anxious not to allow the issue to get out of hand. He had to accept that Greg Murphy's head was not in a good place. He was still reeling from the shock of what had happened to his new sister-in-law at his own wedding and perhaps leaping to his pal's defence was helping him to cope with the brutal reality of a situation that was causing him so much anguish.

'I fully appreciate how you must feel about it since Mr Slade is a close friend,' James said, 'but you must not get involved with our investigation. It's up to us to determine what did or didn't happen and whether or not it had a bearing on Miss Elliott's death. In all likelihood, it'll prove to be an unnecessary distraction at a time when you should be fully focused on helping your wife to get through this ordeal.'

James braced himself for a sharp retort, but it didn't come. Instead, Murphy made a thoughtful noise in his throat and his demeanour shifted suddenly.

'Well, I've made my point so I'll leave it at that,' he said. 'But I'm telling you that Mark did not murder Rachel. If, as you believe, it happened between half five and half seven then he couldn't have because he stayed close to me during those two hours, first in the Garden Room and then in the main hall where he sat at our table. And as far as I can recall, he didn't wander off at any point.'

'Then I'm glad you've told me,' James said. 'It's useful information and I'll take it into account.'

'I trust you won't waste any more time trying to pin it on Mark then. Instead, you should be putting all your efforts into finding that fucking Italian bloke Rachel was planning to run off with. Surely he's the one who killed her otherwise you would have heard from him by now.'

'Rest assured we're doing all we can to find him, Mr Murphy. And when we do, we'll get to the bottom of what happened between them.'

'What about until then? Have you finished up here yet, or do you still think that one of the other guests, or one of my staff, could have been responsible?'

'It's too soon to rule anyone out,' James replied. 'But we've spoken to everyone and taken statements so people are now free to leave the hotel. However, our forensic work will have to continue, as I'm sure you can understand. In the meantime, how is your wife coping?'

'She's still struggling so I intend to take her home soon,' Murphy said. 'I'll come back later, but while I'm gone you can liaise with my manager, Karen. She's agreed to remain on duty for the rest of the day.'

'That's good to know, Mr Murphy.'

'I've also asked her to cancel our honeymoon for us. We were due to fly to Dubai on Thursday.'

'It's all such a terrible shame,' James said.

'I know, and I don't know how any of us will ever be able to get over it.'

Murphy stole a look at his watch, which prompted James to say, 'Look, before you go, I'd like to ask you what you know about Douglas Hannigan.'

'You mean the guy Rachel was engaged to?'

'Yes.'

Murphy shrugged. 'I've never met him, but I know what he did to her and I read about how he screwed up his own bid to become a local MP. Why is he of interest to you? He wasn't here yesterday.'

'We're looking into anyone who has played a significant part in Rachel's life,' James said. 'And he's definitely one of them.'

After leaving the Garden Room, James went in search of DC Abbott. He found her waiting for the lift in reception.

'I'm glad I caught you,' he said. 'There's something I'd like you to do before you go.'

'What is it, guv?'

He told her what Greg Murphy had said about Mark Slade and how Murphy had gone to Belinda Travers's room.

'It upset her, which is hardly surprising,' James said, 'so I'd appreciate it if you could go and check on her – assuming she's still here – to see if she's all right.'

'I'll go straight there.'

'Thanks, Jessica. And then get Sean to take you home and have a well-earned rest. We can touch base later, but I don't expect to see you back on the job until tomorrow.'

'What about you, guv? You've been at it all night too.'

'There are things I need to sort before I can sign off, but I will head home as soon as I get the chance.'

James strode out of the hotel and got into his car. He switched the engine on and let it idle to warm up the interior while he put in a call to his wife.

'I'm sorry I haven't been able to speak to you before now,' he said when she answered. 'It's been full on without a break.'

'I heard about the murder on the news,' Annie replied. 'You wouldn't think that something so dreadful could happen at a wedding, and in such a beautiful place.'

'I know. It's really tragic.'

'Are you close to finding out who did it?'

'Not yet. There are a couple of suspects, but I fear it's going to be a tricky one to solve. I'll tell you more about it when I get home.'

'Will that be soon?'

'Afraid not. Probably early evening. How's Bella?'

He sensed a slight hesitation. 'I think she might have a cold coming on. She's got a bit of a temperature and a bit of a cough.'

'Does she need to see a doctor?'

'Not yet, but if she gets worse, I'll pop her along to the surgery.'

'Keep me informed then.'

'I will, but please don't worry, James. I know what you're like. I'll take good care of her.'

'I know you will. I'll call later then. And Happy New Year, by the way.'

'The same to you, my love.'

After hanging up, James sat for a while with his eyes closed, thinking about his daughter. Where Bella was concerned, he was inclined to be over-anxious. He couldn't bear the thought that she might become ill and so he tended to panic if she cried too much, slept too much or showed signs that things weren't progressing as they should.

Annie was always trying to reassure him that they had a happy, healthy daughter and there was no need for him to worry so much. But he couldn't help it and he supposed it was partly due to the fact that his job exposed him to so much pain and suffering on an almost daily basis.

He often wondered what he was going to be like when Bella started to grow up and ventured out by herself into the big, bad world. A world that was clearly becoming more dangerous and more deadly with every passing year.

CHAPTER THIRTY-TWO

As James drove away from the hotel, the weather was starting to close in with predictable ferocity. The trees along the side of the road swayed and snatched at the sky, and gathering clouds forewarned of snow to come.

He pulled his thoughts away from his daughter in order to concentrate on the case but it wasn't easy because his head was crowded with so many questions.

Was Rachel Elliott killed by one of the people he had spoken to? Or was it her Italian boyfriend, the man she'd been hoping to start a new life with in another country?

There seemed little doubt that the pair had argued in Rachel's room soon after the wedding ceremony ended but what had caused it and could it have triggered a chain of events that led to her death on the jetty?

There were other questions that needed answering in relation to Mark Slade. He and Belinda Travers had obviously been involved in an incident in the garden not long before

Rachel was killed but which of them was telling the truth about who did what to whom? Both James and Abbott believed Belinda's version of events, in part because of Slade's recorded history of violence against women, but could it be proved that he had acted untoward with Belinda?

And why was Greg Murphy so sure that his best man wasn't the aggressor and that he did not go on to kill Rachel? James wasn't convinced that they'd never left each other's side during the two hours between five thirty and seven thirty as Murphy would have been speaking to other guests, eating dinner in front of everyone in the main room, and spending intimate moments with his bride. Surely, he and his best man would have become separated on more than a few occasions, if only briefly. And if so, why was he insisting that wasn't the case?

The other pre-murder incident that involved Libby and Ethan Prescott also raised questions. When James first spoke to Libby, she had said that the last time she saw her sister was at the bar in the hotel's Garden Room. But that wasn't true as she and Ethan were seen confronting Rachel.

And what was it Libby had said when James had brought up her omission? *'I was in shock. I wasn't thinking straight and I just forgot.'*

It was yet another issue that struck James as implausible. No way would she have forgotten the last bitter exchange of words between her and her sister. So why had she chosen not to mention it?

But the questions didn't stop there. Was it Rachel's former fiancé Douglas Hannigan who sent her the birthday card with the threatening message? And if so, did he follow up on the threat and sneak into the hotel knowing she would be there so he could exact revenge?

As he drove, James drummed his fingers impatiently on the steering wheel and told himself to focus on the positives.

Rachel's body had turned up within hours of her disappearance and so they had been able to move quickly. All the hotel guests and staff had now been spoken to and statements taken. Surveillance footage and photographs had been examined and the full forensic sweep of the grounds would hopefully be completed before the weather deteriorated further. And to top it all, there were already a handful of potential suspects.

James heaved a sigh and acknowledged that it wasn't actually a bad start to the investigation, all things considered.

He arrived in the market town of Kendal just after eleven o'clock in the morning. It was one of the most vibrant communities in Cumbria and for visitors coming from the east and south it marked the gateway to the Lake District.

The town had a population of just under thirty thousand and boasted two castles, three museums, a river and plenty of shops, restaurants, pubs and cafes.

James had become extremely fond of the place in the two years since they'd moved up from London.

Constabulary headquarters sat alongside the Fire and Rescue Service building just off the Windermere Road. After parking up, he made his way inside where several people wished him a Happy New Year.

The open-plan office wasn't as lifeless as he'd expected it to be. There were over a dozen people in, including detectives, uniformed officers and civilian support staff.

Phones rang and keyboards clattered, and at least two televisions were switched on and showing rolling news shows.

DCI Tanner still hadn't returned from his Scottish holiday so James was the senior officer, a role he'd grown used to because Tanner often attended meetings, functions and seminars with the bigwigs in Penrith. His desk was piled with various case notes and files, and DS Phil Stevens was standing next to it holding up a takeaway cup.

'DC Abbott rang to let us know that you were on your way, boss, so I got you a coffee,' he said. 'Hopefully it will help you to stay awake.'

James offered him a tired smile and took the cup. 'That's kind of you, Phil. What else did Jessica say?'

'That she's going home to get some sleep and we need to sort out relieving most of the team at the hotel.'

James nodded. 'I'll bring you all up to date in a bit but first I have to make some calls. Thanks for cutting your break short. Was the wife okay about it?'

'Yeah, of course. We were planning to head back home later today anyway. It just meant getting up earlier and cutting back on the drink last night.'

'So, have you got anything to tell me before I get started?'

'I've taken the liberty of assigning detectives Ross and Brady to the other cases we're working on. They'll operate out of one of the other rooms with the help of a couple of support staff. It'll leave the rest of the team free to concentrate on the murder. And I've arranged for the officers at the hotel to be relieved.'

'Great. Are you free to go with me to interview a suspect?

I believe he lives here in Kendal so hopefully we won't have to travel far.'

'I'm at your service,' Stevens said. 'From what I've heard so far, it sounds like we've got our work cut out.'

'We have indeed,' James said.

Though James and Stevens had got off on the wrong foot at the start of their working relationship because James's appointment to the vacant DI position had denied Stevens the promotion he'd been expecting, James had finally won him over and since then they'd got on well.

James tasked a support staffer with getting Douglas Hannigan's address and finding out how many team members would be back at work the following day, and fifteen minutes later, he stood between two large, empty whiteboards. He coughed to clear the dryness in his throat and waited for the hum of conversation to die down before he started the briefing.

He began by describing the scene at The Fells Hotel and explained how the events of the previous day had unfolded. Reading from his notes, he then ran through the names of the family members, wedding guests and hotel staff he had spoken to.

'Our three most viable suspects are Carlo Salvi, Rachel's Italian boyfriend who has disappeared, Mark Slade, the best man who has form for assaulting women, and Douglas Hannigan, Rachel's ex-fiancé, whom I plan on going to interview once we're done here,' he said.

He provided more details about each suspect and mentioned the birthday card with the threatening message that may have come from Hannigan, and the allegation that wedding guest Belinda Travers had made against Mark Slade.

'But I also have suspicions in respect of Ethan Prescott, who dated both sisters, and with Greg Murphy, the groom and hotel owner,' he continued. 'Murphy admitted to me that he didn't like Rachel and she apparently didn't like him either – both she and her parents tried to talk Libby out of marrying him.'

James then ran through a list of other relevant points, including the blood traces on the jetty decking, the fact that no weapon had been found, and the way Libby had at first claimed that her last encounter with her sister was at the bar when in fact it was on the path leading to the lake.

'So far, there's very little in the way of forensic evidence,' he went on. 'However, the techies have yet to go to work on Rachel's mobile phone, which was found in her purse on the jetty, and we also have her laptop and tablet to look at. They were retrieved this morning from her bedroom at home.'

It then fell to DC Dawn Isaac, a Scottish lass with a husky voice, to inform the team that background checks were being carried out on Greg Murphy, his late father, Michael, and Ethan and Claire Prescott.

'We've had nothing back so far on a Carlo Salvi,' she said. 'He's not on our database and nobody matching his description has turned up on social media. We're in the process of checking with the airlines to see if he's on any flights leaving for Italy today and his name will be included in news bulletins along with the photos of him from the hotel, so fingers crossed we'll soon get a result.

'I can also confirm that the Constabulary was never informed by Rachel that she'd received an anonymous threat in a birthday card. That could mean she either didn't take it seriously or she didn't think we'd be able to do anything about it,' Isaac said.

James nodded. 'That's a good start, Isaac. I want you to spend the rest of the day collating the evidence, including all the photos and statements that come back from the hotel. We'll need to have a full team briefing tomorrow morning,' he said. 'By then we should also have the reports in from digital forensics and possibly the post-mortem. And with luck we might have tracked down Salvi.'

As soon as the briefing was over James heard back from the civilian support officer who gave him Douglas Hannigan's address and phone numbers.

'I ran a check on his mobile, sir, and its location appeared to be his home here in Kendal.'

James thanked her then scrolled through his phone contacts for Gordon Carver's mobile number. The *Cumbria Gazette* reporter answered on the second ring.

'Well, this is indeed a coincidence, Detective Inspector Walker,' he said. 'I've just been assigned to the Windermere Lake murder and my editor suggested I give you a ring. I gather it's your case?'

'That's correct,' James replied. 'I've been passing on information to the press office and they're fully up to date with what's happening.'

'And I'm guessing you're calling me either because you're going to offer me something exclusive or you want a favour.'

'It's the latter, Gordon, and if you can help me out, I'll make sure you're one jump ahead of the rest of the press pack as the investigation goes forward.'

'In other words, it's the usual quid pro quo arrangement between us.'

'Exactly.'

'So, what do you want from me then?'

'As you know, the woman murdered at the wedding was the bride's sister and maid-of-honour, Rachel Elliott. Her body was found in the lake and all the evidence suggests she was attacked and beaten about the head while standing on the hotel's private jetty.'

'That much I know. And I also know that your team were there throughout the night questioning guests and staff. Is an arrest imminent?'

'Unfortunately, no. But we are pursuing a number of promising leads. And when there's a breakthrough, you'll be the first to know.'

'Fair enough. Now how can I help?'

James cleared his throat. 'One of the things we've learned about Rachel is that she was once in a serious relationship with Douglas Hannigan, who you exposed as a drug addict last autumn, just as he was standing in a parliamentary by-election.'

'I think I know where you're going with this, Inspector,' Carver said. 'You want me to tell you if it was Rachel who gave us the photos and told us about his habit.'

'That's right.'

'Does it mean he's a suspect in her murder?'

'Not at this stage,' James lied. 'But it's an avenue of enquiry that I'm obliged to pursue.'

After a short pause, Carver said, 'Well, since Rachel is no longer alive, I see no harm in confirming for you that it was her. She came to us because she didn't want the guy to become the local MP. She took the photos of him herself at a party and she was up front about the fact that she wanted to get revenge because he'd dumped her just before their planned wedding. Naturally, we jumped at the chance to run the story and promised never to reveal who it came from.'

CHAPTER THIRTY-THREE

Douglas Hannigan lived on the other side of town, close to the Westmorland Hospital. It took James only minutes to drive there, and on the way, he told DS Stevens what Gordon Carver had revealed to him.

'My guess is that Hannigan either knew or suspected that Rachel was the one who stitched him up,' he said. 'The first question we need answered is whether he was so pissed off with her that he sent that card. The second question is whether he actually went to the hotel and carried out his threat.'

'It shouldn't be that difficult to get to the truth,' Stevens said. 'We just have to find out if he has an alibi and compare his handwriting with the message on the card.'

'Let's hope it proves to be that easy,' James replied.

Hannigan's end-of-terrace house was in a street that was clean and quiet, with neatly trimmed privet hedges and speed bumps in the road. There was no driveway and cars were parked along the kerbs on both sides but James managed to find a gap about twenty yards from Hannigan's front door. As they walked back to it the first flakes of snow started to fall.

'That's all we bloody need,' Stevens said. 'I was hoping it wouldn't reach us until this evening.'

James blew out a breath that clouded in the cold air. 'After two years up here, I'm still not used to how quickly the weather can go from one extreme to another.'

'And you probably never will get used to it, boss. I'm a native northerner and it still never ceases to surprise me.'

There was a light on inside the house but after ringing the bell they had to wait almost a minute before the door was answered.

James recognised Douglas Hannigan immediately from the video and photos he'd seen online. His face was narrow, with a sharp nose and strong jaw. He was wearing tracksuit bottoms and a loose-fitting sweater, and he clearly hadn't showered or shaved recently.

'Good morning, Mr Hannigan,' James said, showing his warrant card. 'I'm Detective Inspector Walker and my colleague here is Detective Sergeant Stevens. We'd like to have a word with you if we may. It's about your former fiancée, Miss Rachel Elliott.'

Hannigan's eyes darted between them before his face folded into a frown.

'I've heard what happened to her and I just can't believe it. But what's it got to do with me? We split up a long time ago.'

'We're aware of that, sir,' James said. 'But it's our understanding that you stayed in contact with her and we need to ask you some questions about that.'

192

'Well, it's simply not true. I haven't seen Rachel in ages, so I don't know where you got your information from.'

'Look, I'd prefer it if we had this conversation inside,' James said. 'So, may we come in? We'll try not to take long.'

With obvious reluctance, Hannigan stepped back and waved them inside, leading them into the living room, which had two long, deep sofas, a view of the small back garden and one wall of exposed brick.

'You'd better sit down then,' he said. 'I'm not properly dressed because I wasn't expecting visitors, and I had a late night.'

'Are you here by yourself?' James asked as he and Stevens perched themselves on one of the sofas.

Hannigan nodded and sat opposite them. 'My girlfriend moved in with me a few months ago, but she's at work.'

James glanced around the room. 'You've got a nice, cosy home, Mr Hannigan. Have you lived here long?'

Hannigan bared his teeth in what passed for a smile. 'Would you please get to the point, Inspector? I want to know what this is all about.'

James leaned forward, elbows on knees. 'Let me begin by saying that I'm heading up the investigation into Rachel's murder and so it's my job to find out as much as I can about her. I've spoken to her parents and during the conversation they told me about your relationship with their daughter and how you broke her heart by calling off the planned wedding.'

Hannigan grimaced. 'I had no choice. I realised we weren't right for each other, though I admit it took me far too long. I do regret leaving it so late to tell her. It made everything so much worse.'

'Were you surprised that she decided to get her revenge when she heard that you were bidding to become an MP?'

'What are you on about?' Hannigan said, shifting uneasily on the sofa.

'You know very well what I'm on about, Mr Hannigan,' James replied. 'We've established that it was Rachel who gave that photo of you snorting cocaine to the *Cumbria Gazette*. Her aim was to embarrass you and trash your bid to become an MP. And you either knew for certain that she was responsible or you guessed it, which was why you sent her that birthday card with the threatening message inside. The one we found in her bedroom.'

Hannigan opened his mouth to respond, but James knew instinctively that he was going to deny it so he raised a hand to stop him, and said, 'I strongly advise you not to lie to us, Mr Hannigan. You must know how serious that will be for you. And you will also know that if you did send that card then we'll almost certainly find out through forensic analysis.'

Hannigan closed his mouth and worked his jaw in circles as he thought through what he was going to say. James sat up straight and waited, satisfied that their suspect was on the back foot.

Eventually, Hannigan threw out a long sigh and gave a tense nod.

'Okay, I'll admit to sending her the card,' he said, his voice slow and measured. 'I did it in a moment of madness because I was so furious with her. I tried phoning her but she wouldn't take my calls. I thought of going to the café where she worked but talked myself out of it because I knew it wouldn't be sensible.'

'So how did you know that it was her?' James asked.

'Nobody else who was at the party would have done that to me,' he said. 'I also know she had other pictures from that night on her phone because she showed me a couple of the two of us together. I didn't know she'd snapped several of me doing stuff. If I had, I would have made her delete them.'

By now a nervous sweat sparkled above Hannigan's top lip and his breathing was rapid.

'So, we've established that you did make a threat against Rachel,' DS Stevens said. 'What we now want to know is: did you go to The Fells Hotel yesterday with the intention of carrying it out?'

A flash of panic passed over Hannigan's face. 'Don't be ridiculous. Yes, I admit I sent the card and that was a stupid thing to have done. But it was only meant to put the wind up her. I felt that was the least she deserved after what she did to me. I would never have done anything to hurt her.'

'Then can you account for your movements yesterday?' Stevens asked him.

'Of course I can. I was at work in the office until six. After work, I had a quick New Year's Eve drink with the team in the pub across the road and left there about seven. After driving home, I showered and changed and then got into a taxi and went to a house party here in Kendal. I came back home at two this morning and went straight to bed.'

'Can anyone corroborate this?' James said.

Hannigan nodded. 'My staff were with me the whole time at work and in the pub. There are three of them. As you probably know, I run my own production company here in

Kendal, which is why I wasn't sacked after the story appeared in the *Gazette*.'

James pushed down his disappointment and got Hannigan to give him the names and contact details of his colleagues, and the name of the pub they went to. If his alibi stood up then they'd lost him as a suspect.

'And what about the girlfriend you mentioned?'

'She was at work. She's in events.'

James went on to ask a few more questions and Hannigan dutifully answered them. Finally, the two detectives got up to leave and James said, 'Thank you for your time, Mr Hannigan. Provided what you've told us is true, I see no reason why we'll need to bother you again.'

They were about to step out of the living room when they all heard the sound of the front door opening and a woman's voice called out, 'It's me. I'm home. We need to talk.'

Hannigan came to a sudden halt and his body seemed to freeze. At the same time, he closed his eyes and swore under his breath.

A moment later the door swung open and James saw what had prompted the man's reaction.

The woman standing there in a long camel-hair coat was none other than Erika Chan, the wedding coordinator at The Fells Hotel.

CHAPTER THIRTY-FOUR

For several long seconds no one knew what to say and it was left to James to break the silence.

'I really didn't expect you to turn up here, Miss Chan,' he said. 'I take it you are Mr Hannigan's girlfriend?'

The woman pressed her lips together in an awkward smile. 'I am, Inspector. I've just come from the hotel. Mr Murphy said I could leave early.'

James turned to Hannigan. 'Why didn't you tell us that your girlfriend worked at The Fells and that she played a major part in organising yesterday's wedding?'

Hannigan twisted his mouth, evidently searching for words, and his body language was suddenly defensive.

'I didn't tell you where she worked because you didn't ask me,' he said, his voice thin and stretched. 'Besides, I don't see how it's relevant. It doesn't change the fact that I did not go there yesterday and I had nothing to do with what happened to Rachel.'

Chan stepped further into the room and James could see the tiredness in her eyes. She looked different to when he'd last spoken to her and he realised it was because her black hair was no longer pulled back in a braid. It hung loose and rested on her shoulders.

'Would someone tell me what's going on?' she demanded, staring at James. 'Why are you here?'

'We came to speak to Mr Hannigan about his relationship with Rachel,' he answered. 'And to ask him where he was yesterday when she was killed.'

Her eyebrows shifted up a fraction. 'But he was at a New Year's Eve party. I know that for a fact because I called him to tell him what had happened.'

'Yes, he's given us an account of his movements, which we'll be following up,' James said. 'But there was another matter we had to discuss with him concerning a birthday card that he sent to Rachel. And I now need to know if you were aware of it, Miss Chan.'

Her hand flew to her mouth and she spun round to face her boyfriend. 'My God. What Rachel told me yesterday was true then. You did send her a card with a threatening message inside it.'

Hannigan's jaw dropped and he quickly reached out to touch her, but she pulled away and gave him a cold, implacable stare. 'I can't believe you did that. It's a horrible thing to have done even if it was her who sent those pictures to the paper.'

There followed another short, frosty silence, and again it fell to James to break it.

'I think we ought to sit down and talk this through,' he

said. 'My colleague and I won't be leaving here until we know exactly what has been going on.'

Seconds later they were back on the sofas. Chan had removed her coat and was sitting next to her boyfriend, but she made sure there was space between them.

James could see she was upset and confused, and that didn't surprise him. The woman who organised the wedding at which the murder took place was now herself a person of interest. It was an unexpected turn of events and one that needed to be thoroughly examined.

James started the ball rolling while Stevens sat beside him with notebook open and pen poised to take down everything that was said.

'My first question is for you, Miss Chan,' James said. 'You've just disclosed the fact that Rachel Elliott confided in you and told you that she'd received a threat from Mr Hannigan. When exactly did this conversation take place?'

Her eyes misted as she began to speak, but despite her obvious nerves her voice was even.

'It was yesterday lunchtime before the wedding ceremony got under way,' she said.

'But you told me earlier that the only time you spoke to her was on the Friday evening,' James pointed out.

Guilt tugged at her features. 'I didn't want you to know about that particular conversation. You see, I wasn't convinced that what she told me was true and I knew that if I mentioned it to you, it would cause problems for Doug.'

'Well, now you need to tell us exactly what was said,' James said.

She coughed to clear her throat before speaking. 'I was in the main hall checking the tables and Rachel approached me. She was by herself and said she wanted a word in private. My heart jumped because I feared she was going to tell me that she'd heard that I'd been seeing Douglas and that I'd moved in with him. And I was right. She said she'd known for some time.'

'Had you been under the impression that she wasn't aware of your relationship with Mr Hannigan?' James said.

She nodded. 'I first met Douglas and Rachel when I was asked to coordinate their wedding, which was due to take place at The Fells. When Douglas cancelled after ending their relationship, I wasn't sure I'd see either of them again. But months later Douglas saw me in a local pub one night. We got talking and one thing led to another, and in no time at all we were a couple. But we both decided early on to keep it fairly quiet, mainly because by then I was involved in preparations for Rachel's sister's wedding and I knew it would be awkward for both of us if Rachel knew that I was with her ex. So only a few close friends were told. I have no idea how she found out.'

'I see,' James said. 'And what else did she say to you?'

'That she had no intention of spoiling Libby's wedding by making an issue of it. She just wanted me to know what a gutless creature Doug is. Those were her words. It put my back up and I told her that she needed to let it go and move on. And I said it was wrong and childish to have sent those damaging pictures to the paper. She denied she had, but I could tell she was lying. And then she asked me if I knew he'd sent her a birthday card with a threat inside. I told her

200

I didn't know anything about a card and that I didn't believe her, but she insisted it was true and said that if he threatened her again, she would go to the police. I was so shocked I didn't really know what to make of it. I tried to get her to say more, but she walked away and left it at that.'

'Why didn't you call to tell me about what she said to you?' Hannigan asked her, his voice unsteady.

'I did, but you didn't answer,' Chan replied.

'But you phoned me after her body was found in the lake. You could have told me then.'

She glared at him, judgement in her eyes. 'I decided it would be best to ask you about it when I got home. Face to face. And that's why I said we needed to talk when I walked through the front door just now.'

'Look, what I did was wrong,' Hannigan said. 'That's why I didn't tell you about it. I knew you'd be mortified.'

Chan turned away from him, gnawing her lower lip, tears in her eyes.

'I'm so sorry, sweetheart,' Hannigan carried on. 'I really am. But I promise you it was a silly empty threat and nothing more.'

She turned back to Hannigan and shook her head at him. 'What else have you done that you haven't told me about? Are you back on the drugs having promised that you'd never touch them again?'

Hannigan spluttered out a response that reeked of desperation. 'There's nothing else. Honest. And I haven't taken any drugs. That's all behind me, and I can't tell you how sorry I am that I sent that card to Rachel. It was stupid.'

Chan held his gaze for a second before her gaze fell to her

lap and she started sobbing. This time, when he reached out and placed a hand on her shoulder, she let him leave it there.

Once she had composed herself, James asked, 'How did you feel about Rachel, knowing she probably sent the photos to the paper?'

'I was angry for sure because I thought Douglas had a good chance of winning that by-election,' she said. 'It was a wretched thing for her to have done just to get back at him for breaking up with her. But equally, what he did to her by sending that birthday card was outrageous and I can't think what possessed him to do it. I know what you're suggesting but I never went to the jetty during the wedding reception and would not have dreamed of causing Rachel any harm.

'On my mother's life, it wasn't me who killed her,' she said tearfully. 'And I really don't know who did.'

CHAPTER THIRTY-FIVE

'Thoughts?' James asked when he was back behind the wheel of his car.

DS Stevens clicked his tongue against the roof of his mouth. 'Hannigan is a grade-A prick, for sure,' he said. 'He should have known better than to have threatened Rachel and he's lucky she didn't come straight to us. But I'll be surprised if his alibi doesn't stand up. He knows it's going to be easy for us to check it out. As for Miss Chan, well, I think she's probably telling the truth about Rachel confronting her at the wedding. But it's easy to imagine that they had more than just a short, civil conversation.'

James nodded. 'I know what you mean. It could also be that she lied to us about exactly when and where this encounter took place, or if it's the only time they spoke. Maybe they actually met up again on the jetty later on and things turned nasty.'

'It'll be worth having another look through the hotel's

surveillance footage, guv. This time see if we can trace Erika Chan's movements during the reception and meal.'

'That's a good shout,' James said. 'DC Hall has been looking after that side of things and he's still at the hotel. Give him a call now and tell him to get started on it.'

James drove while Stevens spoke into his phone. The snow was getting heavier now, big flakes falling from a sky bruised with heavy clouds. He could only hope that this part of Cumbria would escape the worst of what was to come. If it didn't, then their job would be made that much more difficult.

The weight of the investigation, combined with a lack of sleep, was already making it harder for him to concentrate. He could feel the pressure forming behind his eyes and he wasn't able to shake the stiffness in his bones. He was only forty-one and yet he felt much older. He knew it was the same for a lot of coppers at the start of a big, high-profile investigation. Fear of failure and the sheer magnitude of the challenge that lay ahead too often conspired to beef up the pressure.

James rubbed a hand across his unshaven chin and steered a course through the town. The snow was beginning to settle and there were fewer people on the streets.

By the time Stevens ended his call they'd arrived back at headquarters.

'I'm famished,' the DS said. 'My first port of call will be the canteen. Can I get you anything, guv?'

James switched off the engine and replied, 'If you wouldn't mind, something warm to eat and a coffee would be great. Cheers.'

DC Isaac approached James as soon as he walked into the office.

'I've got two messages for you, sir,' she said, before consulting her notebook. 'First, DCI Tanner called to see how things are shaping up. I gave him a summary and told him that you were out conducting an interview. He wants you to ring him when you get the chance.'

'Is he back from Scotland yet?'

'No, but he'll be leaving Dumfries in the next hour or so.'

'And the other message?'

'An update from Sergeant Thomas at the hotel. He wanted us to know that Libby Murphy and her husband have gone home – so has Mark Slade – and the forensic sweep of the grounds has been called off for now because of the weather. They still haven't found a weapon, though. Also, Tony Coppell is on his way here with crime scene photos and notes for the whiteboard.'

'Anything else for me?' James asked.

'Yes, sir. I've had it confirmed that seven more officers should be reporting for duty first thing in the morning. I've sent out a group email informing everyone that there'll be a briefing at nine. Does that suit you?'

'Perfectly.'

'I'll spend what's left of the afternoon collating evidence and I'll make sure it gets updated overnight if anything changes.'

James nodded his thanks. 'Good work, Dawn. When are you knocking off?'

She shrugged. 'My shift ends at five, but I'd be happy to stay if you need me.'

James checked his watch. Three-thirty in the afternoon.

'How many are scheduled to work overnight?' he asked.

'Two detectives and three uniforms, sir.'

'Then you and I will make a point of leaving at five. If I don't call it a day soon, I'll probably fall asleep at the wheel going home.'

They both returned to their desks and the first thing James did was call his boss.

James rated DCI Jeff Tanner highly, but at forty-seven he was at a stage in his career where he seemed to be more turned on by the politics of policing than investigating crimes.

'Hi there, boss,' James said when Tanner picked up. 'DC Isaac passed on your message. I gather you're about to travel back.'

'Indeed, we are,' Tanner said. 'I'm sorry you've been lumbered with what sounds like another scorcher of a case. They always seem to crop up when I'm away from the office.'

Perhaps because you're away from the office more than you ought to be, James thought to himself.

'Can't be helped, sir,' he said. 'How was your Christmas?'

'Hectic, even though it was just me, my wife and our son for a change. But look, that's not what we need to talk about. Have there been any developments since I spoke to Dawn?'

James filled him in on the conversations they'd had with Douglas Hannigan and Erika Chan.

'I'll know soon enough if Hannigan's alibi is legit,' he said, 'but I suspect he was at work or in the pub when the murder took place. Erika Chan, on the other hand, is a more likely suspect. She admits that she had what must have been a difficult conversation with Rachel before the service got under way, and as the hotel's wedding coordinator she would have been able to move around without drawing attention to herself. She doesn't strike me as a killer, but I very much doubt that the murder was premeditated as it seems more likely to have been the unexpected end result of a violent disagreement.'

James gave Tanner a brief description of the other suspects and ran through the various leads that were being pursued. He then sang the praises of DC Abbott.

'The way she got on with the job as soon as the alarm was raised was highly commendable and she proved to be a useful source of information.'

'I'll make a point of thanking her when I'm in tomorrow,' Tanner said. 'Meanwhile, I've been speaking to media liaison about perhaps holding a press conference at some point. It could be useful to us.'

'Agreed, sir. There'll be a full briefing at nine in the morning. We'll hopefully have made further progress by then and all the background checks will have been carried out.'

'Well, it seems that you've got everything under control as usual, James. But before the briefing tomorrow I'd like to have a quiet word with you in my office about a personal matter. Can you aim to be in at around eight?'

'Of course.'

'Good stuff. Sorry to dangle the proverbial carrot but I'll have more time to go into it properly tomorrow. For now, I can assure you it's nothing to worry about. I'll see you then.'

James hadn't a clue what Tanner wanted to talk to him about and decided that there was no point dwelling on it now. As soon as he ended the call, he made another one, this time to the number Fraser Elliott had given him for Mary Wilson, the owner of the café where Rachel had worked. But it went to voicemail so he left a message asking her to ring him.

James was contemplating what to do next when Stevens arrived back from the canteen.

'Lunch is on me, boss,' he said. 'While you get stuck in, I'll go and check Hannigan's alibi with his team.'

Stevens had got him a burger that went down a treat along with a bruised banana and a cup of hot coffee.

James immediately felt the benefit of having eaten something and it perked him up a little.

A few minutes later, Stevens returned to say that Hannigan's employees had confirmed that he was with them in their office until just after six on New Year's Eve. He then went to the pub with them and set off for home about seven.

James shrugged his shoulders. It wasn't an unexpected result but it still served to fuel the frustration that was growing inside him.

He spent the next hour typing up a report and discussing the case with Isaac and Stevens. He was determined to leave at five and by then the nightshift was in place.

There was only one thing left to do before he exited the office, and that was to take a couple of paracetamol to combat the ache that had started raging in his head.

CHAPTER THIRTY-SIX

James's headaches were usually at their most severe when they first came on, and they tended to fade quickly once the paracetamol started to work its magic, so he was hoping that he'd be pain free by the time he'd driven the twenty-five miles to Kirkby Abbey.

Before leaving headquarters, he sent a message to Annie telling her that he was on his way home and asked how Bella was. She replied instantly.

Bella's about the same. Cough, sniffles and slight temperature. I made your favourite stew and it's in the oven.

It was dark now and road conditions had worsened as the snow was still falling and the wind had started to pick up again.

James felt physically and emotionally drained, and the case continued to play on his mind as he drove.

Two calls came through the Bluetooth during the journey. The first was from Officer Hartley, the FLO assigned to Rachel's parents. She wanted him to know that they had asked her to leave their house in Bowness so they could spend the evening by themselves.

'They have my number and I told them I'd pop over in the morning,' she said. 'They're still in a terrible state and not very communicative, sir, so I'm afraid I didn't learn anything about their daughter that we don't already know.'

The second call was from DC Abbott who was responding to a text he had sent to her earlier, asking for an update on Belinda Travers.

'I went to see her just as you asked me to,' she said. 'She was angry rather than upset with Greg Murphy for accusing her of lying. She said it didn't surprise her that he chose to believe Slade because she claimed they always stick by one another.'

'Is she still at the hotel?'

'I phoned her an hour ago and she told me she'd left. I also took the liberty of running a check through the database. She's as clean as a whistle with no priors.'

'Do you still believe she told us the truth about what happened?' James asked.

'No question in my mind, guv. Mark Slade comes across as an arrogant bastard with an inflated opinion of himself. And it really wouldn't surprise me if he turns out to be our killer.'

A thin layer of snow had settled over Kirkby Abbey and it was still coming down when James arrived in the village.

He drove past the small Catholic church and the White Hart pub, and when he came to the market square, he saw that the large Christmas tree at its centre still hadn't been taken down.

Their four-bedroom cottage was close to the primary school that Annie had attended as a pupil and now worked in as a teacher. Across the road, a gate led into a field that had spectacular views of some of the surrounding fells.

He was feeling like a flat battery when he let himself in through the front door, but the mere sight of Annie in the hallway lifted his spirits. A full-wattage smile lit up her face as he walked towards her.

'I can't believe I haven't seen you since about this time yesterday,' she said. 'What a way to start the new year.'

He slid his arm around her waist and they shared a long, lingering kiss that charged up James's battery.

'You must be absolutely knackered,' she said as he removed his coat and shoes. 'Dinner is about ready and there's a drink waiting for you in the kitchen.'

'And Bella?'

'Fast asleep on the sofa. I haven't dared move her because I don't want to wake her.'

'Has she still got a temperature?'

'A slight one, as I said in the message, but I'm sure it's nothing to worry about. We just have to keep an eye on her.'

He went straight into the living room where the radiators were blasting out a fierce heat.

Bella was lying under a blanket with only her head showing. Her mouth was open and she was breathing silently through it.

James crouched down and gave her a gentle peck on the

forehead, which felt warm against his lips. She might have had a temperature but other than that she appeared to be perfectly okay. As cute and cuddly as ever.

James left her there and went into the kitchen where Annie was ladling his favourite chicken stew into a bowl.

'Your drink is over there on the table,' she said.

She'd poured him a large whisky with ice and it was just what he needed after the day he'd had. As he fired it down, he felt it bite the back of his throat.

'You can tell me all about your day and night while we eat this,' Annie said. 'Then you can shower and change while I clean up, if you like.'

Annie evidently knew quite a bit already about the murder of Rachel Elliott because she'd been following the story on the news throughout the day, but having him describe how it had impacted on Rachel's family and friends almost moved her to tears. Several times she closed her eyes and shook her head as though she were trying to banish whatever image had formed in her mind.

'I was surprised to learn that Rachel's parents used to live here in the village,' he told her. 'They moved to Bowness just over thirty years ago before their girls were born.'

'My mum and dad probably knew them then,' Annie said. 'What are they like?'

'They seem a nice, down-to-earth couple. It's such a terrible shame what's happened.'

James revealed what the couple had said about the sibling rivalry between Rachel and her elder sister.

'I feel sorry for Libby,' he said. 'The parents don't like Greg Murphy and they tried to talk her out of marrying him. Her mother even snapped at her in front of me and told her that if she hadn't gone ahead with the wedding then her sister would still be alive.'

Annie was aghast. 'Oh, that is truly awful. The poor woman.'

James chose not to go into too much more detail about the case. He feared that the more he talked about it the less likely it was that either of them would get a good night's sleep.

After dinner, he went upstairs and had a hot shower, then put on jeans and a jumper. When he came back down Annie had finished cleaning up and was sitting on the sofa with Bella on her lap.

'She's just woken up,' Annie said. 'Would you like to have a cuddle before I see if she's hungry?'

Bella's eyes were wide open and she was chewing on her dummy. James was eager to enfold her in his arms, but just as he was about to take her his phone buzzed.

'Damn it,' he said, stepping back and reaching for it in his back pocket. 'I'd better take this. Sorry.'

He recognised the number as soon as he saw it on the screen.

'Is that Detective Inspector Walker?' Mary Wilson said when he answered.

'It is. And you're Miss Wilson, I take it.'

'It's Mrs Wilson, but no matter. I'm sorry I missed your call earlier. My husband and I are spending a few days at a hotel in Keswick and when we went for a walk, I forgot to take my phone. When I heard your voice message, I guessed it was about Rachel. I've been in tears since I heard about what's happened to her. She was such a lovely girl and a hard worker. It just doesn't seem possible that I'll never see her again.'

Mrs Wilson's voice had the rasp of a heavy smoker and James got the impression that she probably wasn't a young woman.

'I understand she worked in your café, Mrs Wilson,' James said.

'She did indeed. She was one of three young ladies who've been with me since we took it over several years ago. She served behind the counter, waited tables and helped with the cleaning. She'll be greatly missed.'

'When was she last in?'

'That would be on Thursday. She had Friday off to prepare for her sister's wedding.'

'And how was she on that day?'

'Same as always. Quiet, but pleasant. Got on with the job.'

'How much do you know about what happened yesterday?'

'I didn't know anything until one of the other girls, Trish, phoned my husband because she couldn't get through to me. We hurried back to the hotel we're staying at until tomorrow and switched on the television.'

'Then you'll have heard that we're trying to trace her boyfriend, a man named Carlo Salvi.'

'Yes, I saw that, but I assumed you'd have spoken to him by now. Please don't tell me you think he killed her.'

'We don't know who killed Rachel yet, Mrs Wilson,' James said. 'However, we do know that Mr Salvi was at the wedding with her and left before the police arrived. Unfortunately, we haven't had an opportunity to speak to him yet.'

'Well, I can't believe he would have been responsible. He doesn't strike me as a murderer.'

'You know him then?'

'Of course. He's been a regular customer in the café for some time. That's how they met. He comes in a couple of times a week for coffee and sometimes a sandwich.'

'And when did they start seeing each other?'

'A few months ago. She would always chat to him and made it obvious that she fancied him and he eventually asked her out. She told me she really liked him but that she didn't want to get too involved because she knew he was going to return to Italy. In fact, he was due to go this week. It's the end of his work contract or something.'

James moved swiftly into the kitchen to make use of the notebook and pen he knew was on one of the worktops.

'Can you tell me all you know about Mr Salvi?' he asked her.

'I only know what Rachel told me about him,' she said. 'I rarely engaged him in conversation and most of the time he sat quietly by himself at one of the window tables reading the paper or a book. He never stayed long because he had to get back to work.'

'Where does he work?'

'At the university in Ambleside. He's a teacher or a visiting professor or something like that. Rachel did tell me once but I've forgotten what he does.'

As James made notes, he could feel his pulse quicken.

'Do you know where he lives, Mrs Wilson?' he said.

'I don't, I'm afraid. It must be in Ambleside though because Rachel stayed with him some nights and she walked to his place, leaving her Mini in the car park behind the café.'

'Were you aware that she didn't tell her parents or sister that she was in a relationship?' James said.

'No, I wasn't,' she replied. 'But as I already told you, she said she didn't want it to get too serious because he wasn't staying long.'

'Well, that is strange. You see, she told one of her pals that she was going to introduce him to everyone at the wedding as her boyfriend, and that she intended to announce that she was going to move to Italy with him.'

He heard the woman catch her breath.

'Gosh, I had no idea she'd fallen for him so hard. She never mentioned that to me. I feel awful now ...'

'You can't blame yourself, Mrs Wilson.'

'No, it's not that. It's just ... well, if I had known that she was planning to run off with him, I would have warned her against it. You see, a few weeks ago, I saw Carlo snogging another girl outside a pub one evening after Rachel had gone home to Bowness. I didn't mention it to her because I didn't see the point in upsetting her as he was soon going to be out of her life anyway.'

'Is it possible she found out about it?'

'I have no idea. But if she did, I'm sure she wouldn't have been happy about it.'

CHAPTER THIRTY-SEVEN

New Year's Day was coming to an end and James was about to go to bed. His body felt numb and hollowed out, and his brain was aching with the effort of thinking.

He'd been hoping that the evening would give him an opportunity to wind down and relax, but it hadn't worked out that way.

What Mrs Wilson had told him about their prime suspect, Carlo Salvi, was significant, and he'd had to pass it straight on to HQ.

But to his surprise it wasn't news to DS Stevens, who was still in the office when James called. He told James that two people had responded after seeing Salvi's photo on the TV news, both of them claiming he was a visiting research fellow at Cumbria University in Ambleside.

'We're chasing it up, boss,' Stevens had said. 'But it being a bank holiday will probably slow the process.'

It was now ten o'clock and James still hadn't heard anything further. Under normal circumstances, he would have chased Stevens up, but he'd felt that it was more important to spend some quality time with his wife and daughter.

Bella clearly wasn't well and he could see that it was now beginning to worry Annie even though she was trying to hide it.

'I'll take her along to the surgery if she's still like this tomorrow,' she'd said earlier. 'I'm hoping that all she needs is a good night's sleep.'

Bella still had a slight fever and a cough, but she did take her feed and smiled when James made faces at her. She was now in her cot and spark out, and Annie was sleeping on the sofa in Bella's room to keep an eye on her.

James had their bed to himself and they'd agreed that if he had to leave early in the morning and they were still sleeping, he wouldn't wake them.

As he slipped beneath the duvet, he felt limp with fatigue and his thoughts were muddy. The full weight of the day's events hit him when he closed his eyes and he felt a surge of anxiety.

He was still lying there some ten minutes later when he heard a text message ping on his phone, which was lying as usual on the bedside table. It was from Stevens asking him if he was still awake.

James rang him straight back and when he answered, said, 'What would you have done if I hadn't responded?'

'I'd have assumed that you were asleep and left you a message,' Stevens replied. 'What I have to tell you can wait but I thought you'd prefer to know asap.'

'Okay, fire away then.'

'Well, it took us a while to get to the relevant people at the university and that's why I couldn't get back to you any earlier,' Stevens said. 'We found out that Carlo Salvi is indeed a research fellow at the university – specifically a geographer specialising in the study of the landscape and climate change. He's been on a year's secondment, which actually came to an end last Friday, and he was due to return to Italy in a week's time.'

'And have you tracked him down?'

'No, we haven't. He's been living off campus in a rented flat in Ambleside, which is where I am now. His landlady, a Mrs Banister, owns the building and lives in the flat above. She's just told me that he packed up and left today. She's not sure what time because she spent New Year's Eve with her brother and his family in Carlisle. Salvi was gone when she arrived back late this afternoon and he'd left a note thanking her for making him feel so welcome this past year. She said his rent is paid up until the end of the week so it surprised her that he'd gone and hadn't even bothered to phone her.'

'Does she know where he is now?'

'She thinks he must be on his way home to Italy, though he gave no hint that he was going to leave early. She also told us he's been leasing a car from a local firm.'

'Have you got the registration?'

'She doesn't know it so we'll have to check all the car hire companies around here.'

'Is there anything in his flat that'll help us find him?' James asked.

'It's a very small place. Just one bedroom, a kitchen and a lounge. I've had a good look round and there's nothing. He's taken all his personal belongings with him. Forensics can't get here for a while and we'll have to wait until morning to get access to local traffic cameras, if there are any.'

'What about his phone?'

'The landlady has given me his number and I've tried it, but it's switched off.'

'Did she know that he went to a wedding?'

'She did, but she doesn't know whether he arrived back on Saturday night or early today because she wasn't here.'

'And what has she told you about him?'

'She reckons he was a good tenant and very pleasant, and she said that several different women stayed overnight with him. I showed her a photo of Rachel Elliott and she confirmed that she was one of them.'

James mulled this over. 'Then it seems we were right to think the guy has done a runner,' he said after a few moments.

'I agree,' Stevens said. 'And why would he do that if he hasn't done anything wrong?'

James stifled a yawn and told Stevens he'd see him in the morning.

'I need to get at least a few hours' sleep,' he said. 'And you should as well. We're both going to need it. Hand over to the uniforms to finish up there and go home. It's going to be another long day tomorrow.'

CHAPTER THIRTY-EIGHT

James was out of bed, shaved, showered and dressed by six o'clock the next morning. He'd had a restless night, during which he'd managed to sleep for barely four hours.

And it wasn't just thoughts about the case that had kept him awake. It was also the wind that battered the windows until the early hours.

Outside, the village was shrouded in snow, which looked to be a couple of inches deep. He wasn't looking forward to driving to Kendal.

He decided not to bother with breakfast or even a coffee, but he wasn't prepared to leave the house without checking on Annie and Bella.

He eased the door open and saw that his daughter was snug in her cot. Annie was lying on the sofa and he thought she was asleep until she spoke to him.

'Are you off then? What time is it?'

'Just after six,' he whispered. 'I'm sorry if I woke you.'

'You didn't. I've been awake for what seems like ages. The weather sounds awful so be careful out there.'

'I will. What kind of night did Bella have?'

'Well, she woke up coughing once, but apart from that she seems to have slept well. Fingers crossed I won't have to take her to the doctor.'

James leaned over and kissed his wife's forehead.

'You will call me if there's a problem?'

'Of course. But I'm sure she's fine. And good luck today. This sounds like one of those investigations where you're going to need plenty of it.'

Since moving to Cumbria, James had got used to driving in inclement weather. Thankfully, today wasn't as bad as he had initially feared it would be.

The snow had stopped falling and the wind had eased so that what had already come down wasn't being whipped into a frenzy. Plus, the gritters had already been out clearing the worst hit stretches of road.

He listened to the radio as he drove and the murder of Rachel Elliott was still being covered on the news. There were no new developments to report, but there were sound-bites from a few of Rachel's friends who had attended the wedding. They described what had happened to her as a complete mystery and one appealed to her boyfriend, Carlo Salvi, to contact the police and help them with their enquiries.

There was no mention of Salvi being a research fellow at the university in Ambleside, but James knew that it wouldn't be long before the media got wind of it.

He arrived at the office just after seven and there were

quite a few people already in, including DC Abbott, who along with DC Isaac was pinning pieces of evidence to the two whiteboards.

'Looks like I wasn't the only one who woke up early and couldn't get back to sleep,' he said to both of them.

It was Abbott who responded. 'No point in lying in bed when there's so much that needs to be done, guv. Did you manage to rest your weary bones?'

'Enough to see me through today without flaking out, I reckon,' he replied.

He left them to get on with it and crossed the room to touch base with the two detectives who had worked through the night. When he saw that they were both glued to their phones he grabbed a coffee and snack bar from the vending machine and then went to his desk to prepare for the nine o'clock briefing.

There was plenty to discuss and lots of tasks to assign, and he wanted to make preparations before his eight o'clock meeting with DCI Tanner.

He was still none the wiser as to what it was going to be about or why the boss had been so cagey. He just hoped it wasn't something that would prove to be a distraction.

His desktop was covered with paperwork and Post-it notes, but the first thing his eyes alighted upon was the page from the *Cumbria Gazette* magazine that he'd picked up in Rachel's bedroom yesterday.

James had completely forgotten to phone the psychic to find out if Rachel had gone to see her for a reading so he added it to his list of things to do and began preparing his notes. He didn't get far, however, before he felt a firm hand on his shoulder and turned to see DCI Tanner standing over him.

'Morning, James,' he said. 'I'm here earlier than expected, so we might as well have that chat now before the rest of the troops arrive. Come into my office.'

James felt an uncomfortable tightness in his chest as he sat across the desk from Tanner.

The DCI was a thick-set man with cropped grey hair and a slightly crooked nose. He was looking smart as always in a well-pressed suit, and his wide brown eyes were giving nothing away.

'This won't take long, James,' he said. 'I just want to make you aware of what's happening before you hear it from someone else.'

'That's usually what people say when they're about to dish out some bad news, boss,' James replied.

Tanner pinched his face into a tight smile. 'I suppose it will be bad news for you and the rest of the team if you've all enjoyed working with me.'

James felt his jaw drop. 'Are you leaving us?'

Tanner nodded. 'I'm moving up the ladder. You'll know about the superintendent vacancy that cropped up at constabulary headquarters in Penrith? Well, I applied for it and was told on Thursday that the job is mine.'

James stood up and reached across the desk to shake Tanner's hand.

'My congratulations to you, sir. It's well deserved and I, for one, will most certainly miss reporting to you.'

'That's kind of you to say so, but you need to keep it to

224

yourself for now. An official announcement won't be made for at least a few days.'

'When will you be starting your new role?'

'At the end of March. The wife is over the moon because, as you know, we live in the town and our place is within walking distance of Carleton Hall.'

James sat back in his chair and folded his arms across his chest.

'Who'll be taking over from you here?' he asked.

Tanner arched his brow and smiled again. 'I'm hoping it'll be you. It's about time you were promoted to Detective Chief Inspector.'

James was thrown off balance. He sat there in silent thought for a moment as Tanner tapped a pen against his teeth while waiting for a response.

Eventually, James said, 'I take it you're serious?'

'Too right I am. I was asked to recommend a replacement and I put your name forward. There will be other candidates, but if you want the job, I'm a hundred per cent sure you'll get it.'

James felt his chest expand as he took a breath. 'There's no question about me wanting it,' he said. 'It's just come as a shock. I've only been with the constabulary for two years.'

'But you've been a copper for over twenty. And since coming here you've made a good impression, cracked some tough cases, and earned the support and respect of the team.'

James grinned. 'Thank you, sir.'

'So, think about it and when you give the word, I'll start the process,' Tanner replied. 'But don't take too long. The powers that be want this sorted as soon as possible.' He put his pen down and leaned across the desk. 'Now, I want you to bring me up to speed on where we are with this case before the briefing begins. You will remain in charge, of course, and I'll have your back. My first contribution will be to front a press conference later today. I know you hate doing them.'

'I'd appreciate that,' James said.

'It's already obvious that there's a lot of public interest in this case. It will stretch our resources and test our resolve but it'll also give you another chance to prove yourself and gain more kudos.'

James was about to respond when someone tapped on the office door and then pushed it open without being invited to.

It was Detective Constable Ahmed Sharma, one of the newest recruits to the team. He was a thin, wiry man whom James considered a diligent investigator with a sharp eye.

'I'm really sorry to disturb you both,' he said. 'But we've had a breakthrough and I thought I should draw it to your attention straight away.'

CHAPTER THIRTY-NINE

James jumped to his feet and gestured for Sharma to step further into Tanner's office.

The detective's use of the word 'breakthrough' had sent a ripple of excitement rushing through him. It was what they desperately needed if any significant progress was to be made with the investigation into Rachel Elliott's murder.

Sharma stood in the middle of the room clutching a note-book, his posture straight and confident.

'So, what have you got for us, lad?' Tanner said. 'Out with it.'

Sharma's brow creased in concentration as he glanced at his notes before speaking.

'It's to do with the boyfriend, Carlo Salvi,' he said. 'We believe he's in London and is due to fly to Italy from Heathrow on a plane that's scheduled to leave in just over an hour.'

James felt a stab of panic. 'Jesus, then we need to stop him.'

Sharma nodded. 'That's what we're aiming to do, guv. We're

in contact with the Met and have passed on his name and the flight number, but we wondered if one of you should get in touch with someone higher up the chain of command to make sure they respond without delay.'

'I'll get onto that,' Tanner said. 'Write down the flight number for me and the name of the person we're liaising with. Then, while I'm on the blower, you can explain to Detective Inspector Walker how you got us to this point.'

'Start at the beginning,' James said as he and Sharma stepped out of Tanner's office. 'The last I heard we'd found out where Salvi lived and worked, but his landlady told us he'd moved out suddenly.'

'We've been chasing it throughout the night, guv,' Sharma said. 'The landlady didn't know the registration of Salvi's car so we had to contact all the hire companies in the area and eventually we got lucky. It's a firm in Ambleside and it turns out he dropped it off there yesterday afternoon. He then got them to call him a taxi to take him to the nearest railway station, which is the one in Windermere. Uniforms were dispatched to check CCTV there and while they were doing that it occurred to me that he might be heading for Manchester Airport, from which there are regular flights to Italy.

'There was one late yesterday, but it was full and he wasn't on it. I checked flights for the coming days though, and found he's booked on a flight next Monday to Milan Malpensa airport.'

'So, why is he in London? Ah, I see. He's desperate to leave the country and as there are no flights from Manchester for a few days he decided to head for London,' James said, thinking it through aloud.

'Exactly, and the CCTV from Windermere Station confirmed it for us a short time ago. Salvi was shown boarding a train for the capital. The journey time is about five and a half hours to Euston so he would have arrived last evening.

'The obvious thing to do then was check all Heathrow flights and that's when his name cropped up on the one to Milan Malpensa that leaves soon.'

'You've done a brilliant job, Ahmed,' James said. 'Well done. We now just have to hope that the team at Heathrow will stop him boarding that plane.'

Just before nine o'clock, DC Sharma came off the phone with an update for James.

'Carlo Salvi has been apprehended by the police at Heathrow, sir,' he said. 'He was waiting to board the flight to Milan when they got him. He didn't put up any resistance and has confirmed to officers that he'd travelled to London from Cumbria yesterday. His three suitcases are being removed from the hold and arrangements are now being made to have him brought north to Kendal.'

'That's great news, Ahmed,' James said. 'Hopefully we'll be able to put him on the spot this afternoon. Can you make sure there's a duty solicitor on standby?'

CHAPTER FORTY

The morning briefing got under way on time and James began by holding up a copy of the post-mortem report on Rachel Elliott that Dr Pam Flint had sent over during the night. He explained that a senior officer based in Carlisle had attended the PM and had passed on his observations in an email.

'The pathologist has confirmed that Rachel died from a severe blow to the back of the head, sustained when she fell or was pushed onto one of the jetty posts,' he said. 'It resulted in internal haemorrhaging and led to irreparable brain damage. She also suffered two blows to her face – one on her forehead and the other below her left eye – and the bruises on her arms were defence wounds, inflicted by a blunt instrument that could have been a heavy torch, a crowbar or even a large stone.

'We have two other significant factors of note. The first is that there were no deposits under her nails, which suggests that she probably didn't manage to grab her assailant, and the second is that blood tests show she'd consumed high levels of alcohol.

'We still don't know why she ended up on the jetty during the wedding reception. It could have been because she wanted to be by herself to have a think or because she hoped the breeze from the lake would help her to sober up. It could also be that she arranged to meet someone there. Maybe the person who killed her.'

The room was packed, the atmosphere charged, and as James spoke every nerve in his body was buzzing. This was the first time the whole team had got together since the murder investigation began and now that the holiday weekend was behind them, he was hoping they'd start to make real progress.

He moved on to Rachel's boyfriend, Carlo Salvi. The word had already spread that the Met had collared him at Heathrow.

'He became our prime suspect because they were seen to have had an argument of some sort during the wedding reception and he subsequently disappeared from the hotel. It's clear now that he was trying to flee the country and so I'm cautiously optimistic that he is our man. That said, there's always still a chance that he isn't, which means we have to continue pursuing other leads.'

He got DC Sharma to run through what they knew about Salvi and how they had managed to track him to London.

'It seems he was popular among the local women while he lived here,' Sharma said. 'Rachel Elliott met him when he became a customer in the café where she worked and she was one of several different women who his landlady saw stay over in his flat. We don't know if Rachel knew about the others but it is possible that she found out about them during her sister's wedding and that's why they argued.'

This was James's cue to explain for those who didn't know that it was DC Abbott who saw Salvi storm out of Rachel's room.

'We also have hotel surveillance footage showing Salvi going off on his own after leaving the room. Following this, it appears that Rachel tried to drown her sorrows and got a bit drunk. This apparently upset the groom, Greg Murphy, who told his new wife to sort her sister out. However, it served to make things worse after Libby confronted her as they had words and Rachel rushed off. That was the last time Rachel was seen in the hall with the rest of the guests.'

James tilted his head towards the whiteboards, which were dominated by photographs of the victim. They showed Rachel in her maid-of-honour dress at the marriage ceremony and posing with others in the garden. The bright, cheerful images were in stark contrast to the shots of her body taken from various angles after it had been hauled out of the lake.

James mentioned the sibling rivalry between the sisters and how Rachel had been jealous of Libby's success with men and in her career.

'As you should all now be aware, our victim was not happy that Libby's wedding was taking place at The Fells Hotel because she had been due to get married there herself early last year,' James said. 'However, the wedding was called off by the groom, Douglas Hannigan, who dumped Rachel and broke her heart.

'Rachel sought revenge against Hannigan by handing photos of him snorting cocaine to the *Cumbria Gazette*. Her objective was to stop him becoming a local MP and she succeeded. Hannigan guessed it was her and he retaliated by sending her a birthday card with a threatening message inside. It initially made him a suspect in our eyes but he has since provided us with a solid alibi for New Year's Eve. He didn't go to the hotel and he didn't kill Rachel.'

James then pointed to a photograph of Erika Chan. 'This woman is the hotel's wedding coordinator, and also happens to be Hannigan's live-in girlfriend. Rachel approached her on the day of the wedding and told her to tell Hannigan that she'd go to the police if he threatened her again. Miss Chan insists she did not come into contact with Rachel after that conversation and denies killing her, but it's possible she's lying and they did meet up again on the jetty. I therefore want a full background check carried out on Miss Chan. Let's see what turns up.

'DC Hall, was Chan with Rachel in any of the surveillance footage or guest photos?' James asked.

'I spotted her several times in the footage but she was always alone and in the background,' Hall answered.

James passed the verbal baton to DC Abbott who explained why best man Mark Slade was also on their list of suspects.

'Mr Slade denies Miss Travers's claim of harassment,' she concluded, 'but we need to take into account his history of violence against women, which I've detailed in the notes that I've circulated. We also need to consider the possibility that Slade went looking for someone else to have a go at and found Rachel alone by the lake. One thing to note is that Slade and

Greg Murphy are best buddies and Murphy has already made an effort to discredit Miss Travers's story.'

James thanked DC Abbott and then drew the team's attention to yet another photo on the whiteboard.

'Ethan Prescott,' he said. 'This man is the son of Claire Prescott, who used to be nanny to the Elliott sisters. He's a contender because he dated both women. First, he had a relationship with Rachel, but then he left her and moved on to Libby, which caused understandable friction between the sisters. He and Libby were together for about six months and it was after they split up that she met Greg Murphy.

'We have an eyewitness who saw Prescott and Libby confront Rachel on the garden path during the reception, just before she must have ventured down to the jetty. Libby notably didn't mention this encounter when we first interviewed her and then later, when asked about it, said she'd simply forgot.'

'But what motive would Ethan Prescott have had for killing Rachel?' DS Stevens asked.

'That's a good question,' James answered. 'Though he doesn't appear to have had one, it could be that he followed her to the jetty and they got into an argument. Maybe he went there to have a moan about her drinking and it turned violent, or perhaps he tried it on with her. At this point we need to consider all possibilities.'

'He's never appeared on our radar before and he doesn't have a police record,' DC Isaac offered. 'He lives with his mother in Windermere and runs a gift shop there. Enquiries have turned up one interesting fact though: the man's got himself into serious debt. He's behind on rent payments for the shop and is struggling to pay back a bank loan he took out to set the business up. His problems are mainly due to the fact that he overstretched himself in order to get started and then trade was slow during his first year.'

'Do we know if he's in a relationship?' James asked.

Isaac shook her head. 'According to his Facebook page he's single, but that doesn't mean he isn't in a relationship.'

It was then the turn of Tony Coppell, the Chief Forensic Officer, to update the team. He chose to do so by using the new interactive whiteboard, which enabled him to project and manipulate files and images onto the wall-mounted screen.

Using a remote control, he started by flicking through photos of the crime scene.

'Despite a thorough search of the grounds and the water around the jetty we still haven't come across a murder weapon, and as the grounds are now covered in snow the search has had to be halted. It should be noted that the area was severely compromised even before the storm by people searching for the victim before we got there.'

He brought up images of Rachel's mobile phone, laptop and tablet.

'The phone was in her purse at the scene and we took the other two devices from her bedroom at home. The technical team are in the process of extracting the digital data from those, however, we've already managed to gain access to her phone and have discovered that the last time she used it was at five-forty on New Year's Eve, which must have been just before she was killed. She sent a WhatsApp message to her sister.'

'That would have been just minutes after Libby and Ethan Prescott tried to talk to her on the garden path,' James said.

Coppell nodded. 'That's why I thought you would find it of particular interest and perhaps relevance. Check it out.'

Another press of the remote and the message appeared on the screen. As James read it, he felt the blood stir in his veins.

CHAPTER FORTY-ONE

A hush descended on the room as the team stared at the message on the big screen.

You disgust me, Libby. I'm not going to keep your sordid secret so make the most of today. And tell that slimy bastard Ethan that if he ever lays a hand on me again, I'll have him put away.

A low murmur spread around the room and someone let out a loud whistle.

'This could be a potential game changer,' James said so that everyone could hear. 'What sordid secret is her sister supposed to be keeping and did Rachel place herself in danger by threatening to reveal it?'

'I can confirm that the message was read only seconds after it was sent,' Coppell chipped in.

'That would mean Libby saw it just before she and Prescott took their seats in the main hall for the wedding breakfast,' DC Abbott pointed out.

James nodded. 'You have to wonder then if one or both of them found the time to go looking for Rachel so they could plead with her to keep her mouth shut.'

'I find it hard to believe that Libby would have killed her own sister,' Abbott said. 'Surely, whatever the secret is, it can't be that serious.'

James shrugged. 'As the crime scene evidence suggests, it was most likely a crime of passion and murder was never the intended result. A verbal tussle may suddenly have become physical. Libby – or Ethan, for that matter – may have lost control and hit out with whatever they were holding, knocking Rachel backwards onto the post.'

'It appears from what Rachel said in the message that Ethan had already got physical with her,' Abbott replied. 'He must have laid a hand on her either before or after they were seen by the staff member arguing in the garden.'

'We'll need to ask him about it. Right, Abbott and I will go to speak with Libby and Ethan again. They've both got a lot of explaining to do,' James said. 'Libby lives in Burnside and Ethan in Windermere, so we should be back in good time to welcome Carlo Salvi to Kendal.

'Tony, was there anything else of interest on Rachel's phone?'

'Most of the calls she made in recent months are to a number I now know belongs to the boyfriend,' he said. 'He called her back but not nearly as often as she called him. They also exchanged messages, mostly about when and where they would meet up and whether she could stay at his flat overnight. It's worth noting that she expressed her feelings more than he did, often telling him how much she enjoyed being with him and how she wished he didn't have to go back to Italy. And she ended every message with four or five kisses. The nearest he ever came to showing affection was by telling her he'd had a good time and was looking forward to seeing her again.'

'That's probably because he was seeing other women while dating her,' Abbott said.

James looked down at his notebook and the list he'd drawn up of all the topics he wanted to raise before he started to assign tasks. He reminded the team that he wanted to know more about Mark Slade and Greg Murphy and was told that little progress had been made yesterday because so few people were in, but these enquiries were now in hand.

'One thing to note is that Libby and Greg were having problems in their relationship some months ago and she was apparently having second thoughts about marrying him. But after his father died, she couldn't bring herself to do it and it would appear they were able to work through their differences. This was much to the disappointment of her parents and sister who have no time for Greg. I don't know if any of this had a bearing on what happened at the wedding, but we need to explore all possibilities. And we should also go along to the university and speak to staff there about Salvi. Find out as much as we can about him.'

James finished the briefing by announcing that DCI Tanner would be staging a press conference this afternoon at Carleton Hall.

CHAPTER FORTY-TWO

'We'll leave in fifteen minutes,' James said to Abbott as soon as the briefing was over. 'I need to make a call. While I do that can you get the addresses for Libby and Ethan Prescott so we can put them into the satnav?'

James went back to his desk and looked up the number for the psychic medium, Lisa Doyle. He had last spoken to her at the end of the investigation into the farmhouse massacre a year ago and what she'd said to him back then he would never forget.

She'd claimed she'd had a vision of James standing over someone's blood-covered body and said that a voice in her head had told her that he and his colleagues would soon be having to confront another tidal wave of death and destruction.

She turned out to be right in one respect as it wasn't long before he was staring down at the body of a man who'd been brutally stabbed to death. But since then, he'd investigated three more murders, not including the current case, and he didn't reckon that amounted to a tidal wave of death and destruction.

Before he met the widow Doyle, he'd never believed in all that psychic stuff. But she made such an impression on him that he now maintained an open mind on the subject.

His number must have been saved in her phone because she greeted him by name.

'Well, hello Detective Inspector Walker. Believe it or not, I've been wondering whether or not I should ring you.'

'Really?' James said, surprised.

'Yes. I caught up with the news last night and learned about that terrible murder at the hotel on Lake Windermere. They said you were leading the investigation.'

'I am. In fact, that's why I'm calling.'

'Let me guess. You've been told that poor Miss Elliott came to see me just after Christmas.'

'That's right. She'd cut out a feature about you that appeared in *Cumbria Life* magazine and had scrawled what I assumed was an appointment note on it.'

'I remember it well, Detective Walker, mainly because she got quite upset. That was why after I saw what had happened to her it occurred to me that perhaps I should tell you about it.'

'Okay, well, start at the beginning. Did she come all the way to your home in Sedbergh for a session?'

'She didn't have to. I spent that day doing tarot card readings at a hall in Ambleside as a post-Christmas event. It was mentioned in the article.'

'Had she met with you before?'

'No, it was the first time, and I got the impression she'd never seen a psychic before.'

'Well, we're in the process of trying to find out all there is to know about Rachel. So, can you tell me why she made an appointment? Was it for any particular reason or just out of curiosity?'

'Like most people who come to me, she wanted to know what the future held for her,' Lisa replied. 'She told me she was about to embark on a new and precarious phase in her life and it was making her anxious.'

'What exactly did she say to you?'

'That she was moving to another country. It was actually hard work getting her to open up, but she did say that she was happier than she'd been for many years because she was in love.'

'Did she say with whom?'

'Her boyfriend. She said his name was Carlo and he was Italian.'

'And what were you able to tell her from the cards?'

'Not much, unfortunately. You see, not long after the reading began, she got a shock when I turned over the notorious death card.'

'How did she react?'

'Badly. She jumped up from the chair and I thought she was going to cry. She asked me if it meant she was going to die and if so when it would be. I tried to explain to her that the card doesn't represent physical death. That is signifies transformation and a time of a significant change in one's life – an end to one phase and the start of another. But I failed to convince her. She did eventually sit down again though

243

and we carried on for a bit, but she'd stopped paying attention and I found it hard to concentrate. So, we both agreed to end the session prematurely. I offered her a refund but she said to keep the money because it was her fault.'

'And was that the end of it?'

'Yes, but before she left, she did say something that struck me as odd.'

'Oh?'

'She said that if things didn't work out as she was hoping they would, then she would rather be dead anyway.'

James told Abbott about Rachel's visit to Lisa Doyle as they set off in a pool car for Libby and Greg Murphy's house in Burnside.

'She was obviously desperate to seize what she saw was an opportunity to change her life,' Abbott said. 'It suggests to me that before she met this Salvi bloke, she must have been terribly unhappy.'

James nodded. 'And seeing that death card obviously freaked her out and made her believe that fate was going to be unkind to her yet again. And sadly, it was.'

'It reminds me of someone Sean knew when he was living and working in York some years ago,' Abbott said. 'The guy went and had a tarot reading with some of his mates on Halloween for a laugh. But he too was confronted with the death card and it scared him shitless.'

'You're not going to tell me that something bad happened to him as well, are you?'

'He died three weeks later when he stepped into the road without looking and was hit by a bus.'

'Christ. It does make you wonder if sometimes they can actually predict the future.'

Abbott pulled a face. 'And that's why you'll never catch me going to a fortune-teller. I don't want to know in advance when I'm going to be shown the exit.'

Despite himself, James couldn't hold back a smile. 'I think we should change the subject or stop talking altogether so that I can concentrate on this bloody road.'

The snow was still holding off and the sun had at last managed to struggle through the murky clouds but the icy surface created hazardous driving conditions.

Luckily, they didn't have far to go as the village of Burnside was only two and a half miles north of Kendal and Greg Murphy's house was just off the main road. They hadn't bothered to call ahead but James thought it likely that the couple would be home.

'We're almost there,' he said. 'It's just up the hill beyond the cricket club.'

In less than a minute they spotted the large, detached house and James eased his foot off the accelerator as they approached the entrance, which was sandwiched between high hedges.

But when they turned into the wide, tarmacked driveway the sight that greeted them was totally unexpected. A fight was taking place between two men who were rolling around on the snow-covered forecourt in front of the house. And two women – one of them Libby Murphy – were standing off to one side yelling for them to stop.

CHAPTER FORTY-THREE

James brought the car to a screeching halt on the forecourt, and as soon as the engine was switched off, he and Abbott leapt out.

At the same time, the two men involved in the brawl on the ground suddenly pulled themselves apart and jumped up.

It wasn't until James got to within a few feet of the pair that he recognised them as Mark Slade, Greg Murphy's best man, and Gordon Carver, the reporter with the *Cumbria Gazette* who James had spoken to only the day before. They were both panting heavily, but neither of them appeared to be injured.

James stopped walking towards them and said, 'What the hell is going on here?'

It was Slade who responded as he wiped snow from the cagoule he was wearing over a T-shirt.

'This hack and his photographer sidekick thought they could come to my friend's house and take liberties, Inspector,' he said, jabbing a finger at Carver. 'And no way was I going to let them get away with it.'

James and Abbott shared a look before James turned and quickly took in the scene.

Libby had stopped shouting and was now shaking her head as though she couldn't believe what she'd just witnessed. To her left stood a girl with exuberant red hair who looked to be barely out of her teens. James recognised her as Elena Devonshire, a photographer employed by the *Gazette*. She was staring at Slade, her thin body shaking beneath a tight, padded black jacket.

Next to her was Gordon Carver, who was rubbing his fingers through his closely cropped hair. James knew he was in his early thirties and whenever they'd met before he had always appeared cool, calm and composed. Now he looked shocked and flustered in a long, beige overcoat that was stained with mud and slush.

'Care to explain exactly what led to the pair of you fighting like a couple of kids in a school playground?' James said, his eyes firmly fixed on Carver.

The reporter's face tightened as he struggled to regain his composure and get his breath back.

'Slade here lost his temper and snatched Elena's camera from her,' he said. 'I tried to take it back and we came to blows, then ended up on the ground just before you arrived.'

'Now tell the detectives why I took the camera from you,' Slade snapped.

Carver was about to respond but stopped himself when Libby let out a giant sob, then turned and rushed into the house through the open front door.

James told Abbott to go and check on her, then turned his attention back to Carver.

'That poor woman has been through enough and this is the last thing she needs,' he said. 'So, finish what you were going to say and then you and Elena need to leave here, assuming I'm not going to be expected to take any formal action against anyone.'

Carver wrapped his arms around his upper body and said, 'We came to see if we could interview Mr and Mrs Murphy about what happened at their wedding. Mrs Murphy came to the door and told us that her husband was out and she didn't want to speak to me. I tried to persuade her as gently as I could to change her mind because that's my job. But while I was doing that, Slade appeared behind her and yelled at me to go away. When I asked Mrs Murphy another question, he stepped over the threshold and gave me a shove. But as he did so Elena snapped a photo of him and that was when it turned nasty.'

'She had no right to take a picture of me,' Slade said. 'It was out of order.'

'And I would have apologised to you if you'd given me a chance,' Elena said, her voice small and unsteady. 'I just acted on impulse and pressed the button.'

James was relieved that the altercation hadn't been sparked by something far more serious. And at least the pair hadn't physically harmed each other.

'Look, can I suggest you both call it quits and put this unfortunate incident behind you?' he said. 'I'm here to talk to Mrs Murphy, so I'll make sure she's all right.'

'I was about to leave anyway before these two arrived,'

Slade said. 'I only popped over to check on Greg and Libby.' He turned to Elena, adding, 'If the camera's damaged you can send me the repair bill. And I'm sorry if I was a bit rough. Like you, I acted on impulse.'

When she didn't respond, he turned to go back into the house.

'I would rather you didn't go inside, Mr Slade,' James said. 'It's probably best if you go now and if you've left anything behind, I can get it for you.'

Slade contrived a weak smile and shrugged his shoulders. 'No, that's fine. I'll be on my way. The last thing I want is for you to think any less of me than you already do.'

Without another word, he strode towards a silver BMW that was parked next to a grey Range Rover on the forecourt.

'It's not the first time I've come across Mark Slade,' Carver said as he stepped up beside James. 'I was the court reporter when he pleaded guilty to breaking his girlfriend's nose at their flat in Keswick. And I read about another case where he smashed a woman's windscreen with a golf club. The man is a nasty piece of work and I had no idea that he was Greg Murphy's friend.'

'He owns the golf club where Mr Murphy is a member,' James said. 'And he was best man at the couple's wedding.'

'I see. I suppose that's his excuse for losing it the way he just did. He was completely over the top, and he gave Elena a real fright.'

'It could have been a lot worse.'

'You're right about that. And I'm bloody glad that you turned up when you did because I can't remember the last time that I had a fight, and I'm no match for the crazy bastard.'

James grinned. 'Is the camera broken?'

'Thankfully, no. And don't worry. We won't be using the picture or mentioning this little incident in the paper.'

They both watched Slade pull off the forecourt and onto the driveway.

'Before we go, is there anything new with the case?' Carver asked.

James nodded. 'I owe you one so I can tell you that this morning we tracked down Rachel Elliott's boyfriend, Carlo Salvi. He was at Heathrow airport waiting to fly to Italy. He's being brought back here now so that we can question him later today.'

'And is he still your prime suspect?'

'He is.'

CHAPTER FORTY-FOUR

After watching Carver and Elena drive away in the Range Rover, James took a moment to pull his thoughts together before going into the house.

He'd come here to speak to Libby about the WhatsApp message she'd received from her sister and had worked out in his head how he was going to approach the interview, but the ruckus between Slade and Carver had thrown up more disturbing questions.

Did Slade's behaviour suggest that the anger management course he was ordered to attend by the court had done little to help him control his fiery temper? And if so, then surely that gave further credence to Belinda Travers's claim that he threatened to slap her in the hotel garden.

James also wondered if anything was to be made of the fact that Slade had been alone in the house with Libby when Carver arrived. Was it true that he had simply dropped by to see how the couple were coping? Or did he know beforehand that Greg was out and he decided to come here because, for whatever reason, he'd wanted to see Libby by herself? These were matters that potentially complicated an already complex case.

Before going into the house, James looked around him to get the measure of the property. It was a big Georgian affair with a garden that wrapped itself around three sides. The slightly elevated location provided striking views of nearby Burnside village and the hills beyond.

As he entered the house, he saw that the interior was just as impressive, with period features including a sweeping staircase in the hallway. He called out to announce his presence and Abbott appeared in a doorway.

'We're in here, guv,' she said.

He followed his DC into a large living room, which had a stone fireplace and a striking bay window overlooking the rear garden.

Libby was sitting on an armchair holding a mug of something hot in both hands. She looked at James and he saw that there wasn't a trace of make-up on her face, which was pale and almost translucent.

She was wearing a blue fleece cardigan and jogging pants, and her long, dark hair was pulled back in a severe ponytail.

'Your visitors have all gone, Mrs Murphy,' he said. 'That must have been very upsetting for you.'

She nodded. 'It was. Mark was only trying to help me, though. But as usual he took it too far and let his temper get the better of him.'

'How long had he been here before they arrived?'

'Only about half an hour. He wasn't expected, and when I told him Greg had gone out, I didn't think he'd want to stay.

But he asked if he could come in so I let him. Big mistake.'

'Did he want to talk to you about something in particular?'

'He wanted me to know that it wasn't true what Belinda was saying about him and that she was the one who accosted him at the wedding.'

As James sat down on the sofa facing Libby, Abbott offered to make him a coffee. He declined because he wanted her to stay in the room and be a witness to whatever Libby was going to say.

'Do you believe Mr Slade's version of what happened with Belinda? Even more importantly, do you think he could be your sister's killer?' James asked.

Libby drew in an anguished breath and shook her head.

'I've already told you that I don't like the man and I know that he's been physically abusive to women in the past,' she replied. 'But I'm sure it wasn't him. He was fond of Rachel and when he sat with us during the meal, he didn't act like someone who had just murdered the bride's sister. He was also among the first of the guests to start looking for her when we told everyone she was missing. Regarding the thing with Belinda, I wouldn't like to say who's telling the truth. But she's been a friend of mine for years and I know that if something or someone takes her fancy, she'll go for it. And sometimes her behaviour has bordered on the inappropriate.'

This surprised James, and from the look on Abbott's face it surprised her too.

Libby finished what she was drinking and placed the mug on the small table next to her.

'Detective Constable Abbott told me you came here to

253

update me on the investigation,' she said. 'It doesn't appear from the television news that you've made much progress, but Dad rang late last night to say that Doug Hannigan was a suspect now as well as Rachel's mysterious boyfriend.'

'You've spoken to your parents then?'

'Only my dad. Mum wouldn't come to the phone. He wanted me to know that, unlike her, he doesn't hold me in any way responsible for what happened, even though I do. So, is it true about Hannigan? Dad told me about the birthday card and the photos that Rachel sent to the paper.'

James explained why they had interviewed Hannigan, but pointed out that he had an alibi and had been ruled out as a suspect.

'I only met him a couple of times and I never got what Rachel saw in him.'

'Did you tell her that when they were together?' James asked.

'No way. She would have told me I was jealous and it would have caused a row.'

'Are you aware that Mr Hannigan is now in a relationship with Erika Chan, the wedding coordinator at The Fells?'

She narrowed her eyes at him, clearly surprised.

'I didn't know that, but she seems a nice person and so I hope it works out for them long term.'

James decided it was time to raise the subject of the WhatsApp message that Rachel sent to her. But first he asked Libby when she was expecting her husband back.

'I don't know,' she replied. 'He called a meeting of his board of directors to discuss the impact of what's happened on the business and how they might limit the damage. Loads of bookings have already been cancelled apparently.'

'I expect that will only be a short-term issue,' James said. 'And the fact that Mr Murphy isn't here might make it easier for you to answer my next question. It relates to the last message you received from your sister before she was killed. We've now accessed her mobile phone and seen it on her WhatsApp log. So, can you tell us what she was referring to when she said she wasn't going to keep your sordid secret?'

Libby expelled a loud sigh and hung her head.

'I was hoping you wouldn't find that,' she said. 'But before I explain what led to it, would you please promise me that you won't show it to my husband?'

CHAPTER FORTY-FIVE

James made it clear to Libby that he had no intention of showing the WhatsApp message to Greg at this stage.

He then took out his notebook so that he could remind her, and himself, of exactly what Rachel wrote.

'You disgust me, Libby,' he said, reading from the note he'd made. 'I'm not going to keep your sordid secret so make the most of today. And tell that slimy bastard Ethan that if he ever lays a hand on me again, I'll have him put away.'

Libby blinked back tears and after a short pause, said, 'You didn't have to read it out to me, Inspector. How can I ever forget what Rachel's last words to me were? But that message was based on a misunderstanding. She jumped to the wrong conclusion and if I have to explain myself to Greg, I know he'll do the same.'

James gave her a long, searching look and wondered if what she was about to tell them would open up a whole new line of enquiry.

'We're listening,' he said. 'Please tell us what the message is about.'

Libby trained her eyes on a spot above James's head and huffed out a breath before speaking.

'I wasn't entirely truthful with you before when I said that I was talking to Ethan on the terrace when we saw Rachel walking down the path towards the lake. The truth is, Rachel upset me with her drinking and attitude so I went outside to have a cry. Ethan was on the terrace and spotted me walking down the path. He came over to see if I was okay, but I wasn't. It had all got too much. The two of us stepped off the path and were standing behind a bush when Rachel came along and saw us. He was giving me a harmless cuddle, but she was still pretty drunk then and immediately assumed it was more than that. She took delight in accusing me of cheating on Greg on my own wedding day. When I tried to explain to her that she'd got it wrong, she refused to listen and stormed off, threatening to tell everyone. Ethan hurried after her and grabbed her arm, and that's what she meant by him laying a hand on her. It wasn't a violent gesture by any stretch of the imagination.'

'Why didn't you tell us this before?' James asked her.

'Because I knew that you and everyone else would get the wrong idea. At the time, though, it didn't occur to me that you'd eventually see the message on her phone.'

'Did you show the message to Ethan?'

She nodded. 'He was still with me when it came through. Neither of us could believe what she'd written and that she referred to it as my "sordid secret". It was almost laughable and, to be honest, we didn't think she'd tell anyone even if she was convinced that I'd done something I shouldn't have.'

'And did Ethan stay with you after you showed him the message?'

'I walked back into the hotel and joined Greg who was with Mark at the bar. And obviously I didn't mention it to them. Ethan went to be with Claire who was on the terrace.'

'So, you don't know if Ethan went back outside to try to speak to Rachel about the message?'

Her eyes shot wide. 'Are you implying that Ethan is the one who killed my sister?'

'I'm only raising it as a possibility,' James said, wishing he'd phrased the question differently.

'There's no way Ethan would have gone after Rachel. We both knew what she'd seen was innocent, and she was over-reacting,' she said. 'I don't believe for a second that he would have attacked her, no matter what she was threatening, and I don't understand why …'

The words dried on her lips and she closed her eyes, squeezing out a couple of tears, which rolled down her cheeks.

'Would you like me to make you another coffee, Mrs Murphy?' Abbott asked her. 'It would be no trouble.'

Libby opened her eyes and gave a sharp shake of her head.

'I just want you to go now,' she said. 'I need to be by myself for a while. If there's something else you want to tell me, or if you've got more questions, then would you please get on with it?'

'I completely understand how hard this must be for you, so we'll be as quick as we can,' James said. He cleared his throat before continuing. 'Another reason for our visit was to inform you that we've managed to trace Rachel's boyfriend, Carlo Salvi, and will be interviewing him later today. He's still very much a suspect and if he does turn out to be Rachel's killer you and your parents will be the first to know.'

He brow shifted upwards. 'Is there anything you can you tell me about him?'

James told her what they knew and that he'd been planning to leave the country.

'What we still don't know is why he argued with your sister in the hotel and if he's the person who killed her. But we will find out.

'Speaking of arguments, it has come to our attention that your relationship with Greg has not always run smoothly. In fact, I've been told that you split up and got back together several times, and that you were going to end it for good just before the wedding but changed your mind after Greg's father died.'

'I'm guessing you got all that from my parents,' she replied. 'They've never been keen on Greg and they didn't want me to marry him because they think he's a control freak and a bully. But he's not like that, or at least he isn't with me. Of course, we fall out from time to time, but I love him and no way was I going to leave him while he was grieving for his dad. But now I almost wish I *had* called it off … because if I had, Rachel would still be alive.'

She broke down then and James felt a blast of guilt as he stood and put his notebook away.

'We'll leave it at that for now, Mrs Murphy,' he said. 'Would you like me to call your husband before we leave?'

'No, just go,' she sobbed. 'And please don't come back unless it's to tell me that you've caught the person who murdered my sister.'

CHAPTER FORTY-SIX

'Well, that's given us a lot more to think about, guv,' Abbott said when they were back on the road and heading towards Windermere. 'Do you reckon she spun us a lie about what really happened on the path?'

James nodded. 'I think it's entirely possible, yes. Don't forget she told us at first that the last time she spoke to her sister was at the bar. But then the encounter on the garden path came to light and her excuse was that she forgot about it. I reckon we need to up our game in respect of both her and Ethan Prescott, but especially Prescott. Perhaps Rachel didn't jump to the wrong conclusion. If so, it's important we get to the truth as quickly as possible.'

'They do have history, guv, so maybe it was just a cuddle for old times' sake.'

'That's quite possible, I suppose. After all, they did remain friends after splitting up, by all accounts. I wonder if she's on the phone to Prescott now telling him that we've been to see her and know about the message?'

'If she is, then he'll probably be expecting us to drop by. But we should do more than just talk to him. Can we call the office and get someone to secure a warrant so that we can take his phone? That should tell us what, if anything, he's been up to. And we have just cause to be suspicious as we now know that he had a reason to go and look for Rachel. What we don't know is if he found her on the jetty and pleaded with her not to tell anyone what she'd seen. As she was bladdered, it likely wouldn't have taken much for things to turn ugly.'

While Abbott made the call, James focused on driving the seven miles to Windermere along a more or less straight road. Conditions were still unfavourable, but it wasn't snowing and the day was brighter now that there were fewer clouds.

When Abbott came off the phone, she said, 'The warrant's being chased and it'll be dealt with as a matter of urgency. Meanwhile, what are your thoughts on Mark Slade?'

'He stays in the frame for now,' James said. 'His hot temper is a factor we can't ignore. It obviously doesn't take much to set him off and we know he was in the hotel garden not long before Rachel was attacked.'

'And yet Libby seems pretty sure that it wasn't him who killed her.'

'Maybe Greg convinced her of that. Although, it was a good point she made about how he seemed perfectly normal during the meal and didn't act as though he'd just committed a murder.'

'He'd have had no problem doing that if he's a raving psychopath,' Abbott pointed out.

'That's true,' James said. 'But I keep coming back to the circumstances that led up to the attack, and the crime scene itself. I'm sure that it wasn't a premeditated murder as there's no evidence of prior intent.'

'And that's why we have so many suspects, guv,' Abbott said. 'It could literally have been anyone who attended the wedding.'

The town of Windermere lay about half a mile east of the lake and James made a point of going to Ethan Prescott's gift shop in the centre first.

He was unsurprised to find it closed and noticed there was no sign on the door telling customers when it would re-open.

The satnav then guided them to a quiet cul-de-sac of small, dated bungalows. Ethan and his mother lived in the one that looked in most need of attention. It was a small property with white, weather-beaten walls and a driveway with an ageing Vauxhall Corsa parked on it.

Claire answered the door and it appeared to James as though she had shrunk since he last spoke to her at the hotel.

She was wearing an oversized jumper and leggings, and grief was scored into her gaunt features. She seemed surprised to see them so perhaps her son hadn't yet received a call from Libby.

'Oh my, it's you, Detective Inspector Walker,' she exclaimed. 'What is it? Have you found out who killed Rachel? Please tell me that you have, for all our sakes.'

'The investigation is still ongoing, Mrs Prescott, but we are making progress,' he said.

'Then why are you here?'

'We'd like to speak to Ethan if that's okay. Is he home?'

The furrows in her brow deepened. 'He's in his bedroom. What do you want him for?'

'We need to ask him some questions. May we come in?'

Claire fixed James with a steely gaze and he noticed that red veins laced the whites of her eyes.

'Of course you can,' she said after a pause. 'I'll get Ethan and then put the kettle on. He's getting ready to go out.'

She turned and called her son's name as she limped along the short hallway. James waved Abbott ahead of him and closed the front door behind them.

Ethan appeared then, stepping out of one of the rooms clutching his mobile phone in one hand and a pair of leather gloves in the other. He was wearing a crisp, white shirt, the sleeves rolled to the elbows, exposing tattoos on both arms.

When he saw who had come calling, he stopped dead, a shocked expression on his face.

'The detectives have come to ask you some questions,' his mother told him. 'They can do it in the kitchen while I make some tea.'

'I'm sorry we weren't able to let you know we were coming, Mr Prescott,' James said. 'A lot has happened this morning and we've had to make some sudden changes to our schedule.'

'That's not a problem, Inspector,' Ethan said. 'You're lucky you caught me in. I was just about to go and do some work at the shop before I re-open tomorrow.'

'We'll try not to keep you long then.'

As they followed Claire into the kitchen, Ethan said, 'Have you solved the case yet? Do you know who killed Rachel?'

263

'No, we don't,' James answered. 'But we're pursuing various promising lines of enquiry.'

'Thank God for that. Do you think the boyfriend did it?'

'We won't know until we've talked to him.'

The kitchen was large and well equipped, with a table and chairs and a door leading to the patio. Claire invited them to be seated before she started filling the kettle.

'So, what is it you want to ask me?' Ethan said as he placed his phone and gloves on the table in front of him.

'First, I'd like to know if you've heard from Mrs Murphy this morning,' James replied.

Ethan frowned, but then smiled. 'Oh, I see. You mean Libby. I haven't got used to her being referred to as "Mrs Murphy". And the answer is no, she hasn't been in touch with me. Why would she?'

'We've just come from her house in Burnside and I thought she might have called to tell you that we went there to ask her about the WhatsApp message that Rachel sent to her just before she was killed.'

The corners of Ethan's mouth turned down and he muttered a curse under his breath.

'Libby confessed to lying about that encounter with her sister on the path and how it came about,' James said. 'And you lied to us as well, Mr Prescott. You told us that you and Libby were on the terrace when you spotted her on the path and went after her.'

Ethan gave a perfunctory nod. 'Look, I went along with it because Libby asked me to. She didn't want Greg to know about what Rachel had written. And I couldn't blame her because it sounded so bad. Saying Libby had a sordid secret and accusing me of hitting her … It was ridiculous. But we didn't stop to think that the police would probably find it.'

'Rachel obviously read too much into what she saw,' Claire said as she moved across the room to stand next to her son. 'Ethan was just consoling Libby because she was upset over Rachel getting drunk. Both Libby and Ethan say it was nothing more than that, and I believe them.'

'So, you knew about the WhatsApp message?' This from Abbott.

'Ethan told me about it after he was interviewed at the hotel,' Claire said. 'I tried to convince them both to put the record straight, but they didn't want to and made me promise not to say anything.'

'It's not Mum's fault,' Ethan said. 'It was our mistake and it's now come back to bite us.'

Claire placed a hand on his shoulder and he sat back in the chair, his shirt stretching tight across his torso.

'Would you be willing the swear under oath that you were giving Libby a harmless cuddle and that Rachel misunderstood it, Mr Prescott?' James asked him.

He nodded. 'Of course. I'm so sorry that I didn't tell you the truth when you first asked me about it. But we were all in a right mess and not thinking straight.'

'Libby has told me that after your encounter with Rachel, and after she sent that message, the pair of you split up before returning to the reception. Is that correct?'

'Yes. She went back into the hotel and met up with Greg at the bar.'

'And where did you go?'

'I went back to the terrace to join Mum.'

'But how can we be sure of that, Mr Prescott?' James pressed.

'What's that supposed to mean?' Ethan asked sharply.

'Well, you told us one lie so maybe this is another one. Maybe you took it upon yourself to go after Rachel in order to put the record straight and to warn her not to ruin the occasion?'

Ethan's jaw stiffened and he was about to speak, but his mother stopped him.

'How dare you make wild accusations about my son in his own home?' she snapped at James. 'My boy had nothing to do with Rachel's murder and yet you're trying to twist what happened in the garden to make it look as though he might have. It's a disgrace.'

'I can speak for myself, Mum,' Ethan said, but she ignored him and carried on.

'After they spoke to Rachel, Ethan came to me on the terrace and told me about it. We then stayed together and had a drink before going inside to our table for the meal. We didn't leave each other's sight until Greg told everyone that Rachel was missing and Ethan joined in the search for her, so there is no way he could have gone down to the jetty. If you're not prepared to accept that, we'll be forced to consult a lawyer.'

James puffed out a breath and said, 'You should both do whatever you think is best. I'm sorry if I've upset you, Mrs Prescott, but my job is to ask questions, some of which can be uncomfortable. It's how we get to the truth.'

'We've told you the truth about what happened that day,' Claire said. 'And I'm not sure what more we can say to make you believe it.'

'I'm not saying I don't believe you,' James said. 'But we have to take into account the fact that your son and Libby weren't honest with us when we first spoke to them.' He switched his gaze to Ethan. 'You should know that I've applied for a warrant to seize your phone and other digital devices. So, if there's something you're still holding back about what happened on New Year's Eve, or about your relationship with Libby, then now is the time to tell us.'

'We're not holding anything back,' Ethan replied. 'You now know what happened and I accept that we should have been up front to start with. But trust me, I'm not going to make the same mistake again.'

He reached for his mobile phone and slid it across the table towards James. 'I've got nothing to hide so if you want to check who I've been calling and texting then take this and see for yourself. There's a laptop in my room so you can take that as well. As long as I get them back. Business is not so great right now so I can't splash out on new ones.'

James took up his offer and placed the phone in an evidence bag he took from his pocket. They then waited while Ethan went to his room to get his laptop.

After he gave them the pin and password, James said, 'Thank you for these. We'll return them as soon as possible. And thank you both for your cooperation.'

It was Claire who responded with a single, sharp sentence.

'You can see yourselves out.'

CHAPTER FORTY-SEVEN

It was midday when James and Abbott left the Prescott residence.

'There's no need to rush back to the station,' James said. 'The Fells Hotel is nearby so let's take the opportunity to go and see what's going on there. You can have a quick look through Ethan's phone on the way. Do you know Libby's mobile number?'

'I wrote it down along with the others,' Abbott said, and quickly consulted her notes.

Once she had it, she put on a pair of gloves and plucked the phone out of the evidence bag, tapping in the password Ethan had given them.

'So, what's your take on what they told us, guv?' she said.

James shrugged. 'I have my doubts that they were completely honest with us. Surely either Libby or Ethan would have gone looking for Rachel after the WhatsApp message came through.

I can't imagine they just left it at that knowing she was drunk and liable to spout her mouth off.'

'Me neither. It just doesn't make sense. And my money would be on Ethan. We only have his mum's word for it that he went back onto the terrace and they stayed together after that.'

'Claire strikes me as the type of mother who'd lie to protect her son whatever crime he might have committed.'

'We should have another look at the hotel surveillance footage,' Abbott said. 'See if we can spot Libby at the bar with Greg and Mark Slade after the incident on the path. But we won't be able to confirm that Ethan went onto the terrace because of the dodgy outside camera.'

'What about during the meal? Do you know if we can see mum and son at whatever table they were on?'

'I can't remember. I'll ask DC Hall when we get back to the station and have a look myself. Meanwhile, I now have access to his phone.'

'Check the call log first,' James told her. 'See how often Libby and him have been in contact with each other.'

James cruised towards the lake while Abbott studied the data on Prescott's phone. After a minute, she said, 'I've gone back ten months and there are no calls to or from Libby. And no text messages either. She's listed as a contact, though.'

'So, either they've not been in touch since they stopped dating, which would be well over a year ago now, or if they have been, then he used another phone.'

'Which is why we'll probably have to execute the warrant

when it comes through and see what else turns up in the bungalow.'

'That will depend on whether we're able to pin Rachel's murder on her boyfriend when we get to question him later,' James said. 'If so, then I won't give a toss if there's something going on between Libby and Ethan Prescott.'

Now that The Fells Hotel was basked in bright winter sunshine it was hard to imagine that something so terrible had happened there.

It looked so warm and welcoming, with its striking red brick façade, extended chimney stacks and smart dormer windows. Not to mention the stunning backdrop of the lake and the distant fells.

'This has to be one of the most spectacular venues in the whole of Cumbria,' Abbott said as they approached it. 'It's easily the most impressive hotel in the Murphy chain.'

'Will you be getting married in one of them?' James asked.

'You've got to be joking, guv. We're opting for the registry office followed by a reception at the local pub, and even that will cost a tidy sum.'

There were no longer any reporters, photographers or news satellite trucks outside the entrance but there was a uniformed officer who waved them through when he saw who was in the car.

'Any idea how many of us are still here?' James asked as he parked up.

'Less than ten, I believe, plus a couple of SOCOs who are finishing up,' Abbott replied. 'I should think we'll be pulling out altogether by the end of the day. The guests have all gone home and there's no point having people here if they've got nothing to do.'

The reception area was very different to how it had been when James was last here. The Christmas tree had been taken down and staff were busy removing decorations.

They crossed over to the front desk and James showed his ID to the receptionist and asked her if he could speak to the manager.

'Miss Cornwall is in her office,' she said. 'Would you like me to tell her you're here?'

'Don't worry. I know where her office is so we'll make our way there.'

The door to Karen Cornwall's office was open and she was sitting behind her desk shuffling through paperwork. When James tapped on the door she looked up and waved them in.

'I didn't expect to see you today, Inspector,' she said, rising to her feet. 'I spoke to Greg only a short while ago and he never mentioned that you were coming.'

'It wasn't planned,' James said. 'We were in the area so I thought we should drop by to check on how things are going. Is Mr Murphy here then?'

She nodded. 'He's holding an impromptu board meeting on the first floor. It's been going on for most of the morning. Do you need to speak to him?'

'Not right now. Which member of our team have you been liaising with?'

'Sergeant Thomas. He told me he doesn't expect to be here much longer.'

'And do you know where he is now?'

'He was making notes in the lounge when I last spoke to him.'

James asked Abbott to go and let the sergeant know they were here and find out if he had anything new to report.

Turning back to the manager, he said, 'Have you been here the whole time, Miss Cornwall?'

'I have. I feel it'd be wrong to go home while all this is going on. I'm staying in one of the rooms. You see, even without the guests, the hotel still has to function. We have to keep the kitchen open to feed the staff and the phones have to be answered. Plus, we're in the process of taking down the Christmas and wedding decorations.'

James noticed then that the heavy make-up the woman had on failed to conceal the darkness under her eyes.

'How has it all impacted on the staff?' he asked.

'Quite badly. Some are so traumatised they're having to take time off.'

'Have you been kept abreast of developments in the investigation?'

'Your officers won't give anything away, but I've been fed bits of news by various people including Greg and Erika, our wedding coordinator. She spoke to me this morning about your visit to her home yesterday. It quite upset her.'

'Is she in today?'

'Indeed, she is. She's helping to sort out the wedding para-phernalia. Most of it belongs to the hotel and needs to be put in storage.'

'And what exactly did she say to you about our visit?'

She rolled her eyes. 'She told me that you went there to see her boyfriend and she arrived home unexpectedly just as you were about to leave. Frankly, it was news to me that she's been living with Doug Hannigan. Erika hasn't mentioned any changes in her private life to me and now I realise why. She felt she needed to let me know what had happened between Hannigan and Rachel before it becomes public knowledge as she fears it will. And she plans to tell Greg when he's out of his meeting.'

'I suppose that makes sense,' James said.

'She assured me that she's left Hannigan. She walked out on him this morning after telling him she needed to be by herself for a while. She packed some of her belongings in her car and I said she could stay in one of our rooms for a few nights while she sorts herself out.'

'Well, that's probably for the best,' James said.

'That's what I told her, but she wouldn't say whether she thinks she might go back after a break. She's in a bit of a mess after what happened on New Year's Eve. As usual, she put her heart and soul into organising the wedding, and of all my staff she's the one who's been most affected by what happened. And to make matters worse, she believes you now regard her as a suspect in Rachel's murder.'

James rolled out his bottom lip. 'Not everyone we speak to is a suspect, Miss Cornwall. Most are just helping us with our enquiries.'

She flashed an uncertain smile. 'You might want to make that clear to her then, Inspector, before she meets with Greg. I very much doubt that he'll be as sympathetic as I am when she opens up to him and I don't think he'll take kindly to the fact that he didn't know about her relationship with the man who dumped his wife's sister. I just hope he doesn't refuse to let her stay here.'

CHAPTER FORTY-EIGHT

James went first to the lounge to pass on to Abbott what Karen Cornwall had told him. She was deep in conversation with Sergeant Dale Thomas and they were the only people in there.

'I want to look around the grounds so I'll seek out Erika Chan while I'm at it,' he said. Turning to Thomas, he added, 'How's it going?'

'As I was just saying to DC Abbott, sir, there's not much more for us to do here,' he replied. 'All those staff who were on duty during the wedding have gone home and I don't believe there's any more forensic evidence to be found.'

'Then I don't see why we shouldn't scale the operation back still further,' James said. 'But I want us to maintain a minimal presence here for at least another day or two. Just a couple of officers who can act as a point of contact between us and the management.'

'I'll get onto it,' Thomas said.

James left Abbott with him and ventured out into the deserted garden. He could feel the pinch of cold through his coat as he strolled across the snow-blanketed lawn towards the lake. The sky was a flawless blue now and a light breeze stirred the branches of the trees around him.

He'd had every intention of returning to the scene of the crime at some point to refresh his memory of the location. And there was always the possibility that he'd spot something he hadn't noticed before, something that would offer up a new clue as to what happened on New Year's Eve.

He looked around for Erika Chan but she was nowhere in sight and he suspected she might have already returned to the hotel.

He paused to look at the path where Rachel was last seen and wondered which of the bushes Libby and Prescott had been standing behind when she spotted them. Then he glanced across at the rear gate that led to the overflow car park where Carlo Salvi must have parked his car.

As he carried on walking, the jetty came into view and he was reminded of that awful moment when Rachel's body was pulled out of the water. Cordon tape was still stretched across the end of the jetty and a sign had been placed there warning people not to step over it.

He was about to turn around and go back to the hotel when he spotted a lone figure standing on the shoreline to the left of the jetty, staring out across the lake.

It was Erika Chan. He knew because she was wearing the same camel-hair coat she'd had on when she arrived at Hannigan's house the day before.

James walked over to her and she snapped her head

towards him when she heard his shoes crunching on the stones.

'Don't be alarmed, Miss Chan,' he said. 'It's only me.'

Her eyes were wide, pupils dilated, and he could tell she'd been crying.

'How did you know I was here?' she asked him, her voice fragile.

'I was speaking to your boss, Miss Cornwall, about various matters and she told me. She also told me that you've left Mr Hannigan.'

Her expression darkened. 'I was awake most of the night thinking about it and decided this morning that we needed some time apart. It's actually been a long time coming. I'm convinced he's still taking drugs when I'm not around, despite his denials. And finding out about the threat he sent to Rachel has finally made me realise that he's not the man I thought he was. I'm not sure I could ever trust him again or if I'll ever go back.'

'I got the impression yesterday that you were prepared to forgive him in respect of the card, and that you felt that Rachel had provoked him into sending it,' James said.

She shook her head ruefully. 'You being there threw me. My mind was all over the place and I actually found myself feeling sorry for him. And I'm ashamed to admit that it prompted me to hold back a part of my conversation with Rachel.'

'Why was that?'

'Because what she told me I found so hard to believe. When I confronted Doug with it after you and your colleague had left, he said it was a lie that she'd made up to turn me against him. And I wanted so much to believe him but it's played on my mind overnight, along with everything else. That's why I came out here. I needed to think it through and decide what to do.'

'Then you should get it off your chest, Miss Chan,' James said. 'Tell me what else Rachel said to you.'

She pushed her fringe out of her eyes and nodded. 'Okay, I will, but I'm still not sure that it's the right thing to do.'

'Why don't you let me be the judge of that?' James said, desperate now to get it out of her.

She closed her eyes briefly before continuing. 'It was after she told me about the birthday card Doug foolishly sent to her. I asked her why she didn't go straight to the police if she was so concerned about it. She claimed that she phoned him after she opened it to tell him she knew it was from him and that she was going to do exactly that. According to her, he just laughed and told her that the police would never be able to prove it was from him. And then he warned her that if she made an issue of it, or even threatened to, he'd pay someone to do something bad to her so that the police wouldn't be able to link it to him.'

CHAPTER FORTY-NINE

Douglas Hannigan was now back on James's list of credible suspects despite his cast-iron alibi. Because if what Rachel told Erika Chan was true, then Hannigan had threatened her not once, but twice.

Of course, it would be hard, if not impossible, to prove that he'd warned Rachel that '*he'd pay someone to do something bad to her so that the police wouldn't be able to link it to him.*'

James could well understand why Rachel decided not to go to the police if Hannigan did say that. But what if he hadn't? What if Rachel made it up solely for Erika's benefit? Sweet revenge on her ex for sending her the birthday card with the chilling threat inside.

'I intend to speak to Mr Hannigan again,' James said as the pair of them walked back towards the hotel. 'And I'll have to confront him with the allegation.'

'Well, don't expect him to admit to saying it, Inspector, even if it's true,' she replied. 'He swore to me on his mother's life that Rachel lied. Perhaps she did. I don't suppose we'll ever know for sure.'

'How did he react when you told him you were moving out?'

'He didn't believe it until I started packing and then he sobbed and begged me to stay.'

'Did he get angry or violent?'

'Oh no. He's never laid as much as a finger on me and rarely loses his temper. And I'm sure he loves me. The problem is, I'm not sure I love him anymore.'

Before they entered the hotel, James asked her if she would allow Sergeant Thomas to take a formal statement from her.

'Of course, but I'd better let Karen know what's going on first.'

'I'll come with you,' James said. 'By the way, while the investigation is ongoing, I'll need to know how to get hold of you if you decide to stay apart from Mr Hannigan for any length of time.'

'My parents live in Carlisle and I can stay with them if needed, but I'm hoping Mr Murphy will let me bed down here at the hotel for a few days while I consider my options. There are plenty of empty rooms.'

Karen Cornwall was still in her office and James explained to her that he wanted Erika to provide a statement, but he didn't go into detail about what it would contain. She had no problem with it and offered the use of her office. Before leaving Erika, he asked her not to tell anyone else what Rachel had said to her, including her boss.

James then went into the lounge where Sergeant Thomas was still talking to Abbott.

He briefed him on what Erika was going to say and then told Abbott that when they got back to the station, they'd find out more about Douglas Hannigan before paying him another visit.

'This is a tricky one,' he said. 'I don't see how we can prove that Hannigan threatened to pay someone to hurt Rachel. But we can certainly try to find out if the person who attacked her on the jetty was motivated by money.'

James didn't want to leave the hotel until he'd caught up with Greg Murphy so when he and Abbott walked back into reception, and he spotted Karen Cornwall behind the front desk, he asked her when the board meeting was likely to end. She said she didn't know but offered to go upstairs to check.

'Why don't you wait in the lounge?' she said. 'I can have someone bring you a bite of lunch if you're hungry.'

'That's very kind of you,' James said. 'I could do with a hot drink and a snack.'

'Me too,' Abbott piped up. 'I made the mistake of skipping breakfast this morning.'

'Then make yourselves comfortable and it'll be along shortly.'

They made their way back into the lounge and this time settled on one of the long, leather sofas.

'Do you know what I find so fascinating about this case, guv?' Abbott asked.

'Do tell,' James said as he sat back and loosened his tie.

'Well, we're not even forty-eight hours into it and it's already throwing up so many secrets, so many lies and so many bloody surprises.'

281

James grinned. 'Not to mention a larger than usual bunch of suspects.'

'I just hope that our killer is among them.'

'Hopefully we'll know soon enough. But all we can do now is go where the evidence takes us.' He raised his hand and started counting on his fingers. 'We know that Douglas Hannigan threatened Rachel after she ruined his bid to become an MP with those photos. I'm not surprised he was angry with her, but did he take it too far and pay someone to assault or even kill her? Then there's Carlo Salvi, the boyfriend. He had a barny with her and then left the hotel in a hurry and tried to leave the country. That puts him firmly in the frame.

'Next, we have Ethan Prescott. Did he go after Rachel to try to stop her telling people what she thought she'd witnessed on the garden path?'

James scrunched up his brow as he briefly forgot who else was on their list.

'Mark Slade, the best man, guv,' Abbott chipped in. 'A convicted violent offender who may have tried it on with one of the other female guests in the garden not long before Rachel was killed. He's a hot favourite as far as I'm concerned.'

James nodded and then tapped his thumb with his pointer finger. 'And finally, there's Greg Murphy, the groom and owner of the hotel. He admits he didn't like Rachel and he knew that she didn't like him either. He was also annoyed with her for drinking heavily. Maybe he saw her going down to the jetty and decided to give her a bollocking himself rather than just leave it to his new wife.'

They were interrupted then by a young staffer who turned

up with a couple of menus. James opted for a cheese and ham sandwich and a mug of coffee. Abbott chose a Cornish pasty and a Diet Coke.

After he left with their order, Karen Cornwall appeared to tell them that she had spoken to her boss and he'd said he'd be winding up the board meeting in about half an hour.

'Can you wait that long?' she asked them.

'We sure can,' James said. 'It'll give us time to eat our lunch.'

When they were alone again, they both reached for their phones. James rang the office while Abbott started scrolling through her messages.

It was DC Dawn Isaac who picked up and James told her where they were and what they'd been up to. He asked if he could speak to DCI Tanner but she said he was on his way to Penrith where the press conference was scheduled to take place at three o'clock.

'We should be back before then,' James said. 'Spread the word that we'll have another briefing.'

Isaac then gave him some updates and crucially she was able to tell him when Carlo Salvi would be arriving in Kendal from London.

When he came off the phone he said to Abbott, 'We should have the boyfriend in the interview room around four. And if we find that he is our man then we might both get to have an early night.'

'Yeah, and pigs might fly, guv,' Abbott said.

CHAPTER FIFTY

When Greg Murphy strode into the lounge, he was casually dressed in a pale blue shirt and navy cords that made him appear much younger than his forty-two years. James couldn't help but notice that he looked tired, his shoulders hunched, eyes heavy.

He sat on the sofa facing James and Abbott and flashed a half-hearted smile at them.

'I'm sorry to have kept you waiting,' he said. 'The board had a lot to discuss, as I'm sure you can appreciate.'

James gestured at the empty plates on the low table in front of them.

'Your manager was kind enough to lay on some lunch so it wasn't a problem. And you weren't to know that we were here anyway.'

'Well, I'm glad you are because it saves me calling you. All the information coming to me about the investigation has been second-hand. I want to know what progress you're making and you said you would keep me updated.'

'We visited your home in Burnside this morning to do just that, Mr Murphy. Has your wife not told you?'

'I haven't had time to speak to her. I was planning to call straight after the meeting. Is she okay?'

James was surprised that Libby hadn't rung to tell her husband about the brawl between Mark Slade and Gordon Carver.

'She was upset when we left your house, so I would suggest you check on her as soon as possible,' he said. 'And you should know that when we arrived there was an altercation taking place between your friend Mark Slade and a local newspaper reporter.'

Murphy's jaw went rigid. 'Are you fucking serious?'

James relayed what he'd been told about what led to the brawl and what he'd witnessed himself. As Murphy listened, his eyes filled with a cold fury.

'I've come across that reporter before,' he said. 'He shouldn't have gone there to hassle my wife. I'm just glad that Mark was with her. If I'd been there, I would have done exactly what he did.'

'Well, at least neither of them was hurt,' James said.

Murphy shook his head. 'That's not the end of it, though. I intend to make a formal complaint to the *Gazette*. It makes me so angry when the press show such contempt for people who are grieving. It's no wonder Libby's upset.'

'Before we left, we told Mrs Murphy about a couple of developments, one of which her father had already mentioned to her,' James said.

'Are you talking about the business with Rachel's ex, Douglas Hannigan?'

'Yes, I am.'

'I was with Libby when Fraser rang last night to talk to her. That bastard Hannigan wants locking up for sending Rachel that card. Have you arrested him?'

'Not yet. He's still under investigation though we have ascertained that he wasn't here on the day of the wedding. The alibi he gave us checks out.'

'Even so, he shouldn't be allowed to get away with threatening her.'

'I hear what you're saying, Mr Murphy, but the Crown Prosecution Service will have to decide whether or not to charge him. And they'll only do that if they believe there's a realistic chance of getting a conviction. In this case, I fear there might not be.'

Murphy clucked his tongue and expelled a puff of air. Eager to change the subject, James said, 'The other piece of news we passed on to your wife was that Rachel's boyfriend, Carlo Salvi, is now in police custody. I'll be interviewing him later this afternoon.'

Murphy's eyes flicked rapidly from James to Abbott and then back to James.

'Where was he and who the fuck is he?' he said.

'He was apprehended in London before he was able to board a flight bound for Italy. He's a research fellow who has spent the last year working at the university in Ambleside and he struck up a friendship with Rachel when he visited the café she worked in.'

'So, he's obviously the one who killed her,' Murphy responded. 'The bastard must have rushed away from here straight afterwards and was trying to flee the country. He

286

probably thought he wouldn't become a suspect because most of us didn't even know he'd come to the wedding.'

'We'll find out what he's got to say for himself soon enough,' James said. 'And please be aware that we're still continuing to chase up other lines of enquiry.'

For now, James chose not to mention the suspicion surrounding Ethan Prescott or the WhatsApp message that Rachel sent to Libby.

'And when will your officers be leaving the hotel? I'd rather be spending time with Libby instead of overseeing the business,' he said, 'but until we can get things moving again, I don't have much of a choice. People will lose their jobs if we don't quickly recover from this. Three forthcoming weddings have already been cancelled, along with a string of other events and lots of weekend reservations. I'm not sure what we can do to counter the bad publicity but we've got to try.'

'I expect all the officers will have left the premises within two to three days,' James told him.

'That's good to know,' he replied, then looked at his watch. 'Is there anything else, Inspector, or can I go and give my wife a ring now?'

James thought about mentioning Erika Chan but decided not to. She would speak to him when she was ready.

'No, we're all done for now, Mr Murphy,' James said. 'It's time we returned to the station.'

The weather started to close in again during the drive back to Kendal. Heavy clouds were blowing across Cumbria from the north and the blue sky had all but disappeared.

More snow was heading their way after what had been a

brief and welcome respite, and at this stage even the forecasters weren't able to predict how bad it would get.

James had asked Abbott to take the wheel so that he could bring his notes up to date and as she drove he wrote down lists of questions, action points and thoughts on where they were with the investigation.

'I reckon Greg Murphy and his board will have a tough job reviving the reputation of the hotel in the short term,' Abbott said as they continued south along the A591. 'I don't imagine many other couples will want to tie the knot there any time soon.'

'I think you're right on that,' James said. 'The media will be all over this for months, covering the moment we charge someone, then the trial, followed by the jury's verdict. And along the way I guarantee it'll be the subject of newspaper and magazine features. I expect the safety of guests at lakeside hotels will also become an issue that'll be hotly debated and will ensure The Fells remains in the spotlight.'

'So, have you given any more thought to Murphy as a suspect, guv? Do you think he could be our man?'

James glanced up from his notes and chewed on the inside of his cheek for a few seconds as he considered the question.

Then he said, 'Let me put it this way, I don't regard him as a front runner and if I was a betting man, I wouldn't put money on him.'

'I've come to the same conclusion,' Abbott said. 'I know that he and Rachel had no time for each other, but I just can't see him attacking her with a weapon just because she got drunk at his wedding. We know her behaviour made him angry, but he responded by asking Libby to speak to her, which strikes me as reasonable. Plus, this whole saga has clearly had an impact on business … which doesn't seem like something he would risk lightly.'

James nodded. 'That's a good point. And no one has said they saw him heading towards the lake at any point during the reception. But that doesn't mean he didn't do it, of course, which is why he needs to remain on the list for the time being.'

They arrived at the station just in time to watch the press conference that was going out live on the news from Carleton Hall in Penrith and the team were gathered round the various TV monitors when James and Abbott walked into the office.

'Good timing, guys,' DS Stevens said to them. 'We're all geared up for the briefing when this is over and I've made sure there's an interview room ready and waiting for when Carlo Salvi gets here. I've also arranged for a duty solicitor to be on hand to represent him.'

On screen, Tanner was sitting behind the table that was usually wheeled out for pressers and a woman from the media department was next to him.

The DCI was in his element on these occasions and James was reminded that if he got promoted, he would have to front more of them, a prospect that most definitely did not appeal to him.

Tanner kicked off with a short statement in which he described what they believed had happened to Rachel Elliott during her sister's wedding on New Year's Eve. Most of it was already in the public domain, but that didn't make it sound any less chilling.

'This was a tragic event that has devastated Rachel's family,' he said, 'and it's the last thing one would expect during a wedding on our beautiful Lake Windermere. Our team of investigators have been at the scene since soon after it happened and dozens of people have already been questioned. I would like to assure Rachel's family and friends that we'll leave no stone unturned in our quest to bring her killer to justice.'

He then invited questions and it came as no surprise to James when Gordon Carver stood up and asked the first on behalf of the *Cumbria Gazette*.

'Your officers appealed for information on the whereabouts of Rachel's boyfriend, a Mr Carlo Salvi,' he said. 'We understand that he was with her at the wedding but left the hotel before the police arrived. Can you confirm that he's now been found?'

'I can confirm that, yes,' Tanner replied. 'Mr Salvi will be helping us with our enquiries.'

'Is it true that he was arrested at Heathrow Airport before he was able to board a flight to Italy?' Carver asked.

Tanner held up his hands. 'Look, it wouldn't be appropriate for me to go into any great detail about the circumstances surrounding it at this time. Suffice to say, we're glad that we're now able to speak to him and we're hoping that he can shed more light on what happened to Rachel.'

Before Carver could ask a follow-up question, Tanner pointed to another reporter who identified himself as being with the BBC. He wanted to know if Salvi should be described as a potential witness or a potential suspect.

'At this point in time we regard him as a witness,' Tanner answered.

More questions followed and the DCI answered them as best he could. None of the other suspects were mentioned by name and James felt that Tanner had been given a relatively easy ride by the hacks.

When it was over, James announced that a team briefing would take place in half an hour, which would give him just enough time to prepare.

CHAPTER FIFTY-ONE

As soon as James returned to his desk his phone rang. It was Tanner.

'Did you catch any of the press conference?' the DCI asked him.

'I watched all of it, boss,' James said. 'It went as well as could have been expected.'

'That's what I thought. I was a little thrown by the first question, though. I wasn't aware that we'd released the information about Carlo Salvi being apprehended at Heathrow.'

'We haven't, but Gordon Carver is a sharp operator and he's got a lot of contacts in the Constabulary. Still, there's no harm done.'

'So is Salvi there yet?'

'No, but he won't be long. I'll be holding a briefing first.'

'Has anything new come up?'

James told him about his conversations with Libby Murphy, Ethan Prescott and Erika Chan.

'We'll follow up with Hannigan on what he allegedly said to Rachel, but I doubt he'll admit that he told her he was prepared to pay someone to do something bad to her.'

'Apply for a warrant then,' Tanner said. 'If the guy is stupid enough to write a threat in a birthday card, then his phone and email accounts are bound to contain other misjudgements.'

'It's already in hand.'

'Good. I'll be staying here for a while before going home. Call if you need me and I'll expect an update after you've interviewed the boyfriend.'

Tanner then asked James if he'd managed to give some thought to having his name put forward for the DCI job.

'While I'm here in Carleton Hall I'm going to be bending the ears of a couple of the decision makers,' he went on. 'They're bound to ask me if I've approached you yet.'

James didn't have to think about it. 'Then tell them you have and that I'm keen to take over from you if they want me to.'

Before calling the team together, James phoned Annie to check on Bella.

'You'll be glad to hear she no longer has a temperature or the sniffles,' his wife said. 'And she's all smiles again. So, there was no need for me to take her to the doctor.'

'That's great news, love. Such a relief.'

'I did tell you that it was probably nothing to worry about. Like any small child, she won't be in tip-top condition all of the time and that's something you'll have to get used to.'

He grinned into the phone. 'Give me time and I will. Probably.'

'Anyway, how are things going with you? Are you making much progress?'

'Slowly, but surely. I've got a big interview coming up with Rachel Elliott's boyfriend. We found him just before he was able to leave the country. It means I can't tell you when I'll be home.'

'Well, try to give me fair warning and if it's not too late I'll keep Bella up.'

'Okay, give her a kiss for me then.'

'I always do.'

James picked up his notes and went and stood in front of the two whiteboards. As soon as his colleagues saw him, they dropped what they were doing and a buzz of anticipation rippled through the room.

'Okay, listen up everyone,' he said. 'As you know, DC Abbott and I went to see Libby Murphy and Ethan Prescott this morning. We then paid a visit to The Fells Hotel. To say it was an eventful trip would be an understatement. But I'll come onto that in a moment. First, Carlo Salvi is due to arrive here at any minute from London. As it stands, he remains our prime suspect. Not only did he appear to get into an argument with Rachel at the wedding before she disappeared, but he also tried to fly out of the country in a hurry. So, we have good reason to believe he killed her. Have we dug up any more information on him?'

It was DC Sharma who answered. 'I spoke to several of his university colleagues today, sir. They mostly described him as an ambitious and intelligent guy who was good at his job. He's never given them any cause for concern, but they were aware that off campus he's earned himself a reputation as a bit of a player when it comes to women. But he never got involved with any of his students, to their knowledge, so it wasn't seen as a problem.'

'Were they aware that he was dating our victim?'

'No, sir. And it appears not to have been common knowledge that he was attending the wedding at The Fells on New Year's Eve.'

'Do we know if he formed any particularly close friendships with any of his colleagues?'

Sharma nodded. 'A Professor Mike Kennedy. I had a phone conversation with him an hour ago. The pair socialised occasionally and got on well. He also met several women Salvi took out over the course of the past year, but none of them was Rachel. He told me he last spoke to Salvi on Monday of last week and told him that his colleagues and some of his students were planning a leaving do for him this Thursday. Salvi gave no indication that he intended to change his plans and return to Italy sooner than expected.'

DC Isaac picked up on this and said she'd been in touch with the police in Milan.

'Carlo Salvi has never come to their notice,' she said. 'His family live just outside the city and the local precinct contacted them on our behalf. Salvi apparently called them late on New Year's Day to tell them he was flying back today.'

'There seems little doubt then that he was doing a runner,' James said. 'I'm just glad we collared him before he got on that plane. Did Salvi's hire car turn up on any traffic cameras between the hotel and his flat in Ambleside? If he drove to the hotel for the wedding and parked in the overflow car park, as we suspect, we need to know what time he left there and headed back to Ambleside.'

One of the support staff raised a hand and said, 'Camera checks are still ongoing, sir, but so far nothing has been flagged.'

James then ran through what was happening outside the Murphy home when they got there.

'I don't know how serious the brawl would have become if we hadn't arrived when we did,' he said. 'But it provided us with more evidence that best man Mark Slade is a hot-tempered individual.'

James went on to describe how Libby had reacted when he raised the issue of the WhatsApp message from her sister.

'She claims Rachel wrongly interpreted what was happening and Ethan Prescott gave the same account. They also both denied that they went looking for Rachel after her message came through on Libby's phone but I want us to check back through the hotel security footage to see if we can confirm for ourselves that they're telling the truth about that.'

'DC Abbott has spoken to me about that and I'm on it, sir,' DC Hall called out.

'Let me know as soon as possible if you find anything,' James said. 'Meanwhile, back to our chat with Prescott. I told him we were going to seek a warrant to gain access to his phone and his response was to give it to us, along with his laptop. DC Abbott had a quick look through his call history but saw none to or from Libby. The techies can analyse both devices properly though. I think we should also get a warrant for the gift shop he runs in Windermere. If the guy is hiding something, that's where we might find it.'

Next, James went through what Erika Chan had told him about the conversation she had with Rachel on the day of the wedding.

'She owned up to holding back the details of part of the exchange when we first spoke to her,' he said. 'Given what she shared, I intend to have another chat with him before the day is out. I don't think there's any question that he'll deny it but it does give us grounds to target him with a warrant.

The briefing was cut short then as word came through that Carlo Salvi had at last arrived.

CHAPTER FIFTY-TWO

As they made their way to the interview room, James felt an adrenaline rush take hold of his body. He could tell that Abbott was just as keen as he was to confront Rachel's boyfriend.

This was set to be a defining moment in the investigation, and one that would hopefully bring it to a swift conclusion.

Salvi and the duty solicitor appointed to him were already sitting at the table when they entered. James introduced himself and Abbott, and as they sat he placed a large folder on the table.

The solicitor, a middle-aged man named Clive Edgar, was a familiar face at the station and held in high regard by all the officers. James acknowledged him with a nod before fixing his client with a hard stare.

Carlo Salvi was wearing a black leather bomber jacker over a crew-neck sweater and pale blue jeans. There was no question he was good looking, with sharp features and dark brown eyes that had a piercing quality. But at the same time his face was pale and his mouth was pinched and drawn tight.

It was Abbott who went through the motions of saying the interview was being recorded and who was present in the room. Throughout this, Salvi remained silent and avoided eye contact with the two detectives, staring down at his hands, which were clasped together on top of the table.

When Abbott was finished, James said, 'For the benefit of the tape, I'd like you to tell me if you know why you're here, Mr Salvi.'

Salvi nodded, but it was Edgar who answered for him. 'My client knows full well that you want to question him in connection with the death of Rachel Elliott. But I've only had time for a brief conversation with Mr Salvi and therefore it might be necessary for me to request a halt to the proceedings if I need to take instructions.'

'That shouldn't be a problem,' James said, turning to Salvi who met his eyes for the first time.

'I'd like to start by asking you a few questions about yourself, Mr Salvi,' James said. 'Can you tell us how old you are and where you've been living this past year?'

Salvi inhaled a long, loud breath before responding. 'I'm thirty-one and my home has been in Ambleside.' His Italian accent was strong, his voice low and raspy.

'And you've worked as a visiting research fellow at the university there. Is that right?'

'Yes. But my tenure has come to an end, which is why I was returning to Italy.'

James could see the tension in the man's neck and he was clearly finding it hard to sit still.

299

'Now, would you tell us how long you were in a relationship with Rachel Elliott?' James said.

'About four months, but it was fairly casual,' he replied. 'We met at the café where she worked. I used to go there for coffee and lunch. She was a really nice person, and I am devastated about what's happened to her, but I honestly had nothing to do with it. I would never have harmed her.'

'We'll come to that, Mr Salvi. First, I'd like to find out more about your relationship with Rachel. How often did you meet up?'

'Two, sometimes three times a week.'

'And she regularly stayed overnight in your flat?'

He nodded. 'We enjoyed each other's company very much and had lots of fun together.'

'Are you aware that she never told her family and friends that she had a boyfriend? For some reason she kept it from them.'

'I knew this. She said she didn't like lots of people to know about her private life, especially her sister who was always critical of any relationships she entered into.'

'Did that not strike you as odd?'

'Not really. It was up to her to tell whoever she wanted to.'

'Fair enough. Now, my next question is this, Mr Salvi: did Rachel know you were seeing other women at the same time as her?'

His eyes seemed to go out of focus for a second and he had to pause to gulp in air before answering.

'There was no need for her to know,' he said. 'She never

asked me if she was my only female friend so I didn't tell her that she wasn't.'

Abbott couldn't resist responding to that one. 'But if you loved her then surely you should have been faithful to her?' she said.

'But I did not love her and I never told her that I did,' he replied. 'I liked her a lot – more than any of the other women – but it wasn't love.'

James pitched in at this point with, 'But were you not aware that she was planning to introduce you as her boyfriend at her sister's wedding and also announce that she was moving to Italy with you? Presumably that was why she invited you.'

He shook his head. '*Moving with me?* No, we hadn't discussed that. She invited me because she didn't want to go by herself and she sold me on the idea of spending one of our few remaining nights together in a grand hotel where we could eat and drink as much as we wanted.'

As James was processing this last answer, Abbott asked Salvi what time he had arrived at the hotel and whether he drove there in his car.

'I drove and I arrived just before the marriage ceremony began at three o'clock,' he said.

'And where did you park?'

'Around the back of the hotel, in a field. The front car park was full.'

James picked up on this. 'When we searched Rachel's room there was nothing belonging to you in there. And yet when you were seen leaving the room you weren't carrying anything. Why was that?'

'I left my rucksack and change of clothes in the car because there was no time to take them to the room before the ceremony,' he answered. 'I was going to get them later.'

'Okay, now talk us through what happened after you arrived,' James said.

'I met up with Rachel. She was excited and got me a drink. She looked beautiful in her dress and I told her so. Then I sat down and watched her sister get married. Afterwards, I got myself another drink while Rachel had her photograph taken. Nobody spoke to me but I was quite happy with that because I didn't know anyone there. When the photographer was finished taking pictures, Rachel asked me to go with her to see the room.'

'And what happened when you got there?'

Salvi paused before answering. 'We talked about stuff and—'

'Let me step in there, Mr Salvi,' James interrupted. 'We have reason to believe that you had an argument in the room. Can you confirm that?'

His face showed surprise. 'How do you know about that?'

'Because I saw you storm out of the room,' Abbott told him. 'I also saw Rachel follow you down the stairs. She was obviously upset. Minutes later, you were captured on one of the hotel's surveillance cameras hurrying across reception towards the rear of the hotel.'

'Not long after that, Rachel was murdered down by the lake,' James said, as he took a photograph from the folder in front of him and pushed it across the table towards Salvi. 'That picture was taken after her body was hauled out of the water. We believe you did that to her and we want to know why and how it happened.'

Salvi took one look at the photo and his eyes swelled. A second later his mouth fell open and he threw up on the table.

CHAPTER FIFTY-THREE

The interview had to be suspended while Salvi was taken to the bathroom to be cleaned up. At the same time, James arranged for another room to be made available for when they reconvened.

While the man's reaction to seeing the photograph had been unexpected, it wasn't uncommon. Over the years James had seen many suspects respond in the same dramatic way when confronted with the unsightly image of a murder victim. And they included individuals who it later turned out had committed the heinous crime.

'It might have been wise to have warned him what to expect, Detective Inspector Walker,' Salvi's solicitor said while they were waiting for the custody officer to bring his client back to them. 'It's clear to me that he's in a fragile state, both physically as well as emotionally. He apparently had no sleep last night and has eaten nothing since this morning.'

'He arrived in London yesterday,' James said. 'Do you know where he stayed overnight?'

'At the airport. He'd been planning to book into a hotel but when he got off the train he decided not to and went straight to Heathrow where he stretched out across some seats.'

Ten minutes later, the interview was ready to begin again.

'I'm sorry about that,' Salvi said when he was seated. 'That photograph turned my stomach and I just couldn't hold it in.'

'I won't show you any more images of the victim,' James said, 'but I'd like you to look at two pictures of the crime scene itself.'

James placed the photos on the table between Salvi and his lawyer.

'The first is of the jetty,' he said. 'We believe Rachel was standing on it when she was attacked. The second is a close up showing her broken glasses and her purse.'

Salvi swiped the heel of his hand across his face. 'Please believe me when I tell you again that I did not do that to her,' he said, his breath rattling hoarsely in his throat. 'I am not a killer.'

'But look at it from our viewpoint, Mr Salvi,' James told him. 'You argued with her and then she went missing and was fatally attacked. It's not a stretch to conclude that your argument could have continued down by the lake and it got so heated that you lost your temper and struck her several times with whatever object you had to hand. When you realised that she was dead, you pushed her over the side of the jetty and hurriedly fled the scene through the back gate.'

Salvi's whole body stiffened and his voice became more

strident. 'No, no, it was not me! After I walked out of the hotel I went straight to my car and drove home.'

There was something about the way he said it that didn't ring true with James, and it prompted him to say, 'I don't think you're being entirely honest with us there, Mr Salvi. There were lots of people around and we're still sifting through the property's surveillance camera footage, so if you're bending the truth for whatever reason we will soon know about it.'

Salvi swallowed hard and then blinked as if coming out of a trance.

'Okay, look, when I told you I went straight to the car I forgot that I did walk down to the shoreline on the way,' he said. 'But I didn't step onto the jetty. And that's the truth.'

'So why did you go there?' James asked.

Salvi let out a weighty sigh. 'After walking out of the hotel, I felt guilty and sorry for Rachel. I couldn't decide whether to go back and talk to her or drive home so instead of going to the car park, I carried on to the lake to think about it and calm down. It was quiet there and I was completely alone. I stayed for about fifteen minutes before I made up my mind that it would be best for the both of us if I just left. And that's what I did, and all the time I was there I didn't see Rachel or anyone else.'

Salvi was sweating now and his breathing was laboured. His solicitor asked him if he felt well enough to continue and he insisted that he did.

'I need to prove that I am innocent,' he said, looking hard at James. 'I did not do that to Rachel. Please, you must believe me.'

The next question came from Abbott. She asked him what he and Rachel had argued about in her room.

'She told me that she didn't want me to go back to Italy without her,' he replied. 'She said she loved me and wanted us to get married. She also said she was going to tell everyone that we were in love and that we were going away together.'

'And what was your reaction?' Abbott asked.

'I was totally shocked. I'd had no warning. I knew she was besotted with me, and she'd asked me more than once not to return to Italy, but I made it clear to her that I had to. I thought she'd come to accept that what we had was nothing more than a fling. When I told her I didn't love her and that it was over between us, she begged me not to end it and pleaded with me to take her to Italy. She was really hysterical and it was scary so I walked out and told her not to follow me or contact me again.'

'And after you left the room, you went to the lake and then straight home?' James said.

Salvi nodded. 'That's right. It wasn't until the next day that I heard on the radio that a woman had died during the wedding. I followed the story as it developed and learned that it was Rachel. That's when I panicked. I didn't want to be drawn into it so I changed my plans and decided to leave for Italy as soon as possible.'

'Did you know we'd put out an appeal for information on your whereabouts?' James asked him.

'Yes. I saw it. I also saw that the police were saying Rachel had been murdered. But by then I was on my way to London and I wasn't prepared to take the chance of staying here and going to prison for a crime I did not commit.'

James couldn't be sure that Salvi was telling the truth, but he was sure that the evidence they had was not enough to secure a conviction. They would need to either wear him down to prompt a confession or come up with a way to disprove his version of events.

Perhaps they would find something incriminating among his belongings or maybe footage from traffic cameras would show that he drove home after Rachel vanished and not before, proving he'd lied.

'We'll terminate the interview there,' James said, 'but you will be held in custody while our inquiry continues, Mr Salvi. It will give you time to think about what you've told us and decide if there's anything you want to change or add. We'll resume our questioning tomorrow, but you should be aware that, as it stands, we're seriously considering charging you with Rachel Elliott's murder.'

Salvi didn't respond. He just sat there staring at James with a fearful expression on his face.

CHAPTER FIFTY-FOUR

'My instinct is to believe him, guv,' Abbott said as they walked back into the office. 'But I'm guessing that's not what you think.'

'I'm not sure what to think,' James said. 'I admit he gave a plausible answer to every question, but he's had a long time to think about it. And he did initially lie about going straight to his car after the argument with Rachel. It means we should regard everything else he told us with a degree of caution.'

Abbott nodded. 'I agree, but if what he said about why they argued is true, then I can understand why Rachel decided to drown her sorrows in drink. It must have come as a bitter blow to discover that their relationship was so one-sided.'

'I know it's a cliché, but it sounds like she was blinded by her love for him,' James said. 'She probably did come to accept that he wasn't going to stay in this country, but then convinced herself that if she offered to go with him to Italy, he'd be all for it and they could then keep their relationship alive. But it proved to be a mistake.'

The team were waiting anxiously to hear how the interview had gone, and they were disappointed to learn that Salvi hadn't confessed to the murder.

'We'll let him stew overnight and have another go at him tomorrow,' James said. 'Meanwhile, let's continue going through traffic camera footage to pin down exactly when he left the hotel and drove home.'

Glancing at the big clock on the wall, James saw that it was half five already. Another working day was coming to an end and it appeared the case was still a long way from being solved. He said as much to the team and urged them to try to pick up the pace.

'Where are we with the warrants?' he asked.

'Just got word that they've been signed off, sir,' DC Isaac informed him. 'The paperwork is being sent across.'

'Excellent. DC Hall, do you have an update on the hotel surveillance footage?'

'I've gone back over it and can confirm that Libby Murphy did join her husband and Mark Slade at the bar after her encounter with her sister in the garden. They stayed there for about fifteen minutes before all three moved away and out of shot. Mr and Mrs Murphy then took their places at the top table for the wedding breakfast at about ten minutes past six. But Slade didn't join them for another twenty minutes.'

'Which means he could have been up to no good down on the jetty,' James said.

Isaac nodded before continuing. 'As you know, the surveillance camera on the terrace was malfunctioning so we don't know if Ethan Prescott joined his mother there after he left the garden. And we don't know exactly what time he and his mum took their seats in the main hall because their table was one of quite a few that were situated in camera blind spots.'

'This clearly means that all our suspects are still in play,' James said. 'And now we're in a position to execute the warrants we can see if there's anything to be found in the homes of Douglas Hannigan and Ethan Prescott. In the meantime, can you report back, Jessica, on what, if anything, the techies find on Prescott's phone and laptop? I also want us to have another word with Mark Slade. Ruffle his feathers and see if anything comes of it. But at the same time we need to ensure that Belinda isn't subjected to any form of harassment from him or Murphy.

'As for Douglas Hannigan, Phil and I will go and see him after this meeting and put him on the spot over his alleged threat to pay someone to harm Rachel. Have we managed to get any more info on him?'

'We're still working on it, sir,' Isaac said. 'Apart from the drugs scandal he's never been brought to our attention.'

James went on to assign various jobs to individual detectives. He then told Abbott to brief the nightshift before she left the office.

'Tomorrow will be another full-on day,' he said to the team. 'So, don't hang around unless you really have to. Go home, get some well-earned rest, and come back in the morning fully charged.'

James saw no point in delaying a second visit to Douglas Hannigan's house since he lived so close to the station. It was dark when he and Stevens set off in the pool car, but at least it wasn't snowing.

311

They were halfway there when the DS inadvertently put James on the spot.

'There's a rumour doing the rounds that Tanner is in line for the vacant superintendent job at Carleton Hall. Were you aware of that, boss?'

James felt a flash of heat in his chest. Tanner had specifically asked him to keep it to himself until the official announcement and he wasn't about to break his boss's confidence.

'No, I wasn't, but it doesn't surprise me,' he lied. 'He's an obvious candidate. Plus, he lives in Penrith.'

'It'll be just up his street too, since he won't have to come out from behind his desk too often.'

James summoned a smile.

'It might interest you to know that the team are already having bets on who'll replace him,' Stevens went on. 'And you are far and away the favourite.'

James feigned surprise. 'Really? I'm flattered, but they could always decide to bring in someone from outside.'

'I hope not, guv, and you should know that I'll be rooting for you. Sure, we got off to a rocky start, but you've never let me down or disappointed me these past two years. You're a credit to the team and the last thing any of us wants is for an outsider to come in and start throwing their weight around.'

There were fewer cars parked in the street when they got there and they were able to pull into a spot on the kerb in front of Hannigan's house.

'Do we tell him we have a warrant to search the place?' Stevens asked.

James shook his head. 'Let's play it by ear. See what he's got to say for himself first and then, if we think it's necessary, we can call in the team.'

'I don't think there's any doubt what he'll say. It's his word against that of a woman who's dead.'

The lights were on inside the house and as they climbed out of the car, James felt the wind bite at his face.

The snow-covered path up to the front door was innocent of shoeprints and James hoped they hadn't missed Hannigan completely.

James rang the bell and when there was no response after thirty seconds, he rang it again.

Still no answer.

'What do you reckon?' Stevens said. 'Is he out or hiding away in there?'

James banged his fist against the door several times and then bent over with the intention of shouting through the letterbox. He lifted the flap and peered into the hallway.

It took a moment for his eyes to adjust to the soft lighting, and when they did his heart lurched in his chest.

'Oh shit,' he blurted. 'We need to break in.'

'What is it?' Stevens responded.

'It's Hannigan. He's flat out on his back on the floor at the bottom of the stairs. I can't tell if he's unconscious or dead.'

CHAPTER FIFTY-FIVE

'You call an ambulance and backup and I'll see if there's a way in at the rear,' James said. 'Hopefully that will be quicker than trying to force open the front door.'

He rushed towards the side gate, which was thankfully unlocked, and tension gripped him as he hurried through it and along a path that ran between the property wall and the high boundary fence.

Just before reaching the rear garden, he came across a door, which had a large glass panel in it. There were vertical blinds on the inside with gaps between them through which he could see into the kitchen. He tried the handle first but it was locked.

James knew that many people with an external kitchen door tended to leave the key in the lock and he hoped that Hannigan was one of them.

He looked around and spotted several empty clay pots in the flower bed just up ahead. He picked one up and used it to smash the glass door panel, thrusting his arm through and moving his hand around until he felt the key and turned it. Seconds later, he burst into the kitchen and bolted through to the hallway.

Hannigan was still lying on the hardwood floor and James immediately dropped down beside him. The first thing he did was to check that Hannigan was still breathing and relief surged through him when he saw his chest was rising and falling. There was an ugly dark bruise on his forehead but no sign of blood or any other injury, leading James to believe that he'd probably fallen down the stairs and was concussed.

James leapt to his feet and opened the front door. Stevens, who was holding his mobile to his ear, stepped inside.

'He's still with us,' James told him. 'Wound to the forehead and most likely concussion. I think he must have fallen down the stairs.'

Stevens relayed the information to the emergency service operator and then hung up the phone.

'Ambulance is on its way and I'll call for backup now,' he said.

'Okay. Stay here while I have a quick look around to make sure there's no one else in the house.'

James checked upstairs first. There were three bedrooms – one had been converted into a small office – which were all empty and tidy, with no sign of anything markedly out of place or damaged. Back downstairs, he went straight to the living room.

The television was on, the volume low, and there was a near-empty bottle of Jack Daniels and a single glass on the coffee table. Next to them lay a razor blade, a rolled-up ten-pound note and a few small lines of white powder.

Cursing under his breath, James re-entered the hallway to find Stevens in full first-aid mode as he kneeled next to Hannigan. He'd tilted him onto his side and was gently rubbing his back.

'His breathing is strong and regular,' he said. 'Can you get me a cold compress of some kind from the kitchen?'

James fetched a tea towel soaked in cold water and Stevens held it against the bruise on Hannigan's forehead. As he did so, the man's neck muscles twitched involuntarily.

'So, what do you think?' the DS said. 'Was this an accident?'

'That's my guess,' James said. 'The external doors were locked from the inside and I haven't noticed any open windows. Plus, it looks like the guy has been snorting cocaine while working his way through a bottle of JD.'

'That would sure as hell have made the plonker unsteady on his feet,' Stevens said. 'Probably went upstairs and lost his footing.'

James nodded. 'We won't know for certain until he regains consciousness.'

'Let's hope he does. Just because he's breathing it doesn't mean he hasn't fucked up his brain.'

The wail of a siren came from outside on the street and James went to the door to see an ambulance stopped in the middle of the road. He waved at the two paramedics who jumped out and as they ran towards the house a patrol car pulled up behind the ambulance.

James told the paramedics that Hannigan had been on the cocaine and booze and they then assessed the situation for themselves.

'It's a good sign that he's breathing well,' one of them said, 'and it seems as though he's gradually becoming more responsive. We won't know if there's serious internal damage until we get him to the hospital though.'

Stevens offered to go in the ambulance with him and James said that he and the patrol officers would carry out a quick search of the house since the warrant had been granted.

'We need to find contact details for his relatives,' he said. 'And at the same time, we'll take the opportunity to see if there's anything incriminating to be found.'

After Hannigan was stretchered out, James informed the two uniforms that the injured man was a suspect in the murder of Rachel Elliott, and gave a brief explanation as to why.

'We're looking for anything that might be perceived to be relevant,' he added.

He told one of them to search all the downstairs rooms and the other to check the bedrooms.

'I'll take the office upstairs,' he said.

Hannigan's mobile phone was found almost immediately on the sofa in the living room, but it was predictably password-protected.

James had better luck with the laptop on the desk in the office. It was already switched on and when he touched the mouse the screen came to life. He then spent the next twenty minutes going through the man's email and social media accounts, internet search history and deleted files. It was virtually all work-related, though, and there was no mention of Rachel Elliott on anything he opened.

However, her name and telephone number were listed in an address book that James found in one of the desk drawers.

Other contacts in there included Hannigan's parents and Erika Chan.

The first call he made was to the parents, to tell them that their son had been rushed to hospital with a serious head injury. It was a landline number and the father answered.

James identified himself and told him that Douglas was on his way by ambulance to the Accident and Emergency Department at the Lancashire Royal Infirmary. He said it appeared he had fallen down the stairs at home, but made no mention of the cocaine and drink.

Mr Hannigan asked why the police were at their son's house and when James replied that he couldn't speak about it over the phone, the man said, 'Douglas told me you questioned him about Rachel Elliott's murder, Detective Inspector. Is that why you were there again, even though you know he was at a party when it happened?'

'It's more complicated than that, Mr Hannigan,' James said.

'I know about the birthday card he sent to her but he's admitted to you that it was just a stupid mistake so you shouldn't be harassing him.'

'Look, Mr Hannigan, I called to let you know that your son has been hurt. I can't go into—'

James suddenly stopped talking because he realised that the guy had hung up on him.

The next call he made was to DS Stevens to warn him that Hannigan's parents had been informed and would probably turn up at the hospital.

'Phone me as soon as you've got a condition update,' he said.

'He's already showing signs of improvement,' Stevens

replied. 'He opened his eyes briefly and the paramedics are confident he'll pull through.'

'Can they estimate how long he'd been lying there?'

'Not with any degree of accuracy, but they don't think it was very long.'

'Well, I don't expect we'll be able to speak to him at least until tomorrow morning so I'll arrange for a uniform to take over from you there and sort you a lift back to Kendal.'

James then made a third call, this one to Erika Chan. She answered quickly and before James could get a word in, she told him she was still at The Fells Hotel.

'I spoke to Mr Murphy and he surprised me by saying I could keep my job and he's letting me stay here until I sort things out,' she said.

'That's great, Miss Chan,' James said, 'but I'm ringing you with some bad news, I'm afraid.'

'What is it?'

'It's Mr Hannigan. He's had an accident at his home and has been taken to hospital in Lancaster by ambulance. I thought you should know even though your relationship with him may well be over.'

She asked him what had happened and he could tell from her voice that she was both shocked and concerned.

'He might have been drinking, Inspector,' she said. 'I've seen him lose his balance and fall over before when he's had too much. He can't handle it.'

'That's something we'll ask him when he's able to speak to us.'

He went on to tell her that Hannigan's parents had been told.

'I'll go to the hospital,' she said.

James stayed in Hannigan's office for another ten minutes, rifling through papers and files, but found nothing to implicate the guy in Rachel's murder.

The officer who had searched the bedrooms also drew a blank, but when they went downstairs the other officer handed James something he'd found in the kitchen wastebin. It was a large, buff-coloured envelope that had been screwed up and dropped in with the household rubbish.

'Check inside, sir,' the officer said. 'It would appear that Mr Hannigan was involved in some suspicious activity.'

James emptied the contents of the envelope onto the kitchen worktop. There wasn't much of it, but what there was sent a jolt of adrenaline spiking through him.

CHAPTER FIFTY-SIX

'It seems that Douglas Hannigan has been stalking his former fiancée,' James told those members of the team who were still in the office when he returned.

James put latex gloves on before removing the contents of the envelope and spreading it out on the table around which they all stood.

'There are seven sheets of A4 paper here and on five of them are various photographs of Rachel Elliott that were obviously taken without her knowledge,' he said. 'In three of them, she's pictured with Carlo Salvi. One shows them entering the flat where he's been staying, and the other two show them walking together through Ambleside. In the other two images Rachel is pictured leaving the café where she worked and entering her home in Bowness. There is also a photo of Salvi walking into the university.'

James picked up a sheet containing a single head and shoulders shot of Salvi. Below it was a list of his qualifications and academic interests, and a note describing him as 'a visiting research fellow at the University of Cumbria'.

'This sheet was clearly downloaded from the university's website,' James said.

'But why was he so interested in him?' asked one of the support staff.

'It must be because he discovered that Salvi was the new man in Rachel's life and he wanted to know more about him,' James said. 'All this suggests to me that Hannigan began stalking Rachel so that he could collect information on her and work out how best to cause her harm, either physically or through threats and intimidation.'

DC Abbott leaned over the table for a closer look.

'So, despite his denials, he appears to have been dead set on getting revenge on her for sending those photos to the *Gazette*,' she observed. 'And if he did go through with his threat to pay someone to hurt her, this stuff could have been passed on to whoever the perpetrator was.'

James nodded. 'It's possible. But it's also possible that he didn't get to make use of these because someone else beat him to it by killing her, and that's why he binned them. The discovery of the envelope is significant, but it isn't enough to pin Rachel's murder on Hannigan. We still have other suspects who are very much in the mix, and the truth is it could be any or none of them,' he said. 'I don't think we've ever worked on a case that's taken us in so many different directions.'

He went on to inform the team that the patrol officers who turned up at Hannigan's house would remain there overnight and arrangements were being made to repair the broken kitchen window.

It was coming up to 7.30 p.m. when Stevens called from the hospital to tell him that Hannigan had regained consciousness but was now confused and in pain.

'He did manage to respond to some questions from the team who treated him in A&E by moving his head,' Stevens said. 'He confirmed he fell down the stairs and that he'd been drinking and snorting cocaine. I've spoken to a doctor who says he doesn't appear to have any serious internal injuries, but we won't be allowed to interview him until tomorrow at the earliest.'

'That's what I expected. Are his parents there?'

'They just arrived. And so did Erika Chan. Turns out Hannigan hadn't told them that she'd walked out on him this morning. I was with her when she broke the news and it didn't seem to come as any great surprise to them. In fact, I got the impression they had every sympathy for her.'

James told Stevens about the envelope they'd found.

'Mention it to Miss Chan and the parents,' James said. 'I'd like to know if they were aware that their boy had been stalking Rachel.'

Stevens sent James a text ten minutes later just as he was about to leave the office to go home.

Parents and Chan claim not to have been aware of the stalking or that he had an envelope containing pics of Rachel and her boyfriend.

The case continued to play inside James's head as he drove home. It hadn't snowed for a while, and the roads were in much better shape, but tiredness infused his bones, which made it hard for him to concentrate.

Before leaving the office, he'd sent Annie a text to say he was on his way. She messaged back that she would put a ready meal in the oven and keep Bella awake until he got there.

His thoughts continued to spin in all directions and he felt uncertainty beat in his heart. He was annoyed with himself because he still couldn't be sure who had murdered Rachel Elliott and why.

There were so many thoughts tumbling through James's mind that it was making the muscles knot in his stomach.

He tried to drown them out by turning on the radio, but it was bad timing as he caught the tail-end of a news story in which the reporter told listeners that Cumbria police were making slow progress in their hunt for the person who'd been dubbed 'The Winter Killer'.

CHAPTER FIFTY-SEVEN

By the time James arrived home he felt mentally fried and was struggling to ignore the questions that were bunching up inside his head.

But as soon as he walked through the door and saw his daughter beaming at him from her mother's arms, all thoughts of the case vanished from his mind and a warm glow rose in his chest.

'Hello, my little darling,' he said, dropping his case and walking towards them. 'You look so much better than you did this time yesterday.'

'That's kind of you to say, dear,' Annie said with a smile. 'And I'm not even wearing make-up.'

James held his arms out and she handed Bella to him.

'We'll let Mummy think that I was talking to her,' he said to his daughter before giving her a sloppy kiss on the cheek.

She threw her head back as though she'd been tickled and started to laugh.

'It's such a relief to see her back to her jolly old self,' he said. 'I had visions of her ending up in the hospital.'

Annie rolled her eyes at him. 'I'm sure your colleagues have no idea that you're such a worrier. If they did, then they'd look at you in a whole new light.'

They moved towards each other and as they kissed, Bella poked a finger into her mother's ear.

'Your dinner is almost ready,' Annie said. 'Madam here can watch you eat it, then we'll put her down and we can have some us time before we turn in.'

They sat Bella in her highchair while James munched his way through a beef hot pot ready meal. But after only a few minutes she was struggling to keep her eyes open and she was fast asleep even before James had finished his dinner, her head lolling to one side, her mouth open.

'She's been awake for most of the day,' Annie said. 'I reckon she decided to make the most of feeling better.'

'I'll take her up,' James said as he swallowed the last forkful of beef.

Bella stayed asleep as he carried her upstairs and placed her gently in her cot. He kissed her forehead, told her how much he loved her, and realised yet again just how lucky he was. Having her in his life helped him to cope with the horrors he encountered on the job.

Annie was waiting for him in the living room, her legs tucked beneath her on the sofa and her fingers wrapped around a mug of tea.

'There's plenty more boiled water in the kettle if you want to get yourself a hot drink,' she said. 'Though I don't suppose that's what you fancy.'

She was right. Exhausted, he succumbed to the lure of alcohol, pouring himself a large whisky. After he downed a couple of mouthfuls, he felt his cheeks warming as it spread into his bloodstream.

'I don't think I need to ask if you've had a tough day,' Annie said. 'You look shattered.'

'I am.'

She patted the sofa next to her. 'Come and tell me as much as you can then.'

He told her about his day, including how they had traced Rachel Elliott's boyfriend to London and found Douglas Hannigan lying on the floor in his hallway. He was always mindful of police protocol but he rarely held anything back with Annie because he knew that whatever information he shared with her would go no further.

'I'm not surprised you need that drink,' she said, nodding towards his third gulp of whisky. 'This sounds like one convoluted investigation. I really wouldn't like to be in your shoes.'

It was eleven o'clock by the time they finished talking about it and they were both ready for bed, but that was when James realised that he hadn't mentioned his conversation with DCI Tanner.

'Actually, there was one bright spot in the day,' he said. 'The boss is leaving and he wants me to take over from him.'

He told her what Tanner had said and she was delighted, as he knew she would be.

'It will certainly ease the pressure on our finances after my maternity leave ends,' she said.

They spoke about it for a few minutes and he explained what the role would entail.

327

'It won't actually be very different from what I do now,' he said.

'Well, if Tanner is recommending you for the position, you're bound to get it,' Annie said encouragingly.

Though exhausted, it took James hours to get to sleep, and when the darkness finally consumed him, he found himself standing over Rachel Elliott's battered body.

Even though her lips weren't moving, he could hear her voice as she pleaded with him to find *The Winter Killer* for the sake of her friends and family.

CHAPTER FIFTY-EIGHT

Once again, James was up and dressed the following morning before his wife and daughter were awake. Annie didn't stir until he gave her a gentle nudge.

'You asked me to let you know when I'm about to leave,' he said. 'Do you want me to make you a brew?'

'No, don't worry. I'm going to hop in the shower before our little munchkin demands my attention. What time is it?'

'Half seven. I'm driving down to Lancaster Infirmary in the hope I can speak to Douglas Hannigan before going to the office.'

'Well, best of luck with that, and with the rest of it. You'll be in my thoughts.'

It was a twenty-minute drive from Kirkby Abbey to Lancaster and soon after setting off James received a phone call from DS Stevens in response to a text message he'd sent him earlier.

'I just spoke to the hospital and Hannigan is awake and

willing to talk to us,' Stevens said. 'I've already left home so I'll meet you there.'

By the time James got to the hospital he'd worked out an action plan for the day ahead: he would execute the search warrants against both Hannigan and Ethan Prescott; he would haul Carlo Salvi in for another interview under caution; and he'd get the team to go through all the statements taken from wedding guests and hotel staff. He wanted to be sure that they hadn't missed anything.

The murder still featured on the radio news and James was surprised to hear a clip of an interview with Greg Murphy.

'We're still struggling to accept that Rachel is no longer with us,' he said. 'She was such a lovely person who was dear to all our hearts. Mere words can't adequately describe the pain her family is suffering, and that pain is compounded by the fact that she was killed at the wedding of her sister and myself. I know the police are doing all they can to find the person responsible, but if anyone listening has information that might be of help then please, please come forward with it.'

He spoke clearly and with conviction, and James knew listeners would never have deduced that the truth was he and Rachel couldn't stand each other.

The announcer went on to say that Rachel's boyfriend, Carlo Salvi, had been detained overnight at Kendal Police Station after being questioned yesterday, and so far, no charges had been brought against him.

James was glad that the story was still considered newsworthy into day three of the investigation. But he knew that if they didn't get a result soon, the media would either lose interest or start to question whether the detectives leading the investigation were up to the job.

Stevens was waiting for James when he got to the hospital. He was standing with the uniformed officer who'd been stationed outside Hannigan's private room throughout the night.

'I've been given an update by the doctor,' Stevens said. 'Our man has had a comfortable night and they're satisfied he'll make a full recovery. It was a combination of the blow to the head, the cocaine and the booze that rendered him unconscious.'

'What would have happened if we hadn't found him when we did?' James asked.

'According to the doctor, he might not have woken up at all.'

James flicked his head towards the room. 'Then let's go see how grateful he is.'

Hannigan was sitting up in bed reading a newspaper when they entered. He closed it immediately and said, 'I agreed to see you because I wanted to say thanks for turning up when you did. Christ only knows what state I'd be in if you hadn't managed to break in and call an ambulance.'

'All in a day's work, Mr Hannigan,' James said. 'It's good to see that you're on the mend.'

His face was slack, listless, and pitted with grey stubble. The bruise on his forehead also appeared to be much darker and bigger.

'I gather you told the detectives that it was an accident and you fell down the stairs?' James said.

331

Hannigan turned down the corners of his mouth and shrugged. 'I got wasted. It was the only way to stop myself thinking about how I'd fucked up my life. Erika has left me and the stuff with Rachel will haunt me forever.'

'So how did the accident come about?' This from Stevens.

Hannigan blew out his cheeks. 'Everything was fine until I decided to go upstairs and get something from my study. I can't even remember what it was. Then I lost my balance coming down and I don't recall anything until I briefly came to in the ambulance.'

'You're lucky you didn't suffer more than a bruised head,' James said, as he and Stevens moved to either side of the bed.

Hannigan nodded. 'I know. And I also know now why you're paying me a visit. They let Erika and my dad come in and see me during the night. She told me about what else Rachel said to her on the day of the wedding and also about the photos you found in my bin at home. I'm guessing that's why you're here.'

'And you've guessed right,' James said. 'But I'm sure you're going to deny that you were stalking Rachel and say that you didn't threaten to pay someone to hurt her.'

He shook his head and James could see the tension rise in his body.

'On the contrary, Inspector. I've thought long and hard about this and it's time I owned up to being a complete dickhead. I did say that to Rachel when she phoned me. Neither she nor anyone else realised just how upset I was that she fucked up my bid to become an MP. I wanted to get my revenge and so I sent her the card with the threat. And yes, I followed her and took photos in the hope that I could catch her doing something that I could use to humiliate her, just as she'd humiliated me.

'When I discovered she was seeing some bloke who worked at the university I thought I was onto something but then came the wedding and her murder. It made me feel ashamed of myself.'

'Did you pay someone to go to the hotel and teach her a lesson?'

Another shake of the head, and this time when he spoke his voice shook with emotion.

'I swear I did nothing of the kind. It was an empty threat and you need to believe that. And you won't find any evidence to prove that I'm lying because there isn't any. I'll happily confess to being a nasty, vengeful prick, but I'm not a murderer.'

'You should know that we've obtained a warrant to search your house and gain access to your phone and computer,' James said.

'That's fine by me, Inspector. It's time I faced up to the consequences of my actions. Erika has told me it's over between us and I don't blame her. I swore to her that I'd stopped taking drugs and I lied. Even my own parents now know what a poor excuse for a human being I am.'

Hannigan was now sobbing as the words rasped out of his throat. James threw a few more questions at him, but his answers became incomprehensible and a doctor was summoned to come and check on him.

'We'll leave it at that for now, Mr Hannigan,' James said. 'But I'm sure we'll need to speak to you again soon.'

CHAPTER FIFTY-NINE

The morning briefing got under way soon after James and Stevens arrived back in Kendal. The room was filled with fifteen or more weary-looking detectives and support staff, and it was clear that they'd reported for duty having had very little sleep.

DCI Tanner was conspicuous by his absence and James was told he'd been called to a meeting at Carleton Hall.

The first item on the agenda was Douglas Hannigan and James consulted his notes as he ran through what the guy had told them.

'Phil and I are of the same opinion,' he said. 'We believe he told us the truth. The guy is seriously fucked up, but it seems highly unlikely that he would have paid someone to go to the hotel to attack Rachel Elliott. But we won't rule him out entirely until we've searched his house and gone through his phone. DS Stevens will be overseeing that.

'While that's going down, Abbott and I will have another

go at Carlo Salvi before we descend on Ethan and Claire Prescott's house in Bowness with a warrant,' he said.

DC Isaac confirmed that she had spoken the previous evening to both Mark Slade and Belinda Travers.

'They're sticking to their stories,' she said, 'and Travers is furious that he's telling everyone that it was her who behaved inappropriately with him. She's now seriously considering making an official complaint.'

'Did you mention that to Slade?' James asked.

'I did, and he said she was bluffing. But I got the impression that the thought of it made him nervous.'

'Have we come up with anything else on the guy?'

Isaac shook her head. 'Nothing that we don't already know, sir. Unfortunately for us, if he did meet up with Rachel on the jetty then we're not going to know unless a witness suddenly turns up. There's no forensic evidence so far to show he was there.'

It was over to Abbott then to pass on some more disappointing news.

'Digital analysis of Ethan Prescott's phone and laptop has come up with sod all, guv,' she said. 'There's nothing on them to suggest that he's back in a relationship with his old flame, Libby.'

'That doesn't mean we won't find something when we go through his home and belongings,' James said, knowing that his voice conveyed very little optimism. 'I think he was a bit too willing to give us his phone and computer. He knew there was nothing incriminating on them. There's always the chance that if he is our killer, we'll find a speck of Rachel's blood on

335

his clothes or shoes, so let's make sure we get to examine what he was wearing at the wedding.'

At ten thirty James called time on the briefing and he and Abbott went to conduct a second interview with Carlo Salvi.

A night banged up in a cell hadn't done the Italian Lothario any favours. His face looked as though the blood had been sucked out of it, his eyes dull and ringed with fatigue, and he was wearing a sweatshirt and tracksuit bottoms provided by the custody team. Forensics would be examining his clothes and shoes, as well as swabs from his hands and face.

As the two detectives took their seats, he stared at them with undisguised hostility.

Meanwhile, Clive Edgar, the duty solicitor, sat next to him looking as dapper as ever.

'I trust you had a comfortable night?' James said to Salvi, who just pulled a face.

Abbott switched on the tape and announced who was present in the room and why the interview was taking place.

Before any questions were asked the solicitor made it clear that his client was continuing to insist that he did not kill his girlfriend on New Year's Eve.

'Mr Salvi has now been held in custody for almost seventeen hours,' he said, 'and if you've been unable to come up with evidence that will justify continuing to hold him, then I insist that he be allowed to leave so that he can return to his family in Italy.'

James shook his head. 'You're well aware, Mr Edgar, that we can apply for a custody extension, which would almost certainly be granted given that your client is a flight risk.'

The formal questions began then, but Salvi stuck to the same answers he had given the day before.

'I did not murder Rachel,' he said. 'She was alive when I left the hotel.'

James could tell that the frustration was like a storm raging inside the man and some of his words were lost as he struggled to speak.

They were twenty minutes into the interview, and getting nowhere fast, when there came a sharp knock on the door before it was opened by DC Isaac. She signalled to James that she needed to speak to him.

For the benefit of the tape, James announced that the interview was being suspended and apologised to Salvi and his solicitor.

As the detectives stepped out of the room into the corridor, Isaac wasted no time.

'I'm afraid you're not going to like it,' she said. 'We now have proof that Mr Salvi was not at the hotel at the time Rachel was killed.'

CHAPTER SIXTY

Carlo Salvi was in the clear thanks to evidence provided by CCTV footage.

James viewed the footage in the office on a computer screen. The first clip showed the Italian's hire car passing one of several recently installed traffic cameras along the A591 just north of The Fells Hotel. The time was 4.45 p.m. on New Year's Eve – almost half an hour before the last photograph was taken of Rachel on the hotel terrace.

Another clip from a surveillance camera outside a shop had captured the car passing through Ambleside town centre ten minutes later. And when the video was paused you could clearly see that it was Salvi behind the wheel.

'The next clip is the clincher,' Isaac said. 'The camera is on the front of a doctor's surgery across from the building where Salvi was living. We didn't know it was there until a couple of hours ago. It's angled in such a way that it covers the road between them. At five o'clock, Salvi can be seen pulling up to the kerb opposite.'

James stared at the screen, slack-jawed, as a man who was most definitely Carlo Salvi climbed out and walked up to the entrance.

'The car remained there for the rest of the evening,' Isaac said. 'And there's no way he could have got back to the hotel by any other means before Rachel went missing.'

It was a major blow to the investigation, for sure, as two suspects had suddenly been taken out of the equation. The day couldn't have got off to a worse start.

'It's a shame it's taken so long to find this out,' James said.

Isaac shrugged. 'Couldn't be helped, sir. It's been slow going with the system moving at half speed.'

James swallowed back his disappointment and stood. He told Abbott to make the rest of the team aware of the developments.

'I'd better let Tanner know,' he said. 'He'll be none too pleased.'

And he wasn't. The DCI swore into the phone and told James that a press release would have to be put out.

'I'll sort it from this end,' he said. 'It's only fair to the guy to announce as soon as possible that he's been cleared.'

'We could have cleared him much sooner if he hadn't decided to do a runner,' James pointed out. 'We weren't able to look for his car until we identified him and then got the registration from the leasing company.'

'Well, it's not good news, and at this rate it won't be long before we run out of bloody suspects altogether.'

339

Minutes later, James was back in the interview room breaking the news to Salvi and his brief.

The Italian reacted by dropping his face into his hands and mumbling what sounded like a prayer.

James then explained how they had been able to prove that what he'd told them was true.

'You'll be pleased to know that you are now free to go, Mr Salvi. I'll see that your belongings are returned to you and we'll arrange transport for you back to London.'

Salvi sat up straight and pushed his shoulders back. His face was red, and it looked as though he was about to cry.

'I don't blame you for believing that I might have killed Rachel,' he said. 'I should not have panicked and tried to leave the country. It was foolish and unforgivable.'

James nodded. 'I won't argue with you there, Mr Salvi. It caused us to waste a lot of very valuable time.'

'I realise that and I'm sorry. I will have to live with the guilt of leaving her that night and it won't be easy. Rachel was a kind and generous person and I'll never forget what fun we had together while I was here. I really hope that you can now go on and catch the person who did that horrible thing to her. Whoever it was deserves to rot in prison.'

He began to cry then and James left it to his solicitor to console him. When he returned to the office, he asked DC Sharma to make all the arrangements on Salvi's behalf. He then got the team together and gave them a short pep talk.

'We still have other suspects and other leads that need to be followed up,' he said. 'So, let's crack on with the case and not allow ourselves to become too disheartened.'

He fired off a few more instructions before heading back to his desk. Just as he got there, his mobile rang. He pulled it from his pocket and saw it was a call from Victoria Hartley, the Family Liaison Officer assigned to Rachel's parents.

'I'm ringing to update you on a couple of things, guv,' she said. 'Is now a good time?'

'Sure. Fire away.'

'As per your instructions, I've arranged for Mr Elliott to formally identify his daughter's body at ten tomorrow morning. And his other daughter will be going with him.'

'Have you spoken to Libby then?'

'Yes, sir. I came over to the Elliotts' house earlier to see how they were and keep them abreast of things. Not long after I got here, Libby turned up with Claire Prescott, her former nanny. Libby came because she wanted to talk to her mum and picked Claire up on the way.'

'And are mother and daughter back on speaking terms?'

'I'm glad to say they are. But just so you're aware, there was a bit of an incident outside the house when Libby pulled up in her car.'

'What kind of incident?'

'Well, Mr and Mrs Elliott have been pestered since yesterday by various newspapers who are baying for an interview with them about Rachel and the wedding. There was a reporter and a photographer here when they arrived and they pounced on Libby as soon as she climbed out of the car. She refused to speak to them and after helping Claire out, they started towards the house, but in their haste, Claire tripped over the kerb and fell.'

'Shit. Was she hurt?'

'Oh no. It wasn't serious, thankfully, and she managed to get straight up.'

'Where were you?'

'I was watching through the window from inside the living room. It all happened so fast and by the time I'd rushed outside Libby and Claire were hurrying in through the front door.'

'Was that the end of it?' James asked.

'Yes, it was. The photographer and reporter got in their car and drove off.'

'As a matter of interest, were they representing the *Cumbria Gazette*?'

'No, sir. They were there on behalf of the *Daily Mail*.'

James told Hartley that he needed to deliver what would be unwelcome news about the investigation to Mr and Mrs Elliott.

'In view of what's happened, I'll come over to Bowness now and take the opportunity to tell Libby at the same time,' he said.

After hanging up, he passed on what Hartley had told him to the other detectives.

'When I'm finished in Bowness, I want us to descend on Ethan and Claire Prescott's house in Windermere and hopefully find out if they've been hiding something from us. So, have a team on standby and be ready to roll as soon as you receive my call.'

CHAPTER SIXTY-ONE

Someone had been thoughtful enough to bring a tray of coffees into the office so James helped himself to one before he and Abbott set off. He needed it to revive his senses.

This morning's setbacks had left him feeling unsettled and far less positive about the investigation, and uncertainty continued to beat in his heart as Abbott drove them to Bowness.

He wasn't looking forward to telling Rachel's parents that two of their main suspects had fallen by the wayside. Or that their daughter's latest boyfriend had rejected her just as Douglas Hannigan and Ethan Prescott had.

Libby also needed to be brought up to date and made aware of why her sister had drunk more than was good for her at the wedding.

Would it make Libby feel even more guilty than she already did? he wondered. Or would the knowledge that another man had broken Rachel's heart give rise to a sense of anger rather than pity?

'I feel that each time we take a step forward we then have to take two steps back,' Abbott said. 'Where do we go if Ethan Prescott turns out not to be our man? And Mark Slade as well, for that matter?'

'We'll do what we always do in those circumstances and start over again,' James replied. 'That's why I've begun the process of going back over all the statements and notes we've taken. We might have missed something because when those few suspects emerged, we convinced ourselves that the killer had to be one of them. You'll know yourself that it happens with some investigations.'

'You're not wrong there, guv,' Abbott said. 'The nightmare scenario for us, though, would be if Rachel was murdered by someone who just wandered into the hotel through the back gate and wasn't known among the guests and staff.'

James made a noise in his throat and said, 'That, Jessica, just doesn't bear thinking about.'

Officer Hartley opened the door to them when they arrived at the Elliotts' house in Bowness. The first thing she told them was that Libby had just left.

'She knew you were on your way here to provide an update, but after receiving a text message she insisted she had to go,' Hartley said. 'Claire went with her, so I expect she'll drop her off before going on to wherever she needs to be.'

James frowned and couldn't help wondering if Libby had left in order to avoid speaking to them. It seemed odd that she hadn't stayed to find out what was happening with the investigation, but he pushed the thought to one side as he stepped into the house and followed Hartley into the living room.

Rachel's parents were sitting side by side on the sofa waiting for them. They both looked exhausted, their faces gaunt and colourless.

'Good day to you, Mr and Mrs Elliott,' James said. 'May we sit down?'

Fraser Elliott gestured at the two armchairs facing them. 'Of course. Please.'

Officer Hartley remained standing with her back to the door, notepad at the ready.

Denise Elliott was the next to speak, her voice barely above a whisper.

'Have you found out who killed our daughter yet?' she said. 'Please tell us that's the reason you're here.'

James felt a knot tighten in his throat. 'I'm sorry to say that we haven't, Mrs Elliott. However, we are still—'

'But what about the Italian man you arrested yesterday?' she cut in. 'Her so-called "boyfriend". Why haven't you charged him?'

'Because he didn't do it,' James answered. 'Evidence has emerged that proves he was not at the hotel when your daughter was killed. He'd returned to his flat in Ambleside at that point and he remained there for the rest of the evening.'

A shadow crossed her face and she bit her lip. 'But if he didn't do it then who did?'

'We still don't know,' James said. 'The reason we came here today was to provide you with an update on the investigation, just as I promised you I would. And I was hoping that Libby would be here as well.'

'She had to go,' Denise said. 'We told her we would pass on whatever information you gave us.'

'And how is she?'

It was Fraser who answered. 'She's still finding it hard, as we all are, but I think that coming here this morning has helped.'

'I told her that I was sorry for my outburst at the hotel,' Denise explained, 'and that I was wrong to make her feel guilty about what happened to Rachel. It wasn't her fault and I wanted to tell her that to her face. That's why we asked her to come over.'

'I understand there was an incident outside with the press when they arrived,' James said.

Fraser nodded. 'The bloody vultures caused trouble at Libby's house yesterday and here today. They won't leave us alone. We've had phone calls and visits from newspapers, radio and television. But no way are we prepared to be interviewed.'

'Are you aware that Mr Murphy was on the radio this morning?'

'We weren't until our daughter told us. He spoke to them yesterday afternoon when they turned up at the hotel. To be fair to the man, he does keep checking to see if we're all right.'

'And how is Mrs Prescott?' James asked.

'Oh, she was a bit shaken but otherwise okay. Given how frail she is, she was lucky. She did have a cry when she came in here though. But it wasn't over that.'

'What was it over then?'

'The WhatsApp message that Rachel sent to Libby. Libby told us about it and Claire got upset because she said you more or less accused her son of going after Rachel to stop her causing a fuss over nothing.'

'We didn't accuse him of anything,' James said. 'We merely asked some questions because it was a curious message and it was sent perhaps only minutes before Rachel went down to the jetty.'

'Our daughter told us exactly what happened, Inspector,' Fraser said. 'And we have no reason not to believe her. Rachel obviously got it wrong. Libby had only just got married, for heaven's sake. She'd gotten worked up because of her conversation with Rachel and Ethan was there to comfort her. Their fling ended a long time ago but they've remained good friends so there was nothing inappropriate about it.'

James tried not to let the scepticism show on his face and said, 'One of the things we came to tell you is that we now know why Rachel got so upset after the wedding ceremony.'

The couple glanced at each other and Fraser took his wife's hand.

'It would seem that Rachel misunderstood the nature of her relationship with Mr Salvi,' he said. 'I think it's fair to say that when Mr Salvi told her that he didn't love her and that he didn't want her to go to Italy with him, it broke her heart.'

Denise started to weep then and James wished he didn't have more bad news to impart. He waited until she had stopped crying before carrying on.

'There's something else I feel you should be made aware of,' he said. 'It relates to Rachel's former fiancé, Douglas Hannigan.'

'Did he admit to sending her the birthday card with the threat inside it?' Fraser asked.

'He did, but we've also had it confirmed that your daughter is indeed the person who took those photos of him taking drugs and then sent them to the *Gazette*. The threat in the card was in retaliation, but Mr Hannigan insists that he only wanted to scare her. I should also remind you that he was nowhere near the hotel when Rachel died.'

James decided not to reveal that Hannigan had also been stalking their daughter. At this stage, there was no need for them to know.

The final matter he brought up was the formal identification of Rachel's body.

'We already know it's our daughter lying in the morgue, but I know I have to see her,' Fraser said. 'Libby will be coming with me.'

Denise drew an anxious breath. 'I've decided not to go. I think the experience will be too painful for me and I want to remember Rachel as she was when I last saw her. She looked so sweet in that ever so pretty maid-of-honour dress.'

Denise slumped against her husband then, and the tears flowed as James and Abbott got up and left the room.

CHAPTER SIXTY-TWO

'This issue with the WhatsApp message that Rachel sent to her sister is really bugging me,' James said as he and Abbott drove away from Bowness. 'I'm puzzled as to why everyone in the family has been so quick to believe that Rachel misinterpreted what she saw going on between Libby and Ethan in the garden. What if she didn't and the pair of them have lied to us? If so, then maybe they also lied about what happened after that.'

'I've been thinking about it as well, guv, and I'm inclined to believe them,' Abbott said. 'For one thing, we know that Rachel had been on the booze and so could easily have made a mistake. Plus, we've been told that the relationship between the two sisters was strained, and therefore she may have seen it as an opportunity to ruin Libby's wedding and her marriage to Greg Murphy. And that's not all. We also know from what she did to Douglas Hannigan that she was not averse to going to extreme lengths to get revenge.'

'They're all reasonable points to make,' James agreed.

'And there's one other matter that has to be taken into account, and that's the not insignificant fact that Libby had only just got married. Would she really have been stupid enough to become intimate with her ex at her own no-expense-spared wedding?'

James nodded. 'That's a good question. Perhaps we'll get the answer to it when we put more pressure on Ethan.'

'Is that what we're about to do by executing the warrant? If so, we need to tell the team to head to Windermere.'

'I want to hold fire on that until we get there ourselves,' James said. 'Claire Prescott is probably at home by herself now and I don't think we should spook her by going in mob handed when we can give her fair warning of what to expect before calling in the troops.'

Despite all the points Abbott had raised about Rachel's WhatsApp message, James was still troubled by it. His copper's intuition was at work again, and it was telling him not to simply assume that Rachel had made a mistake about what she saw on the path or that she had chosen to lie about it to cause problems for her sister.

James reminded himself of what Rachel wrote: *You disgust me, Libby. I'm not going to keep your sordid secret so make the most of today. And tell that slimy bastard Ethan that if he ever lays a hand on me again, I'll have him put away.*

Whatever the truth, James found it hard to believe that Ethan and Libby would choose to ignore the message, as they'd claimed, and though the hotel surveillance footage showed Libby returning to the bar straight after the pathway encounter, there were no clips to prove that Ethan went onto

the terrace to be with his mum. They only had Claire's word
for it that he stayed with her and therefore could not have
gone looking for Rachel. And that was more than enough to
keep the wheels turning in James's suspicious mind.

They got a surprise when they arrived at the Prescott house
in Windermere as Claire wasn't by herself after all.

There were two cars on the short driveway. One was the
Vauxhall Corsa that had been parked there when they last
visited, which James had assumed belonged to Ethan. The
other was a smart black BMW that was probably Libby
Murphy's.

It was Ethan who opened the door and his face dropped
when he saw them.

'Hello there, Mr Prescott,' James said. 'We didn't expect
you to be here.'

A flash of panic passed over the man's face. 'Mum needed
me so I closed the shop and came home. What do you
want?'

'To have another chat with you. And would I be right in
assuming that Mrs Murphy is here?'

A curt nod. 'She went to see her parents and took Mum
with her, then she brought her back. She'll be leaving soon.'

'Well then, while we're here we can update her on the
investigation. Can we come in?'

After a brief hesitation, he said, 'I suppose so.'

Libby was in the living room sitting next to Claire on the
sofa. She looked drained, her eyes sunken and shadowed.

It was Claire who spoke first, and the agitation was obvious
in the tenor of her voice.

'Are you here to make more unfounded allegations against my son?' she said. 'Or to tell us that you've caught Rachel's killer?'

'First, allow me to ask you if you're okay, Mrs Prescott,' James said. 'We arrived at Mr and Mrs Elliott's house shortly after you'd left and they told us about the incident with the press photographer and reporter.'

'I'm fine,' Claire responded. 'I just lost my balance when I hit the kerb. It shook me up a bit, but that was all.'

He then turned to Libby and told her that he had news to pass on about the investigation.

Libby gnawed at her lower lip and gave him a considered look.

'You had better sit down then,' she said.

There weren't enough chairs for everyone so Ethan sat on the arm of the sofa next to his mother.

James had decided to take it slowly and not to rush into announcing that he was about to trigger the execution of a search warrant. He hadn't expected Libby to be here and so he wanted to seize the opportunity to question all three of them together.

He couldn't help noticing the nervous looks that passed between them and the sense of anticipation that was almost palpable. It made him all the more convinced that there was something they were holding back. Something they were hiding.

Libby appeared to be the most anxious. Her face was tense, jaw locked, and a muscle under her right eye was twitching.

Ethan, for his part, seemed to be finding it hard to keep his body still and kept fidgeting with his shirt collar.

As for Claire, she sat forward on the sofa, hands resting on her walking stick, her pale, watchful eyes filled with something akin to indignation.

'The first thing that you need to know is that two of the men we've been questioning are no longer suspects,' James said. 'It's been established that neither Carlo Salvi nor Douglas Hannigan were at the hotel when she was killed. Hannigan was never there, and Salvi left after he and Rachel argued in her room.'

'Do you know what the argument was over?' Libby asked.

James nodded. 'Rachel had fallen in love with him and she thought he felt the same so she decided to declare her love for him at the wedding and tell him she wanted to move to Italy with him. She thought it was what he wanted too, but he told her that he didn't feel the same way and that it was over between them. That was why she was so down and almost certainly why she consumed a significant amount of alcohol.'

All three of them were shocked into silence, but it was Libby's face that showed the most emotion. She clenched her jaw tight and her eyes filled with tears.

'You probably don't need me to tell you that having lost two of our main suspects, we're now forced to shift the focus of the investigation,' James said. 'Other scenarios will be given more consideration.'

He could tell from the way Claire was looking at him that she knew where he was going with this.

'Get to the point, Inspector,' she said. 'What is it you want us to know?'

James let the question hang in the air for a few moments before he answered her.

'I want you to know that I'm going to serve you and your son with a warrant, Mrs Prescott, and within the next half an hour or so a team of police officers will come here and carry out a thorough search of this house. Your digital devices, clothes and other belongings will be taken away for forensic examination.' He switched his gaze to Ethan, adding. 'We've also secured a warrant to do the same at your gift shop, Mr Prescott.'

Ethan looked fit to explode. 'I don't understand. What do you expect to find that you didn't find on the phone and laptop I gave you?'

'I'm not sure what we'll find,' James said, 'but I need to satisfy myself that you've been entirely honest with us. You see, I'm not convinced that you and Mrs Murphy have told the truth about what happened when Rachel came across the pair of you on the garden path.'

'But we've both explained what happened,' Ethan said. 'And we've told you that there's nothing going on us between us. If you've looked through my phone, you'll know we haven't been calling or messaging each other.'

'But that doesn't mean you haven't been doing so on other devices,' James said.

'Are you actually serious about this?' Claire snapped. 'We've all been at pains to tell you that Rachel got it wrong. And honestly, she clearly wasn't in the best headspace.'

'In that case, you won't object to a search being carried out,' James said. He then turned to Libby. 'We can't ignore the WhatsApp message that your sister sent to you, which you chose not to mention to us. Or the fact that you failed to tell the truth when we first spoke to you about when you last saw her.'

It was Libby's reaction that told James he had been right to pursue the issue. She caught her breath and her eyes swivelled nervously in their sockets to the left, towards Ethan.

Abbott picked up on it too and said, 'You need to understand, Mrs Murphy, that we will explore all avenues in order to get to the truth. And that will include looking through your own personal data too, and speaking to your husband. If there's even a shred of evidence that you haven't been entirely honest with us, we'll find it.'

Claire gave a loud snort of exasperation and her son jumped up.

'This is all wrong,' he raged. 'Why won't you believe us? We've done nothing wrong.'

But Libby just sat there and raised her eyes to the ceiling. It gave James the impression that she was desperate to unburden herself and so he decided to push his luck.

'You owe it to your younger sister to tell us what really happened when you last saw her, Mrs Murphy,' he said. 'We're not here to pass judgement on you. We just want to find out why and how she was killed, and who did it. If you want to help you must tell us the truth.'

Libby lowered her eyes and stared at James. As she opened her mouth to speak Claire grabbed her hand and squeezed it.

'Don't listen to him, Libby,' she said, panic in her voice. 'He'll make you say something that you'll regret.'

But Libby snatched her hand away and shook her head. 'No, Claire. He's right. It's not fair on Rachel to carry on pretending that she got it wrong when she didn't.'

'But you're confused,' Claire said. 'You shouldn't do—'

355

Libby cut Claire off before she could finish her sentence.

'The truth is that Ethan and I are seeing each other, Inspector, and we have been for about five months,' she said. 'And we were kissing when Rachel saw us behind the bush, so I had to tell her what was really going on. My "sordid secret" as she put it. And after I did, she blew a fuse and stormed off.'

It was Abbott who responded, no doubt because she was taken aback by the confession.

'But I don't understand,' she said. 'If you were having an affair with Ethan, why marry Mr Murphy? Why not end things?'

Libby looked at her and raised her brow. 'I was going to do exactly that just over three months ago when Ethan and I took the decision to stop with the affair and make our relationship permanent. We'd never really fallen out of love, you see. But then Greg's father died so I stayed with him.'

Abbott leaned forward, frowning. 'Are you saying that you didn't leave Mr Murphy because you felt sorry for him?'

Libby wiped a tear from her cheek and turned to Claire.

'Are you going to tell them, or shall I?' she said.

By now sweat was beading above Claire's upper lip and veins were bulging out of her neck.

'It was me who persuaded her to remain in the relationship and to go ahead with the wedding,' she said. 'I knew it'd be the best way for her and Ethan to have a great future together.'

CHAPTER SIXTY-THREE

The air in the room was suddenly oscillating with tension. Libby began weeping and Ethan moved to stand behind her so that he could place his hands on her shoulders.

Claire's breathing was getting louder and faster and all the colour left her cheeks.

James, on the other hand, felt pleased with himself, and a fizz of excitement ran through him.

He gave them all a few moments to process what had happened before asking Claire to elaborate on her revelation.

She cleared her throat, licked her lips, said, 'Libby made a terrible mistake entering into a relationship with Greg Murphy. I warned her against it because I knew that he was a bullying control freak, just like his father. And before long she discovered that I was right. He wasn't the man for her and her thoughts turned to ending it with him.'

Libby wiped her eyes with the sleeve of her sweater and took a deep, audible breath.

'Greg is far too possessive,' she said. 'I realised that when he started checking my phone and asking me to account for my movements. I thought I loved him, but it took me a while to realise that I didn't. The only person I told was Claire and I started coming to see her more often. And that's when I started bumping into Ethan and discovered that I still had feelings for him.'

'And I had never stopped loving her,' Ethan said.

'So, you started seeing each other while you and Greg were planning the wedding?' James asked Libby.

'We were very careful,' she answered. 'We both used burner phones to communicate with each other so Greg was none the wiser. Honestly, it didn't take me long to make up my mind to end it with him, but just as I was about to do so his father died suddenly. I decided to wait until after the funeral because I didn't want to add to his pain. That was when Claire got Ethan and me together and things changed.'

'In what way?' Abbott asked.

It was Claire who answered. 'I was told that Greg had inherited his father's business and all his money, which ran into the millions. It provided an opportunity for Libby and my son to ensure they would never have to want for anything. And ... it helped that I would finally be getting my revenge for what his father did to my husband.'

Realisation dawned for James and he said, 'So it was all about the money?'

She nodded. 'I persuaded Libby to go ahead and marry Greg so that she could get her hands on a chunk of his fortune. All she had to do was stick with it for four or five months. Then she could seek a divorce and secure a sizeable settlement.

It ticked all the boxes. Ethan's debts could be paid off and I wouldn't have to worry about ending up in some crappy care home. And the pair of them would be able to live life to the full and never have to worry about money. It was win-win all the way as far as I was concerned. They both thought so too, which is why they were happy to go along with it.'

'And did your parents know about it, Libby?' James asked her.

Libby pursed her lips and shook her head. 'Nobody knew except us. And I beg you not to tell anyone now. It's nothing to do with Rachel's death, and it's nobody's business but ours.'

'I have a question for you,' Abbott said. 'Given the situation, why did you risk everything by kissing Ethan in the hotel garden?'

'I was desperate to speak to him after the marriage became official,' Libby replied. 'I told him to meet me there so that we could talk. I asked him if he still thought we were doing the right thing and he assured me that we were and that we needed to stay focused on the future. We fell into each other's arms because we didn't think anyone could see us. But that's when Rachel appeared.

'I didn't think she'd react the way she did when I told her. She was fuming and I realise now that it must have been partly because her own relationship had just ended. She refused to let me try to justify what I was doing and marched off.'

'And that brings us to the WhatsApp message she sent to you,' James said. 'She made it clear that she was going to tell everyone your "sordid secret", as she put it, and yet you've told us that you didn't try to stop her. And that just doesn't ring true.'

'But it is true,' Libby responded, her voice cracking. 'We didn't think she would actually do it. Not to me, her own sister.'

'But you couldn't possibly have been sure considering the state she was in. And that's why it's hard for me to accept that you didn't go looking for her.'

'I've already told you that I went straight to the bar and met Greg and Mark. And I stayed with them.'

'Yes, you were captured on a surveillance camera, Mrs Murphy.' James turned to Ethan. 'But you weren't, Mr Prescott. So, we can't be sure where you went after Rachel rushed off.'

'I joined Mum on the terrace. You know that. And I didn't go back into the garden.'

'It's true,' Claire said. 'How many times do we have to tell you that?'

'We can't just take your word for it,' James told her. 'How do we know you're not just saying it to protect your son?'

'Because I wouldn't do it if I thought he'd killed Rachel. That should be bloody obvious.'

'No, Mrs Prescott. What's obvious to me is that your son has become our prime suspect. We now know that he had a lot to lose if Rachel revealed what her sister had told her. That gave him a clear motive for wanting to stop her. He also had the opportunity. He was already outside and he knew that she was heading down towards the lake.'

Ethan stood back from the sofa, vigorously shaking his head. 'No, it wasn't me. I didn't go to the jetty and I didn't kill Rachel.'

At the same time, Libby leapt to her feet and spun round to face him.

'Please tell me that you're not lying, Ethan,' she pleaded. 'I can't bear to think that you're the one who hurt my sister. I would never—'

'You've already asked me that, Libby, and I swore that I didn't. I thought you believed me.'

Libby squeezed her hands into fists and pushed them against her temples.

'I did. I mean I do. But now … Oh Jesus, I don't know what to think anymore.'

Claire reached out, grabbed Libby's sleeve, and pulled on it.

'Stop it, Libby. Stop it. You must know in your heart that it wasn't Ethan.'

James decided it was time to take things to the next level and pile the pressure on their latest prime suspect. They needed to get him back to the station and question him under caution as soon as possible.

He got to his feet and said, 'Ethan Prescott, I'm placing you under arrest on suspicion of the murder of Rachel Elliott.'

He started to read him his rights but his voice was drowned out by a scream that came from Claire. It lasted several seconds and when it subsided, she looked up at James, her eyes unflinching and fierce.

Suddenly, shockingly, he knew he'd got it wrong, and that it wasn't Ethan who had killed Rachel.

'You can't do this to my son,' Claire yelled at James. 'He's innocent. It wasn't him who went looking for Rachel. You need to believe that.'

As James looked at her, he felt a shudder run down the length of his spine.

'I think I know that now, Mrs Prescott, because it was you, wasn't it?' he said. 'You're the one who went looking for Rachel and when you found her you killed her.'

Claire's face seemed to fold in on itself and her breathing became a series of violent gasps. In between them she managed to splutter out a confession.

'Yes, yes, it was me. Not Ethan. But I didn't mean for it to happen. It was an accident. She made me lose control.'

CHAPTER SIXTY-FOUR

After Claire's startling confession the room descended into chaos.

Libby's eyes blazed as she grabbed Claire's walking stick out of her hand and tried to hit her with it.

'You killed my sister,' she screamed. 'How could you? I thought you loved her like a daughter.'

James managed to rush forward and get hold of Libby's wrist before she could do any damage and as he pulled her away, she dropped the stick and collapsed onto the floor in a flood of tears.

At the same time, Claire's traumatised son backed up against the wall and started shaking his head in disbelief.

Both James and his DC moved into damage limitation mode. They knew there was no point trying to get more out of Claire with Libby and Ethan in the room.

James told Abbott to help Libby up off the floor and shouted at Claire not to move from the sofa. He didn't think she heard him because she was rocking back and forth with her hands clamped over her ears.

He then crossed the room and took Ethan by the arm before leading him out through the door into the hallway. Ethan didn't try to resist and just kept shaking his head and mumbling to himself.

James led him into the kitchen and got him to sit at the table. He then went back into the living room where Libby was now on her feet and hurling abuse at Claire as Abbott tried to push her gently towards the door.

With James's help they finally managed to get her into the kitchen where she fell into Ethan's arms.

'Stay here with them,' James told Abbott. 'I'll call for backup and then see what more I can get out of Mrs Prescott.'

When he returned to the living room, he was relieved to see that Claire still hadn't moved from the sofa. But now she was sobbing and dabbing at her eyes with a screwed-up hanky.

James stood over her as he phoned Control and summoned backup. Then he sat beside her and asked her if there was anything he could get her.

She shook her head tearily.

'I need to know if you meant what you told us, Mrs Prescott,' he said. 'Or did you say it because you know that your son killed Rachel and you want to take the blame for him?'

She shook her head. 'No, it was me. Not Ethan. And I didn't tell him what I did. I just hoped he would never find out.'

'We'll carry out a formal interview at the station, but can you please explain to me what happened?'

She turned to face him, her lower lip trembling. 'I was with Ethan on the terrace when Libby approached us and told Ethan she wanted to talk to him. She told him she would go and wait behind the bushes next to the path and he went and met her. When he came back, about twenty minutes later, he told me what had happened with Rachel. I was shocked and urged him to go and find her to stop her making mischief. But he didn't think she was serious so he wouldn't. So, I took it upon myself to sort it as I didn't want her to ruin everything. I told him I needed to use the loo, but instead of going inside I slipped into the garden and followed the path all the way to the lake. And that's where she was. It was freezing cold, but she didn't seem to care. She was standing on the jetty and staring out over the water, as still as a statue.'

'What did you do?'

'I walked up to her. She turned and even though it was quite dark I could see she'd been crying. She didn't seem surprised to see me and so I started trying to talk sense into her. I urged her not to betray her sister, but she was having none of it. She said she was fed up with bad things happening to her and not to Libby. And she accused me of being sick and twisted for coming up with the plan to get some of the Murphy money.'

She paused then, as though the words were stuck in her throat.

'Is that when it turned ugly?' James asked.

It took her a few more seconds to find her voice. When she did, she said, 'She flipped suddenly. Told me I'd never loved her and that Libby had always been my favourite, which hurt because it wasn't true. I reached out to take her hand but she responded by pushing me away. I almost lost my balance and it was only thanks to my walking stick that I didn't fall into the lake.

'Rachel then said she hated me and that she wished I was dead. I lost it then and lashed out with the stick. It caught her on the chest and she called me a bitch and tried to punch me. So, I hit her again and as she stumbled backwards, I kept on doing it. She managed to fend off most of the blows with her arms but then I struck her face again and her glasses fell off and she dropped her purse. I should have stopped then but I saw red and I just couldn't. The next blow was hard enough to knock her over and her head landed on one of the jetty posts. I saw she was hurt, but it took a while for me to realise that she was dead. And that was when I panicked. I looked around and there was no one in sight so I did the only thing I could think of doing and pushed her into the lake.'

'And what did you do after that?' James asked.

'I walked back to the hotel, cleaned my stick, and made sure there was no blood on me. It was then that I realised I'd left her purse and broken glasses on the jetty, but it was too late to go back and get them so I went downstairs and back to Ethan, who was still on the terrace. It wasn't easy, but I managed to hold myself together and get through the rest of the evening without breaking down. To be honest, I'm glad I haven't got away with what I did because I really don't deserve to. I loved Rachel as much as I love Libby. But now I've lost both of them and I only have myself to blame.'

After she stopped talking, her shoulders dropped and she withdrew into herself.

James stood and told her she was under arrest for the murder of Rachel Elliott. She didn't respond and that didn't surprise him.

CHAPTER SIXTY-FIVE

Things moved pretty quickly after backup arrived. As Claire was escorted out of the house by uniformed officers who would be taking her to the station in Kendal, James sat down with Ethan and Libby and told them what she had said to him. They were both reduced to tears.

He also made it clear that the plan they'd hatched with Claire could no longer remain a secret.

'It will all have to come out after she's charged,' he said to Libby, 'as your husband and parents will need to be told what led to Rachel's death. There's no way of keeping it from them.'

'I'll tell my father first and then get him to go with me when I break the news to Greg,' she replied. 'I've no doubt he'll expect me to move out right away, but that's the least of my worries.'

'And I think you need to accept that it's highly unlikely

you'll get any kind of divorce settlement in view of what you did, which will come out in court.'

'I know that, Inspector, but I really couldn't care less about that now.'

There was disbelief on the faces of virtually every member of the team, including DCI Tanner, when James got back to the station. He briefed them on everything that had happened at the Prescott house while a doctor spent some time with Claire to ensure that she was in a fit state to be formally interviewed.

James made it clear that she would be charged with murder but that he expected that when it came to trial her legal team would push for it to be reduced to manslaughter.

The briefing ended with a few loose ends being tied up. DS Stevens said that the search of Douglas Hannigan's house had proved fruitless, and the Crown Prosecution Service would have to decide whether it was worth pursuing a case against him for making threats against Rachel. James very much doubted that they would.

And DC Isaac had an update on Mark Slade that amused everyone.

'After we told him that Belinda was considering making an official complaint about his behaviour in the hotel garden, he decided to go and see her,' she said. 'He actually apologised and offered her a financial bribe to do nothing. She told him she'd consider it. But what she didn't tell him was that before answering the door to him she turned on her phone to record the conversation. She sent it to us to prove that she was telling the truth because in the process of bribing her he verbally admitted that he had approached her and kissed her without her consent.'

'Is she going to take it further?' James asked.

'No. She says she can't be bothered.'

EPILOGUE

The snow was falling again over Cumbria but James didn't care because he was on a day off and had spent it at home with his family.

It was a week since Claire Prescott had been charged with Rachel Elliott's murder and the case was ready to proceed to trial. The media frenzy that had surrounded it had quickly died down and the team were already focused on other things.

James was glad it was over, but that wasn't why he and Annie had been in a celebratory mood all day. Tanner had called first thing this morning to tell him that he was officially being promoted to the post of Detective Chief Inspector.

'You take over from me on the last day of March, which is when I move to Penrith,' he'd said. 'So, congratulations to you and I'm sure your colleagues will be delighted at the news.'

It was now early evening and they had just put Bella down for the night.

'It's time to treat ourselves to that tipple,' Annie said as she came into the living room with an uncorked bottle of Prosecco.

James had already placed two glasses on the coffee table and Annie wasted no time filling them.

'Here's a toast to your latest job, my darling,' she said, as they clinked their glasses together. 'It marks yet another milestone for the Walker family and provides you with an opportunity to go on making us proud.'

THE END

ACKNOWLEDGEMENTS

As ever, this book would not have seen the light of day if not for the fabulous team at Avon/HarperCollins. I'd like to thank them all for their continued support, most especially my editor Molly Walker-Sharp, who contributed so much even before I put pen to paper. She's always so tactful and insightful, as well as being a delight to work with.

If you've enjoyed *The Winter Killer*, then why not head back to DI James Walker's first case?

Twelve days.
Twelve murders.

THE CHRISTMAS KILLER

ALEX PINE

A serial killer is on the loose in Kirkby Abbey. And as the snow falls, the body count climbs …

One farmhouse. Two murder cases.
Three bodies.

DI James Walker knows that to catch
this killer, he needs to solve a case long
since gone cold …

Karin
Slaughter's
Killer Reads
Exclusive to
ASDA

EXCLUSIVE ADDITIONAL CONTENT

Dear Readers,

This next read will leave you chilled to the bone! A
Christmas crime novel to die for, *The Winter Killer* is an
atmospheric and twisty thriller set in the remote Lake
District – but even in the fells, nothing stays buried
forever …

DI James Walker has finally made it through the Christmas
period without a drop of blood spilled – or so he thinks.
But as he settles down to ring in the New Year, he's called
to the wedding of the season at a lakeside hotel – where
the bride's sister has disappeared. Before the wedding
night is out, the lake is being scoured for a body …
One guest is a killer, and it's up to DI Walker to crack
the case before the confetti settles.

So … grab yourself a mulled wine and a mince pie – and
delve into this murder!

Karin

READING GROUP QUESTIONS

(Warning: contains spoilers)

1. What three words would you use to describe *The Winter Killer*, and why?

2. This Christmas crime series is set in the Lake District in the depths of winter. Did you get a strong sense of place from the writing? How did the setting impact the crime?

3. Which character did you relate to the most, and why?

4. If you were Detective Inspector on the case, would you do anything differently to James? Why/ why not?

5. Did your opinion of the characters change over the course of the novel? Who was on your list of suspects?

6. What was the biggest red herring for you? Why did it throw you off?

7. Were you able to guess who the killer was before the big reveal? If so, which clues did you uncover that gave it away?

8. This book is the third title in a series. Have you read them in order? How has reading the books in order – or not – affected your reading experience? Which book in the series was your favourite, and why?

A Q&A WITH ALEX PINE

(Warning: contains spoilers)

What inspired the central mystery behind *The Winter Killer*?

It was actually a series of colourful wedding features in *Cumbria Life* magazine that gave me the idea. I was struck by the beautiful photographs of various lakeside ceremonies and the smiling faces of the happy couples. Then my warped crime-writer mind kicked in, and I started to wonder how often people get married for the wrong reasons and what might happen if it causes things to go badly wrong. This thought process led me to consider the worst-case scenario: a murder being committed during the nuptials. I was soon on the phone to my editor and within days we were developing the plot for *The Winter Killer*.

Do you plan your novels in detail before beginning to write, or do you start writing and see where it takes you?

I prefer to make a detailed plan and work out what is going to happen in each chapter. I'm not sure I could approach it any other way! Crime novels are full of twists and turns and these need to be carefully constructed, and I also like to chart the progress of all the characters so that I can determine exactly where and when their paths will cross and collide. And it goes without saying that, when writing a series, careful planning also helps to keep track of the various characters and their respective lives as the series progresses.

Can you tell us a bit about how you started out as a writer?

It's thanks to my late mother that I began writing. She was addicted to Agatha Christie and Mickey Spillane, and she encouraged me to read their books at an early age. When I did, I became hooked and it wasn't long before I was writing my own short stories. At fifteen I completed my first novel. Although it was never published, I enjoyed the experience so much that I put my heart and soul into the next book, which was acquired by a publishing house. The rest, as they say, is history …

How do you approach researching a book like this, with a police detective at its heart?

I always enjoy researching a book and I've made the most of it with this series. It's given me the perfect excuse to spend even more time in the Lake District – one of my favourite parts of the country – in order to scout out locations. The weather and the landscape play a major part in this series, and it was important to me to immerse myself fully. With regards to law enforcement, I've been writing thrillers for years, so I've become familiar with how the police operate. Plus, the internet provides a wealth of information on police forces across the country – true crime stories and real cases with similar themes are immensely useful when it comes to getting the procedure right, and it also helps that I was a crime reporter for a while during my years as a newspaper journalist, giving me valuable insight into big investigations. That said, it's a balancing act between fact and fiction, so there'll always be an element of artistic license to ensure it remains a pacy story.

Outside of the recurring cast, who was your favourite character to write in this book?

That would have to be the bride, Libby Elliott. No matter what, she was going to be a challenging character to create because she's on such an emotional rollercoaster. It's her wedding day and we want her to be on cloud nine at the start. But then we need to see her reacting to her sister's disappearance and murder, while at the same time doing her best not to reveal the secret that she's hiding … A character with so many layers is always fun!

What kind of fiction do you love to read when you aren't writing your own books?

I tend to stick to crime fiction. Not only do I enjoy it, but I also find out about things I didn't know in virtually every book I read. And I think it's fascinating to see how other authors approach familiar subjects such as murders, investigations, autopsies and the motives that drive individuals towards committing heinous crimes. Among my favourite crime and thriller writers are Lynda La Plante, Ian Rankin, Sam Carrington and Amanda Robson.

How do you come up with new and original twists and turns for your novels?

Coming up with something original is not always easy, but it's still possible. You only have to read newspapers regularly to know that criminals continue to surprise us! Every day there are reports of crimes involving unfamiliar methods and motives … I'm often inspired by these and use them when constructing my storylines.

And, finally, what's next for the newly promoted DCI James Walker?

Whilst I know that James would like nothing more than a quiet Christmas at home with Annie and Bella, I have a feeling that his plans for next Christmas and New Year will be disrupted once more … And now that he's been promoted to DCI, I'm sure that he will be more than ready to crack the case. Watch this space!

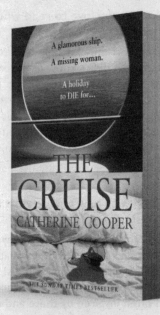

A glamorous ship

During a New Year's Eve party
on a large, luxurious cruise ship in the Caribbean,
the ship's dancer, Lola, goes missing.

Everyone on board has something to hide

Two weeks later, the ship is out of service, laid up far
from land with no more than a skeleton crew on board.
And then more people start disappearing ...

No one is safe

Why are the crew being harmed?
Who is responsible? And who will be next?

**The twisty new thriller from the *Sunday Times*
bestselling author of *The Chalet* and *The Chateau*.**